a good divorce

JOHN E. KEEGAN

the permanent press
sag harbor, ny 11963

Copyright© 2003 by John Keegan

Library of Congress Cataloging-in-Publication Data

Keegan, John
    A good divorce / by John Keegan
    p. cm.
    ISBN 1-57962-092-2
      1.Divorce—Fiction. 2. Divorced men—Fiction. 3. Seattle
    (Wash.)—Fiction. I. Title.

PS 3561.E3374 G6 2003
813'.54—dc21

2002038180

CIP

Printed in The United States of America

THE PERMANENT PRESS
4170 Noyac Road
Sag Harbor, NY 11963

I thank the many people who helped me - critics, sources and supporters - Dennis Adams, Rebecca Brown, Greg Forge, Sharon and Jim Langus, Neil McCluskey, Diane Norkool, Marty and Judith Shepard, Marlene Stone, Bruce Wexler, all of the Rosses, Figys, Dowlings, Hills, Cawleys, Nealeys, Shanti and Riley, my brothers, my parents who lived a long and loving marriage, and especially Carla and David who have been more than any father deserves.

The triggering event for this book is true. I lost the marriage with the woman who is the mother of our children, she found a wonderful and lasting relationship with another person, and we built a good divorce. The story and the characters, however, are fiction, what Ray Bradbury calls gentle lies wishing to be born, the imagining of how it could have been.

JEK

For Mom,

Betsy Ross Keegan, 1922-2003

Once the realization is accepted that even between the closest human beings infinite distances continue to exist, a wonderful living side by side can grow up, if they succeed in loving the distance between them which makes it possible for each to see the other whole against the sky.

Rainier Maria Rilke Letters (1910-1926)

1.

On Sunday, I drove home from the ocean, constipated, still holding onto the last meal I'd eaten before Jude broke the news. And I feared what she'd told the kids.

We'd met in a psychology class in our senior year at the University of Washington in the early sixties. I'd taken the course as a lark; she was minoring in psychology. The first time we walked over to the HUB after class I bought her coffee and the people in the next booth asked if we played bridge.

"Why not?" I said. It couldn't be any more perplexing than Jung.

With her textbook Goren and my cow town bluff, we had a little trouble communicating at first but Jude made a small slam in clubs and we won the first rubber. I was in heaven that spring. This sophisticated, big-city woman was interested in a kid who'd worked in the sugar beet plant and played basketball for the Quincy Jackrabbits. She thought there was something trustworthy about a man who grew up in a town with a grid street pattern and lived in a dormitory.

"We're going to have a big family," she'd told everyone when she found out she was pregnant.

When I reached the front door of our house on Broadway, I didn't know whether to knock or just go in. In the hope that our impasse was temporary, I slipped my key into the door and listened to the tumblers engage, all the while praying she hadn't changed the locks. Derek was on the floor petting Magpie, the kids' Labrador with dalmatian paws, and he looked up at me like I was an apparition. Jude had told them. A column of sunlight teeming with floating dust specks shone from the side window to Derek's rectangle on the rug.

"Hey, buddy, where is everyone?"

He stood up, out of respect it seemed, and brushed the dog hair off the front of his pants. Normally he would have given me a hug, but he seemed uncertain of the rules. "Mom's out in back."

I was still wearing the same clothes I'd left for work in on Friday, except that now the pants were creaseless and my wingtips were speckled with mud. I was grateful the kids hadn't seen me flattened against the sand in the rain like a page of newsprint. I'd promised to take them to the Bumbershoot Festival at the Seattle Center that weekend, and in my panic to get away it hadn't even occurred to me to bring them to the coast. Unconsciously, I'd already conceded them to Jude.

Derek drifted close and I gathered him in. He buried his head against me the way Magpie did when you snuggled her, and his knuckle-whitened hands clung to my jacket pockets. I had to concentrate to keep from crying.

"I better talk to your mom."

He let me go out the back door alone.

I'd replayed our last Friday together a thousand times. Everything had seemed normal enough. Jude skipped rope in the middle of the kitchen like a prizefighter while I ate my breakfast. She was training for a half-marathon and, after that, a triathalon.

"Thirty-four," whap, "thirty-five," whap, "thirty-six . . . . Can you take your nose out of that newspaper for half a minute?" Whap, step. Whap, step.

"Sorry. It's just that . . . ." I was two days behind in the newspapers and trying to finish Thursday's *Times* so that I could see the headlines of Friday's *Post-Intelligencer* before leaving for work. It was a game I played. Jude thought I was too linear.

"Just what?" Whap, step.

"It's hard to talk when you're jumping up and down like that." I found myself chewing toast to the rhythm of her jump rope. She was a metronome.

"I thought you wanted me to lose weight," she said.

"That's your mother."

"You said my butt was getting loose."

"I said I liked something to grab onto . . . I was just . . . it was a compliment." I sipped my Instant Breakfast to wash the crumbs down.

"You're just more subtle than my mother," she said. Whap, step. Whap, step.

I shook my head and folded up the paper. She once called me an emotional archive because I revealed nothing unless someone else looked it up. Here we were in the era of alternative lifestyles and movements—everyone wanted to go somewhere else other than

6

where they were, people were Moonies, Hare Krishnas, Zero Population Growthers—and her husband wasn't moving. Jude's movement was the liberation of women. She was passionate on the subject.

"Are you in the office this afternoon?" she said.

Jude thought men were so lucky. It didn't matter what they looked like, because they had the correct anatomical equipment. Two pregnancies had spread things around, but if you'd asked me that morning I'd have said she was still a turn-on. She was tall, with copper-colored hair that she used to blow dry when we were first married so that it crowded her face and framed her full rose lips. I could still remember the first time she let me hold the weight of her hair in my hand.

She did come by the office that afternoon. She never came to the office. She hated the extravagance of the marble, brass, and blown glass in the reception area. She'd had it with the haves. To her, the law had become the playground of the propertied classes, the aristocracy of orthodontia and uplift bras.

"I can't do it anymore, Cy." She was sitting in my grey overstuffed client chair when she announced it. "Our marriage has become a yoke I have to get off my back."

I fiddled aimlessly with my ballpoint pen. My throat was as stiff as the leather sandals in the back of my closet that I hadn't worn since law school. I'd need a shoehorn to force words through it. Her leaving was the implied threat of every argument we'd ever had. The prospect of divorce gave power to those encounters. "Why didn't you tell me this last night?"

"You don't like to talk about heavy stuff before going to sleep. Remember?"

She was right. I hated it when she unloaded on me at night and then, unburdened, fell fast asleep while I stared at the ceiling until I had to get up and read a book or do push-ups. "What about the kids?"

"I could use a break from them too."

"I meant, have you said anything to them?"

"Not yet."

When I reached the backyard, Jude was kneeling on the grass in her cutoffs, her back to me, stabbing the trowel into the flower beds,

7

pulling the weeds, then shaking the soil off the roots and tossing them into a cardboard box. My shadow reached her before I did. She turned, shading her eyes with a green-gloved hand.

"When did you get home?" She said it like it was still Friday and everything was going to be the same as always. Better. She was wearing one of my old dress shirts, with the sleeves rolled up and the shirttail tied around her middle. There were streaks of mud on the front and a dab like a cat's paw on her cheek.

"Just now," I said.

"Did the kids see you?"

"Derek. Justine must be in her room."

She motioned me closer. "I can't see you against the sun." I squatted on my haunches almost knee-to-knee with her and she lowered her hand. "It's been a little traumatic around here."

"You told the kids."

She puckered her lips. "Justine's in a big funk about it. She's hardly spoken to me since." She shook her head and studied me. "How are you doing with it?"

"Shitty."

"Me too." She reached out and I pinched a single finger through the glove. There were little plastic nubs on the material and I could feel the pad of her finger where a hole had worn through. I wanted to launch into the speech about how this was a good wake-up call, how it had forced me to do a lot of thinking about the changes I needed to make, about how I wanted her to forgive my obtuseness. All the stuff I'd imagined at the ocean.

"I missed you, Jude."

She lowered her head and let her hand fall away to her thigh. I couldn't see her eyes but there was a sadness in the slump of her shoulders and her green-gloved hand was limp. I felt stares in the back of my head and turned around to see Justine watching us from behind the curtain of her bedroom window upstairs. Derek, who must have been sitting on the sink, was watching from the downstairs kitchen window.

When Jude and I announced our engagement, people said it would be the perfect marriage. Our kids would be so smart. We'd breed perfect little Americans, future CEOs and mayors. The kids had turned out fine. Fortunately, neither of them had my big ears. Derek inherited Jude's copper coloring in his hair and his freckles.

Justine was darker-complexioned but she had her mother's flair for standing her ground. Both of them had a dash of my clumsiness and crowded teeth. But the bloodlines that coalesced in the offspring had coagulated in the parents.

I stayed for dinner, which consisted of grilled cheese sandwiches with tomato rice soup and potato chips. It was a solemn affair. Everyone seemed to be weighing their words, trying to deal with the reality of it but at the same time not wanting to set anyone off. Between comments, there was nothing but the crunching of potato chips, the chinking of spoons against the bowls, and the slurping of soup.

"Where are you going to live?" Justine asked.

"Probably at Warren's," I said, knowing that I hadn't even told my brother what had happened yet. As usual, Justine was ahead of me. The kids loved Warren.

After another long pause, Derek spoke. "If Dad's gone, who's going to make up bedtime stories about three-legged dogs?"

"You'll still see your dad," Jude said.

More spooning and slurping.

"Will we still be able to afford my braces?" Justine asked.

"I thought you didn't want braces," I said.

"Da-ad," she said, drawing out the word as if to underscore my thickheadedness.

Jude asked me to stay until the kids were in bed. We took turns tucking them in. I told Derek the thimble version of how Odysseus wandered around after the siege of Troy, escaping the one-eyed Cyclops and Circe, and finally returning to the kingdom of Ithaca and his faithful wife, Penelope. Justine, who we'd baptized along with Derek just in case heaven was really only open to Catholics, hated going to church, but she told me she'd been praying that her mom would change her mind about our marriage, a definite bright spot in the evening.

Jude poured us each a glass of Chardonnay and we sat at the kitchen table in the nook that was surrounded by single-pane windows on three sides. She took out a manilla folder labeled "Divorce from Cyrus" on the tab, and I was curious why she had added the "from Cyrus" part.

"I don't like this any more than you do," she said, "but we can't just leave everything up in the air. The kids are starting school in two days. I think we owe them some stability."

"Isn't it a little sudden?"

"It's not like this is the first time we've talked about it," she said, biting her lip, and then taking a sip of wine as if to wash something down. She put two fingers on the back of my hand and rubbed the veins that ran like catacombs between the wrist and the first set of knuckles.

"Nothing we do tonight has to be forever, right?"

She raised her glass and we clinked gently. "To an amicable . . . and provisional settlement."

We drank, each watching the other, and I was already missing those forthright, unblinking eyes.

"I have an attorney," she said, slipping it in quickly, the way a good dentist gives you the needle while you're finishing a sentence.

"Who?"

"Charles Johnson."

My wince had to be visible. This wasn't just a weekend whim. Divorces were all that Charlie did. He was a mercenary. Now that she'd mentioned him, I remembered her telling me that Charlie was also the divorce attorney for her friend Lill Epstein, the leader of the Sunday night women's group.

"He's just an advisor," she said. "I'd like the two of us to work things out by ourselves."

The subjects on the list she took out of the folder were so rudimentary they were frightening: Kids, Property, Support. Her organization was both impressive and out of character. When the phone company cut off our service and Jude swore they hadn't billed us, I found the unopened statement as a bookmark in the "Gutters and Downspouts" section of the Yellow Pages, which were under the magazines in the wicker basket by the downstairs toilet.

"Let's do Property," I said.

Jude pulled out some pages paper-clipped together that listed our assets and liabilities in two columns, hers and mine. The assets in her column included the checking account, the Smith Barney stocks, and the whole life insurance policy. In my column, she'd listed our savings account, the long-play record collection, the Raleigh ten-speed (which neither one of us had ridden since the gearshift turned to mush), the '73 Plymouth Fury (which needed a brake job and a replacement windshield), and a loan for three thousand five hundred dollars to Warren Stapleton.

"That's not an asset," I said, "he's my brother."

"You mean he's not good for it?"

"That's not the point."

"It was your idea to give it to him."

If Jude only knew how much we'd loaned Warren, she might have moved it to her column. He probably owed us three times what she showed. He needed "cold water" when he was in the Peace Corps to bribe the local police and bail out one of his friends. When he got back to the States, he needed his own bail for staging a one-man demonstration in the Spokane City Council chambers to protest the UN's support for baby formula. In the larger scheme of things, Warren was probably the most humanitarian investment we'd ever made.

I wasn't in the mood to haggle and pretty much went along with her list as well as the initialing of the furniture. The house wasn't in either column. It was assumed that I was the one moving out, and without the house it didn't make sense for me to have a lot of furniture. Jude had such a focused vision as to how life was going to unfold, for both of us. It was like we were getting ready to launch me into outer space and she didn't want to weigh me down with luxuries. I was numb when we moved to the subject of support and quickly agreed to an amount for the monthly payment. After all, this was at least for the benefit of the kids. The cynical side of me wanted to ask her what had happened to equal rights and women's lib, but deep inside I still wanted reconciliation. I couldn't say the division of assets and liabilities in a manner to benefit the wife was out of the ordinary, but it was traditional and, in that respect, unlike Jude.

When we turned to the issue of custody, I came out of my stupor. This mattered. "I'll take the kids."

"You're working full-time. How could you even consider it?"

"You work too," I said. "And they're in school. I could have a babysitter till I came home."

"You don't have a place."

"I thought you were feeling smothered by them. The yoke and all that."

"I know but I couldn't . . ."

"I wouldn't criticize you for it. We could lie to your mom and say they're still with you."

She sighed. "Oh, God, I dread telling her all this."

"I'm serious."

"I'm impressed you would offer."

"You think I'd screw it up and they'd wither from neglect, don't you?"

"It's just that you haven't had that much practice parenting."

"I feel like I'm breaking promises to them."

She studied me and I could tell that she was moved in a way that had seldom happened when we were plain husband and wife instead of putative plaintiff and defendant. "Let me talk to my lawyer," she said.

I grimaced openly. "Let's let the kids decide."

"Cyrus! Derek's eight, Justine's fifteen."

"They're smart kids. Why not?"

"Let's settle the dust first," she said. "Let them stay here until you get a place. Then we can do some visitation and see how it goes." For as much as she loathed the law, she had quickly become conversant in the jargon of domestic relations. Jude closed the folder and I felt a sense of triumph that we'd managed to get through round one of this more or less intact. It had been so long since we'd seen eye-to eye on anything.

"I better pack up a suitcase and call Warren," I said.

She looked over at the clock on the stove. It was eleven-thirty p.m. "Stay 'till the morning. It'll help the kids digest this better."

"Which couch?"

She laughed. "I don't think one more night in the same bed will kill us. Besides, I don't have any clean sheets."

When Jude and I announced we were going to get married, her family threw an engagement party in their Queen Anne mansion on Highland Drive. Mom made Dad buy a new blazer and slacks that he stained with grease from a Dag's Beefy Boy on the way to the Martins. Coming from Quincy, my parents had never been in a house with a dumbwaiter and an intercom. They tip-toed around the Martins' Mexican ceramics and South Pacific tribal masks like the house was a museum. All their prior doubts about my marrying a Seattle girl vanished once they saw Highland Drive. The Stapletons were commoners and the Martins were the Capulets. We'd been elevated and now, with the separation, they were going to be crushed.

Jude was curled around a pillow at her midsection with her face turned into the sheets when I turned off the light and felt my way to the waterbed. It sloshed when I got in despite my best efforts to be weightless. From the throbbing, I knew she was crying, and her tears smelled like the warm washcloth Mom used to hold against my forehead when I had a headache. I reached over and tried to work my fingers between hers but her fist was a Gordian knot.

When Justine was three weeks old and I could still feel the soft spot in her skull, Jude took her grocery shopping at University Village. We had one of those portable beds made of vinyl that folded up into a shoulder bag. The exterior sheathing was red, black, and navy blue plaid, and we took Justine everywhere in it. When they returned from shopping, Jude set Justine's bed next to the car in the parking lot behind our apartment while she unloaded. I was home studying for a Torts exam and Jude yelled at me to come down and help carry the groceries. As I came across the lot, a white Volvo station wagon that needed a wash was backing onto the plaid bed. I hollered and waved my arms, trying to get the attention of the driver. I couldn't believe that Jude had been so careless. The Volvo revved its engine to make it over the obstruction. I imagined Justine's skull being crushed like a cantaloupe. The driver stopped and rolled down the window to see what the matter was. Jude's face was red and sweaty as the two of us knelt down to extricate the port-a-bed from underneath the back of the car. There were dusty tire treads across one side of the crib and on Justine's blue-and-white checkered jumpsuit. The lady in the car was distraught, and Jude kept saying, "It's fine, it's fine." I ran into the apartment with Justine screaming in my arms and we tore off her clothes to feel her bones. I couldn't believe Jude had put her at such risk and I was shivering uncontrollably. There were blood blisters in a thick belt pattern around her waist where the tire had pinched against the diaper and cinched it like a noose, but she seemed to be whole and she was breathing. Both of us fell whimpering onto the bed and cradled her between us the way I wanted to cradle Jude now.

When I awoke during the night, Jude and I were intertwined between the sheets like seaweed. In a night that I knew could be our last, I patched as much surface area together as I could, bone against bone, skin against skin. In the stillness, I tried to memorize that feeling. She was as soft of body as she was hard in spirit and I wished into my wet pillow one more time that I could relive, no, remake this decade.

In the morning, there was light in the window and Jude was folding my clothes from the dresser into a suitcase at the foot of the bed.

Jude didn't want to be there when I left and asked if I'd stay until she and the kids had departed on the overnighter to Lopez Island that we'd promised and never gotten around to doing. The last grains of summer were dropping through the waist of the hourglass.

"It'll be better than seeing you drive off in a car to God knows where."

The kids weren't fooled and neither was I. As they traipsed down the stairway with their duffel bags bumping the walls, my Adam's apple burned and I didn't have enough saliva to douse it. The bravery in Derek's chin was betrayed by the trail of tears sneaking down his cheeks.

"Come on, Magpie."

Breaking the rule that said we were all supposed to act as if this would be better in the long run, I spoke up. "I don't like this."

Derek and Justine stopped. The dog looked up at me with her orphan brown eyes, begging me to throw my arms around the three of them and wrestle on the rug the way we used to after dinner.

"Come on, Derek," Justine said, "Mom's waiting." Jude had pulled the car out of the garage and parked across the street.

"I'm going to miss you," I said.

Justine hiked the bag strap up her shoulder and grabbed the Safeway sack on the couch with her hair dryer and bathroom stuff in it. I held the door and patted them helplessly as they passed. Neither one of them slowed down enough for a kiss. Derek's flashlight fell out of the pocket of his pack and the lens shattered when it hit the cement porch. I stuffed it back under the top flap next to a pair of rolled-up jeans.

"Good luck, Dad," he whispered. He was crying and when I hugged him to my stomach his bag clunked against me. I couldn't help but wonder how much this was going to cost them. And who was going to pay them back?

Justine disappeared down the steps to the street. I watched her, hoping she'd turn back to see me waving, but she plowed ahead, dragging her bag to the protection of her mom's fatherless car.

"Don't forget Odysseus," I told Derek.

He let go of me, descended the steps, looked both ways and ran across the street. Magpie fast-stepped beside him to keep up. When he slowed down, I could still see the hitch in his gait from an old bike wreck.

2.

The University of Washington campus was only a few blocks from Warren's apartment, and I walked over there with Warren some evenings. The boughs of the giant oak trees along the walkways had already shed their easy leaves. The tenacious ones hung on. I told him that I kept hoping Jude would relent, send me a longhand confessional letter or make a late-night phone call.

"She'll wake up in a cold sweat some morning," Warren said, "and realize that her sugar daddy is gone."

"I have the sinking feeling she won't miss me a bit."

"You gotta start dating. Get your mind off Jude."

Although I was only seven years older, it felt like Warren was another generation. I'd inherited our dad's fear of the Depression and wasted no time in moving from college to law school to my first job. By the time Jude and I had Justine, Warren was just starting high school and seemed in no particular hurry to get anywhere. He was less interested in school than in playing guitar and he put together Sergeant Warren's Lonely Hearts Club Band. "So I can speak to the world through my music," he said. Mom and Dad coaxed him into Spokane Falls Community College by promising that he didn't have to work as long as he stayed in school. That gave him time to write poetry that he published in Xeroxed magazines and mailed to coffee houses all over the country.

When he realized how unreceptive Spokane was to his politics and his music, he transferred to Western Washington in Bellingham where he eked out a degree in Humanities after five years. He spent summers in Seattle with me and Jude, living out of our basement, until he enrolled in the Peace Corps, where his flower-child ways hardened into a kind of anti-American missionary zeal during his two years in Turkey supervising the construction of public toilets. We kept up a steady correspondence in which he blamed the perpetuation of poverty in the third world on the United States. He thought we'd lost our way as a nation when we traded the farm for consumerism. We'd forgotten how to grow our own. Warren was skeptical of demagogues and subscribed to Lenny Bruce's philosophy that any man who called himself a religious leader and owned more than one suit was a hustler. Of feminism, he said, the women's movement had sold out for the worst features of masculinity.

I wasn't going to take Warren's advice. I was worried that dating would get in the way of a reconciliation with Jude, which was ironic considering all those times she'd turned her back on me in bed and I lay awake fantasizing how it would have been if I were only single. I'd also wondered whether her apparent indifference to me was because she was being unfaithful.

It was an argument over fidelity that had precipitated her first flight to Lill's. We hadn't seen each other for several evenings. Sunday was her women's group and Monday we traded cooking nights so she could go to the ACLU Board meeting. The next night she said she had to entertain someone from the national organization.

"A he or a she?" I asked.

"Does it really matter?"

I rested on the couch reading *Open Marriage* while I waited up for her. It was one of the books on the reading list Jude had made for me, which also included *The Female Eunuch*, *Fear of Flying*, and the *Whole Earth Catalog*. Reading about people who tried to make promiscuity sound like a spiritual quest and drew no distinction between social and sexual intercourse made me feel worse, but I knew the jealousy would cripple me if I didn't immunize myself against it. Open relationships were the natural evolution of the species, Jude had said. I could either join the survivors or become part of genetic history.

She seemed a little boozy when she came home. Her hair was mussed and she held her coat around her like she'd broken the zipper in her cords. Guilt was written all over her face.

"Kind of a late dinner, wasn't it?"

She hung her coat and fussed in the hall closet. "What's that supposed to mean?"

"I mean it's after midnight and I didn't know where you were."

She stepped into the room and planted her legs with her hands on her hips as if she were Annie Oakley. "You're wondering if I slept with him, aren't you?" I wished she'd moved away from the stairwell so the kids wouldn't hear us. "Why are you so paranoid? Men

17

think the only thing a woman's good for is what's between her legs." Her hair was throwing sparks as she moved toward me. "Well, fuck you all!"

"Is that your long-range plan?" It was mean, but I couldn't help it.

She towered over me on the couch so that I was looking straight at her zipper and she glared at the book in my hand. "Marriage doesn't mean you have to be Tweedledum and Tweedledee." Her breasts bounced under her shirt as she fired off rounds at me. Then she seemed to tire and sat down next to me; her voice changed. "I'm suffocating, Cyrus. We need a break from this."

Tiger Lill, as some of the women called her, was a refuge for frustrated wives, and Jude was one of her projects. But I didn't get it. What kind of an advance for humanity was this if the transformative action consisted of jettisoning your spouse? We'd had this discussion before too. Males didn't know how to bond; all they could do was pat asses and talk sports.

"How long are you going to be gone?"

"A week, maybe longer."

"What will we tell the kids?"

"Tell 'em their mom needs a vacation."

I'd suspected there was someone else—the unexplained extra dishes in the sink, the mysterious telephone calls she pulled into the hall closet to handle—I wasn't naive. By the seventies, who hadn't been cheated on? After Vietnam and Watergate, people were tired of loyalty to institutions. They wanted to break out, find their own space. Sociologists and psychotherapists had painted monogamous couples as slow-witted.

Maybe I was slow-witted. Maybe I should have taken my nose out of the newspapers. Jude would have said I'd become apathetic about our marriage the same way someone let their VW bus get out of tune, putting in more oil instead of getting a ring job, holding the license plates on with duct tape, letting the hinges rust. I'd settled for something that got us there, forsaking the quality of the ride, and ignoring the increased likelihood of total breakdown. But I didn't care as much where we were heading as who I was riding with. Jude desperately wanted me to cut loose of my forty-two long middle-class straightjacket and stop apologizing for the Jerry Falwells and Archie Bunkers of the world. "For a change," she said, "just screw what everyone else is doing."

She came back after two weeks. Warren was convinced she was sleeping around. I assumed that she was and resented her for it but, without proof, I was haunted with the possibility that she was innocent and I was the paranoid, cultural pygmy she'd accused me of being.

Two weeks after Jude's and my separation, I moved out of Warren's apartment and into a two-bedroom basement unit in the Alhambra Arms, a building which bore no more resemblance to Moorish architecture than it did to the Taj Mahal. Warren, dressed in a suit with a black shirt and Cuban heels for a party he was going to afterwards, helped me haul the stuff from the house, and I restrained myself from asking whether he'd bought his outfit with money from Mom and Dad. We siphoned the water out of the waterbed with the garden hose. Although the bed was Jude's idea, she was tired of it and gave it to me. A friend of Warren's had lent us his pickup and we loaded out the back door while Jude and another mother catered a birthday party for one of Derek's buddies in the dining room.

Moving out of your own house was the stuff of tragedies and I didn't particularly want the kids to witness it. Between loads, I'd sneak a look from the hall closet at the festivities in the dining room. It was a masquerade party and everyone had a mask, Jude's a Cinderella face that she pulled down each time she went in the dining room. Derek was Dick Nixon and made a peace sign each time one of the mothers brought them something. I was out of body, hovering, looking back on how they would live without me, and it hurt to see how smoothly things ran. The laughs were just as loud, the lights just as bright, and nobody seemed to notice me and Warren.

Jude and I pretty well avoided each other the night of the move. She'd scotch-taped tags to everything that was mine. I used a plastic drop cloth from the basement to cover the load and secured it with rocks from the flower beds between trips into the house. The wind whipped the plastic loose and impaled it on the antenna. It was just as well she hadn't given me any of the good furniture.

Warren's bachelor's program had included an introductory course in psychology. Whenever he could, he practiced on me. He called around and discovered that there was a men's therapy group

19

starting at Group Health. The first twelve sessions were covered by my medical plan.

"You've got to get in touch with your bitterness," he said. "Own it."

"If I'm neurotic, how does throwing me into a room full of other neurotics help?"

Raised Catholic, I considered confessions private affairs. But in the spirit of new beginnings, I told Warren I'd go once to try it. The sessions were held in a room at the hospital with nothing but couch pillows in a circle on the floor. I never would have imagined that Group Health had such non-medicinal-looking space. As men came in, they saw the sign by the door, took off their shoes, and sat silently on one of the pillows. Everyone was so serious. At five past, with one of the eight pillows still vacant, I knew someone had chickened out.

The guy in a black turtleneck and beaded necklace sitting in a lotus position opened the meeting. "Hello, everyone. I'm Rick." He looked around to make eye contact with each one of us. "I'm a sociologist and I'll be one of your facilitators along with my partner here, Tony." The man next to him nodded in recognition. "Men's groups are one of the most rewarding parts of my work. We see so many breakthroughs." As he looked around the circle again, I turned my gaze to my navel.

When it was Tony's turn to talk, he fidgeted and pulled at his collar like he craved a cigarette. His gray slacks had a small split in the crotch. He told us he was an M.D. and a psychiatrist. I could have killed Warren. He didn't tell me there'd be a shrink. I'd have to start checking "yes" on the forms that asked if I'd undergone psychiatric treatment.

"There's a tradition of men's groups," Rick said, "that goes back to the apostles." He rocked gently and extended his neck as if to stretch out his spinal cord. "Men's groups have existed in tribes and clans on all continents and in all cultures. The industrial revolution and single-family homes have isolated us from each other. We've forgotten how to talk man-to-man."

I didn't need this. As I looked around the room at the other blank faces, I could hardly imagine us sharing a last supper together. If this was men's answer to women's liberation, I felt sorry for us. Jude was right; men didn't know how to relate.

When Tony invited us to go around the room and share our reasons for joining the group, I felt panicky. I suspected I wasn't the only guy in the group to deal with a possible divorce. Big deal. I needed something more juicy.

The guy on Tony's left started and told us he was a data processor for an insurance company. He rubbed his hands over his sock to cover up the hole in the big toe. "I've been married for seven years. We've got two healthy kids, but" — he bent his toes back and his voice was weak — "we're having trouble in the bedroom."

"Down here you mean." Tony cupped his crotch.

"Yeah," the guy whispered.

"It's okay, man," the turtleneck sociologist said.

"Are you on any medications?" Tony said.

"Just aspirin for the headaches." His shame sapped the energy from his voice. "My wife has lost patience with me."

The beatnik with a pullover blouse and Jesus haircut went next. I figured him for a druggie, one Tony could fix with a prescription. "My problem is a little different," he said, in a cowboy twang, with a smirk on his face. "Fact is I don't think it's a problem at all but my woman does. She caught me diddling around on her." He looked around the room; his eyes were beautiful and unshielded. "Actually more'n once. She said she wouldn't care if it were strangers, but I diddled with a couple of her friends. I guess I'm the man who loves to fuck too much." The guy with the hole in his sock stole an admiring glance at him.

I was shocked at the candor. Men weren't supposed to talk like this. As people took turns around the circle, moving closer to me, I changed my story several times. It was the same feeling I used to get in gym when I had to play on the Skins basketball team. My chest never developed the mat of gorilla hair other guys had and I wasn't muscular. I needed to get mad at Jude but I kept thinking of the things I admired about her, how she laughed off scorn, how she treated the kids as adults, how she cut through the crap. I'd expected everyone to be more guarded and hypothetical, especially in the first session. I consoled myself in the fact that I didn't have to see these people again.

"I'm Cyrus and I think I'm getting divorced." I laughed nervously. I'd decided to forego the obligatory penis biography. Rick's was the only friendly face in the room. "My wife, or ex-wife . . . whatever, she's been a good mother and a good wife. We've had a pretty good marriage. Well, up until recently. Things have kind of tapered off." I realized I was running off at the mouth, going nowhere. "If you asked me why we're getting divorced, I couldn't really tell you for sure except that my wife's really gotten into the women's lib thing." It was the worst thing I could think of. When I looked around for some knowing smiles, it was as if I'd said something in Latin. "Women's groups, no bras, all that stuff. I'm not really complaining. I know a lot of it is overdue the way women have been walked on." I'd lost my train of thought, plugged into one of Jude's National Organization for Women tapes. I flashed on the time I gave Jude *"J" The Sensuous Woman*, mistakenly thinking that I was honoring her sexuality, and she ridiculed the butterfly flick. "Another male book on how to titillate the female doll," she'd said. I thought it might resurrect our sex life, but she said, "Good sex starts with what happens between breakfast and bedtime." I felt cheated. Just when I thought I'd overcome the guilt of a Catholic upbringing, a new movement came along that amounted to the same thing. Deny the flesh.

Rick brought me out of my trance. "So how does this make you feel?"

"Confused, I guess."

People laughed.

"How are the children handling it?" Tony asked.

"Fine, I think." I would have said more but nobody here seemed to be into kids.

"Thanks for joining the group," Rick said. I had the impression he was unconvinced I had anything big enough to bother with, that he was patronizing me.

The session lasted an hour and a half. An alcoholic dominated the discussion, and I couldn't imagine some woman staying around for this guy. The more he talked the more I thought it could work out between Jude and me. I'd never laid a hand on her. I'd never broken chairs against the door jamb. Maybe Jude was the one who needed the therapy, to rid herself of the notion that everyone who peed standing up was a Neanderthal. If she could only get a glimpse of this group, she'd grab onto me and never let go.

It was tempting to blame my predicament on the Sunday night meetings at Lill's when Jude came home supercharged with reformist ardor. Women had a way of reaching out and taking care

of each other while men egged each other on, always trying to compete. Men would rather have a good job than a good friend. At first
I'd thought I could get in on the new religion, but whenever I asked
her how the meetings went, she just talked about the problems everyone was having with their husbands. What emerged was a picture of
women continuing to live in the same house with husbands they'd
given up on emotionally. They were living with men they refused to
collaborate with. These weren't guys who were sleeping around;
they were just guys like me who didn't get it. For a while I figured
the women's group was a salutary thing. The more shit that other
husbands pulled, the better I looked, but that had turned out to be
wishful thinking.

On the way out of the therapy session, I ended up at the urinal
next to the diddling Jesus. "This Jude must be some package," he
said. Close up I noticed that his face was pockmarked and he looked
more like Judas Iscariot. He was doing it no hands with his pants
belted. I always unzipped, loosened my belt, and took it over the top
of my underpants. The public urinal was another test of manhood.
When he peered over the divider, I let go, a rebel gesture to show
Jude that she wasn't the only one who could ride the roller coaster,
scream on the steep drops, and go bug-eyed on the corners.
Somehow I was going to get even with her and Gloria Steinem.

The Alhambra was located near the Broadway District within a
triangle formed by the kids' schools and the house, as near the geo-
graphic center of Justine's and Derek's world as I could find. The
Safeway, Deluxe Bar & Grill, and Harvard Exit Theater provided all
of my basic needs. We'd shopped there as a family when Derek was
young enough to ride in the shopping cart with his bare legs hanging
out of the legholes. The Broadway District was a village where the
checkout clerks still chatted with the kids while they punched prices
into the cash register and emptied the buggy onto the counter.

I hated to be the one who had to move out. I loved the old place,
which was an oversized two-story house with an attic, a partially-
finished basement, and a long flight of painted red cement steps from
the street to the porch. The front lawn was so steep that I had to wear
my high school track shoes to push the mower back and forth. We'd
made the fourth bedroom upstairs into a family room and taped
blown-up photos of the kids and their finger paintings, and recycled

23

John Travolta and Shaun Cassidy posters to the veneer oak walls. Jude had said if she moved out, she wanted something in Madison Park, maybe the Edgewater. That would have meant more than twice the rent of the Alhambra. Since I paid the rent no matter who moved, I traded elegance for price, hoping it was only temporary. The Alhambra was also an opportunity to show Jude and the kids that our standard of living was going to take a nosedive with a divorce. No more Gloria Vanderbilt jeans for Justine.

I looked forward to the kids' first weekend with me since the separation and wanted the new apartment to feel like a home. We still hadn't settled temporary custody for the kids. Jude, or maybe it was her attorney, was dragging her feet. I figured I had no chance if it was left up to Jude and her attorney, so I was still lobbying for letting the kids decide. At neighborhood garage sales, I'd found a five-drawer unfinished dresser, a striped couch with a small tear across the back, and a barely dented chrome and vinyl kitchen table set. They'd finally see how the other half of the world lived, how you had to stack your clothesbasket on top of the washer to save your place in line, how you could listen to *Happy Days* through the ceiling without turning on your TV. They'd marvel at the dart holes in the walls, the iron burns on the linoleum drain board, and the warped ceiling tiles with broken corners from previous falls.

"Where is Derek going to sleep?" Justine asked, as she dropped her rainbow overnight bag onto the sagging single bed in the second bedroom. Seven years older than her little brother, she was used to getting her way. At school it was a different story, of course, where deference to peers and popularity were more important. Justine had a natural beauty like her mom's, with good lips and straw-blonde hair that she felt compelled to shampoo every morning. She wore risers to make her look taller.

"You're both in here," I said. "One of you can sleep on the cot until we get another bed. For tonight, you can sleep in the same bed."

"No way," Derek said. "I'm not sleeping with her. She kicks."

Justine bared her teeth like a mule. "I don't either."

"Maybe we need to take the tour one more time," I said, despite Jude's admonition that sarcasm wasn't a good teaching tool. "I only counted the master bedroom and this one."

"You don't need the biggest bedroom," Justine said, "with you and Mom splitting up."

"They might not," Derek said, his Nike athletic bag still on his shoulder. Magpie had parked herself at Derek's feet and was still panting with the excitement of a new set of smells.

Justine sat down on the bed, daring Derek to put his bag on it. She studied the watermarks on the wall where the moisture had flared into a series of rusty stains. "Well Mom's sure not going to live in this dump."

Derek peeked up at me through the reddish shock of hair that had fallen over his right eye to see what I was going to do. Despite Jude's work, he was pure boy, always getting into fights on the playground over yo-yo and spitting contests. A gang of kids had once jumped him for name-calling and banged his forehead against the sidewalk so hard they knocked him out. I knew that Justine's challenge was a defining moment for this new relationship and so did Derek. It was about time for a dose of the real me.

"Think about what you just said, Justine."

She rolled her eyes and folded her legs under her. "What?"

"Do you even remember what you said?"

"Dump," Derek said.

"I know," Justine said. "So?"

I was beginning to realize how much we'd spoiled them, with ski lessons, ski vacations, and their own record players. Of course, Jude had insisted that we gender cross-train them so Justine took drum lessons, Derek the violin, Justine weights, and Derek had a diary with a key. Inadvertently, we'd also taught them to argue in the voices of their mom and dad. "So how many apartments have you been in?" I said.

Justine started counting silently on her fingers as she gazed up at the ceiling. A sooty cobweb clung to the bouquet wallpaper in the corner. "Ugh!"

"She's changing the subject," Derek said.

"No I'm not," she said. "I've been in lots."

"Name them," Derek said.

"Derek," I said, and he sat down on his bag and put his chin in his hands.

I turned back to Justine, who sat stiff-spined. "Do you know that more people live in apartments than houses? Ninety-five percent of the children in the world would beg to live in a place half this nice. Hot and cold running water. Electricity at your fingertips. Paned glass windows. Insulation. Carpeted floors. Refrigeration."

"Do they all smell like burned toast?" she asked, wrinkling her nose.

"It's old eggs," Derek said.

"What are you talking about?" I breathed deeply but all I could smell was the mint of my Gleem toothpaste. "It just needs to be lived in. Brand new houses smell. The point is we have a roof over our heads. And we're together." Derek, chin still in his palms, watched me. "Besides, we don't have to spend all our time inside. There's a courtyard." The only people I'd seen in it were two elderly ladies with sun hats sharing a park bench in the shade.

"So where's Derek sleeping?" Justine asked.

"I think you mean, 'Boy, do Derek and I get this whole bedroom to ourselves?'"

She slumped and pushed her bag onto the floor, and it landed cleats down on the gray concrete floor like a tap dancer, startling Magpie. "Go ahead, Derek."

He leaped onto the bed, spread-eagled, trying to fill it with his eight-year-old frame. Magpie got up and put her head on the bed-spread, testing. Maybe she'd gotten lucky.

"Not so fast," I said. "We're going to learn to negotiate in this family." Contracting with your partner was another one of those feminist tools for demystifying marriage. Jude and I had attended a second wedding for one of the women in her group where they read a marriage contract out loud instead of vows. It covered everything from whether to have children to who does the dishes.

"But she said I could have it," Derek said.

"That was before she knew there was a choice," I said. "In bargaining, there are always choices." I wondered if they could hear Jude's voice.

"I'll sleep with Dad in the waterbed then," Derek said, rolling to the edge, draping one arm over Magpie's neck, and giving me those same beggar-dog eyes. The waterbed had always been clearly marked as the marital bed. No kids allowed.

The next thing Jude would have mentioned was boundaries. Everything had boundaries: people, the solar system, even ecstasy. She said that was one of my problems; my mother had never taught me any. I'd been fed, served, and applauded on demand. "My bed is out of bounds," I said.

26

"Then there aren't any choices," Justine said. "Dad, I'm fifteen. I have a boyfriend. I'm not going to sleep with my little brother."

She knew how to work me. I didn't want to hear boyfriend and sleeping in the same paragraph. It was a mistake to let her have a boyfriend at this age but Jude had insisted. "She can't learn to putty without a trowel," Jude said. So a pointy-headed kid who talked like he needed to blow his nose was her trowel. "You're right. Sleeping together is a bad idea."

When the negotiations ended, Derek had the first weekend on the living room couch in his sleeping bag and Magpie as a consolation prize. In a side deal, Justine secured permanent first rights to the shower in the morning in return for Derek getting his name ahead of hers on the mailbox. But Justine couldn't resist discounting the value of what she'd conceded. "Nobody's going to send you anything at your dad's apartment."

I'd underestimated the burden of raising kids. Jude was pregnant when we decided to get married or, rather, because Jude was pregnant we decided to get married. But if marriage was the moon to me, parenting was Mars. Jude always thought I was too passive and needed to get more involved with the kids. Whenever we had those discussions, it felt as if she was comparing me to my dad and I felt shamed.

Derek woke up with nightmares the first night and he and Magpie showed up in my bedroom. His pajamas were soaked with sweat so I hung them over the shower rod and made a mental note to move them before Justine got up. He changed into yesterday's underpants. As I spread out his sleeping bag at the foot of the bed, I noticed on the manufacturer's tag that it was designed for minus sixteen degrees. No wonder he thought dogs were chasing him around in a burning house.

I couldn't get back to sleep and wondered what Jude was doing on her weekend off. Nothing pleasant came to mind; distance seemed to spawn the worst possibilities. Maybe she'd looked up Jordan, my secretary's boyfriend, whom she'd met at the office picnic at Golden Gardens and surprised me by volunteering for volleyball.

Jordan's torso looked like it had been dipped in Coppertone and he wore a gold neck chain with a male symbol charm and three bulky class rings on his fingers. Jude played on Jordan's team. It wasn't really much of a team because Jordan spiked, scooped, or set every shot we sent over, giving his body to every point. When he dove for a sideline shot and dredged a scoop of sand into his sweatpants, somebody on the sidelines yelled to my secretary. "Is he that good in bed?" Everyone laughed while Jordan sucked his stomach in and reached into his crotch to shake the sand out. Milking the moment, he brushed sand down one leg and then the other. Someone whistled. When I looked through the webbing of the net, I saw that Jude was transfixed with a rapturous smile I hadn't seen since Derek was still in the cradle.

Sometimes I just didn't understand her. I thought she would have detested this highly competitive male with a bulge in his sweatpants. She'd always said that a woman's sexuality was more complex than a man's, that a woman's genitalia were connected to the heart, and men were wired from the penis to the ego. So why was she so fascinated with a guy who could grip his sweatpants between his buttock muscles and had a pouch in his crotch that looked like a sack lunch?

It wasn't that I was any better than Jordan. If Jude had ever stuck her arm down my golf bag, she'd have croaked. That's where I kept a water-stained *Sports Illustrated* swimsuit edition and an old *Playboy*. For emergencies. I could still conjure up the globe-faced girl paddling a canoe in *Sports Illustrated* that reminded me of Jude. Of course, Jude had convinced me there was nothing wrong with nudity *per se*. We had let the kids run through the sprinkler naked when they were little. Jude drilled a small hole and glued a cribbage peg into Derek's GI Joe doll to make him anatomically correct. Justine used to ask me male body questions while I shaved. For a while, Jude even did her jump roping in the raw. Her point was to take the titillation out of the human form. It was like seeing *Wizard of Oz* so many times that you lost your fear of witches. She said it would give us a jump start on the kids' sex education. Derek gained a reputation at day care with his penis questions. We used the correct names in our house; there were no "doodads" or "thingies."

"I didn't know you were such a volleyballer," I had said to Jude on the ride home from the office picnic.

Her head was forward as she brushed her hair from the back to the front, letting particles of sand sprinkle onto her purple cords. "What did you say?"

"I was glad to see you enjoying yourself."

She shook her hair and then picked at it. Somebody behind us blinked their headlights on and off to move me into the right lane. "Is

28

this about the jock?"

"Yeah, what did you think of him?"

She flipped her head back and started brushing it in the other direction. She turned the rearview mirror so that I could see her in it. She was now the car on my ass, but she was smiling. "The truth? I thought he was a hunk." I didn't know if she was serious or just trying to get a rise out of me, but it had the opposite result. Maybe the penis was connected to the ego. She put her hand on my thigh. "But I'd prefer a dollop of tenderness anytime."

The rattle of Magpie's dog tags startled me as Justine stumbled into the bedroom and tripped over her.

"What's the matter?"

"I felt scared."

I put out my arm, felt the flannel of her nightgown, and wrapped my hand around her legs.

"Be quiet you guys," Derek said. His voice was coming from somewhere under the bed.

"Shh," I said, putting my finger across my lips. It was pitch dark. The single window next to the ceiling looked into a corrugated metal window well. I had to turn on the overhead light in the middle of the day if I wanted to match a shirt and tie.

"Can I sleep with you guys?"

I remembered nights when Justine used to fuss because she was teething or had an earache, and she slept between me and Jude. She did kick in her sleep. They weren't so much kicks as territorial spreads. What her mother had taken two and a half years of Sunday night caucuses at Lill's to learn, Justine seemed to know instinctively. Claim a wide berth for yourself. "Sure, sleep here till you settle down," I said.

As she climbed onto the bed, I started dismantling the fortress of pillows and duffel bags that I had stacked around myself at night to reduce the vastness of sleeping alone. Justine kneed me in the ribs. We probably hadn't been in the same bed together for twelve years.

"Dad," she whispered, "I don't really think it's a dump."

I smiled in the dark and rejoiced at the thought that maybe the cross-training hadn't worked after all. She still had some little girl in her.

3.

The handball courts at the YMCA were on the top floor of a six-story brick building in the middle of downtown Seattle. In the freight elevator, on the way up, I leaned against the furniture pads that hung from cleats near the ceiling. Although this was the night of the big meeting at Jude's for the kids to decide who they were going to live with, I had my regular appointment with Warren to play handball first. It had taken some convincing—Jude's attorney was adamantly against it—but Jude had agreed. Now that we were doing it, I'd been haunted with the thought of how it was going to come out and wished we could just back up instead of going forward. If it had just been me and Jude that would have been one thing, but how could we justify screwing up the kids' lives, too? Didn't we at least have to gut it out until Derek was through high school? The washer and dryer Jude's parents gave us were going to last longer than our marriage. I realized I'd never really lost anything that mattered. This feeling of desperation was something new and made me feel more like an animal. I'd decided that Jude was trying to rip something off that wasn't just hers to take. I wanted the kids. Despite all evidence, I had the unwavering feeling that the kids would be better off with me. But Jude had said it herself. She wasn't just weary of our marriage, she was weary of motherhood. I was ready to compete for them. I missed them terribly. And, I hoped, it wasn't just to get back at her.

I could tell when the elevator had reached the floor with the handball courts because the air suddenly became cooler. Although it was only September, the winter rains had started and the weather had moved into that eternal limbo when clouds covered the city in a seamless dome. The elevator shuddered to a stop, bounced up and down, and the doors opened top and bottom like the jaws of a whale. I wished I'd worn sweatpants. It was too easy to pull a muscle when your legs were freezing. I heard the slap of a ball and someone bouncing off the back wall in what was supposed to be our court and peered through the napkin-sized pane in the door at Warren.

I stooped into the court. The white walls, ceiling, and floor gave it the feeling of an igloo that had been dabbed with skid marks. Warren wore black Converse hightops that were laced partway up, cutoffs, a tie-dyed T-shirt, and a red headband that made his hair stick up like a patch of weeds.

"Hey, where you been?" he said.

"Let's see, what have I done today? Lubed the car, earned a living, and called home to cover for my brother."

"How's Mom?"

I slammed the door and pushed the loop latch flush into its notch. "Worried about the divorce."

Warren clutched his heart in mocking agony. "Oh, poor little Cyrus."

I slugged him on the ball of his arm the way my older brother Carl used to do to me. I knew that Mom was still praying for the survival of the marriage and why shouldn't she? There had never been a divorce on her side of the family. Mom's parents had been married fifty-three years when her father died of a heart attack. From my current vantage point, such longevity was stunning. I had no idea what marriages that long were made of. What fresh idea could you bring home in the fifth decade that made up for what had to be flagging energy and emotional complacency? Did they last simply because the convergence of expectations and rewards occurred at a much lower level? Could Jude and I have made it if we'd been born before the Depression?

Warren shoved his hand down the inside of his cutoffs to adjust himself. "You need some handball to unwind."

When I reached down to touch my toes, my hamstrings felt like piano wire and the backs of my legs burned. "Ouch."

"You've got to start playing more. You move like you've got arthritis. You're an item on the market now." Warren's theory was that I was pent-up from sixteen years of monogamy and needed to mess around before I'd be ready to settle down again. Maybe he was just trying to joke me out of the whole thing. It's not that I didn't think of women I could call on in case Jude ever went through with her threat, but the list was short. Sonya Carpenter, who was a year ahead of me at Quincy High when we did *Carousel*, was on it. She was the first person I'd wanted to marry, a gentle Middle Eastern girl, with smooth, almond-colored skin and prominent cheek bones. After the cast party, we climbed the water tower together and I watched the moonlight bounce off her bare calves as she scrambled up the welded ladder ahead of me. But she was in love with the kid who played Billy Bigelow. The day I found out she'd broken up with Billy, I also learned she'd joined the Franciscan nunnery in La Crosse, Wisconsin. Many nights when things weren't going so well with Jude, I'd asked myself how things would have turned out with Sonya Carpenter, which was ludicrous given the fact that she'd chosen a cloister of nuns.

I spread my feet on the handball court, shifted my weight to the right, and sank into a fencing pose. My inside tendons felt like a weak seam in an old pair of pants. The thought of the upcoming meeting at Jude's had stiffened me. My brain and my muscles. Moving to the left, I stuck my arms out and rotated them to warm up the shoulder sockets. Handball was really armball and wristball; everything had to move like a whip. Warren threw the ball against the front wall and caught it on one bounce.

"Hey, come on, I'm freezing my buns off."

"Let me hit a few practice shots."

Warren dropped the ball on the floor next to me and I launched it against the front wall on the upward bounce. He stepped out of the way and let me dig it out of the corner. The ball stung through the leather gloves. I didn't play often enough to develop a callous and had to tape bunion pads over the bones in my palms. "Ready," I said.

"You serve," he said. "No candy ass. I want your best stuff."

When Warren was little, I babysat him. For some reason, Mom and Dad had waited a while after me and my older brother Carl. Maybe Warren was an accident. If so, he was a happy one. Carl was four years ahead of me and always ran with friends I didn't know. When I was getting out of grade school, Carl was already graduating from high school. When I made varsity football, Carl was already married with a kid. By the time I'd earned two letters, Carl had two kids. He was bogged down in night school and a day job to support his family while I was still figuring out how far I could go with a girl.

So Warren was my main brother. I paid attention to his life the way I'd wanted Dad to watch mine. Until I left Quincy, I went to Warren's Little League games and school carnivals. When I went away to the University of Washington, we corresponded. On long weekends and vacations, Mom would put him on the train to stay with me. I snuck him into R-rated movies, gave him sips of beer, and told him how babies were made. When Justine was born, he loved the idea of being an uncle and tried to make it to Seattle for all of her birthdays. Warren had come to me for the big decisions in his life — whether to leave Spokane, smoking dope, girls. I told him that joining the Peace Corps was procrastination and that he should get on with his life but he disregarded my advice.

"I'm not ready for nine-to-five," he'd said.

I'd created another welfare recipient.

What I liked most about Warren was the fact that he made me laugh. We shared the same sense of humor, wisecracks that sprang out of the moment, a neon sign with some of the letters burned out, word associations that ended in the absurd. Although he always got along with Jude and relished her irreverence, he was quick to take my side in the divorce.

I didn't have my heart in the handball, and Warren beat me two games out of three. I had about an hour before the meeting with the kids, and Warren chose McCormick's for his victory beer. McCormick's was a little pricey but the fact that I was now supporting two households was lost on Warren. The bar was decked out in dark mahogany, brass piping, and green linen curtains. There was a Wendell Wilkie for President sign and a moveable numbers calendar on the wall that said _152 Days Until St. Patrick's Day_. The floor was covered with the same miniature white, six-sided tiles that were in the courthouse lavatories. The place was full of guys who'd loosened their ties in hopes that the women had loosened their libidos. The roaming waitress brought Warren a Guinness and me a Coke.

"So how's it going, man?" He had to speak up to be heard over the smokey din. Some people would have said it didn't make sense to air out your lungs in the handball court and then bring them here.

"Ask me after the meeting." I tapped the ends of my fingers against each other and tried to push down the rising taste of acid in my throat that accompanied these kinds of events. "It's like a beautiful woman stepped out of the crowd and asked me to dance, and I had this fleeting moment. Then when I reached my hand out she walked right past and danced with the guy behind me."

"Lose the self-pity," Warren said. "It's a turn-off."

"The scary thing is the marriage with Jude was my best effort. I worked hard so she could stay home with the kids. I went along with all her movements." Warren rolled his eyes. "Now I'm starting to feel cheated. How can she live with me and the kids for sixteen years and then just say, excuse me, I'm supposed to be doing something else? What was wrong with my trying to be on top of things, to worry about money, to want a Sunday dinner once in a while with a tablecloth and candles?" I was beginning to feel heated and looked around to make sure no one was listening.

Warren pushed his glass against my knuckles, which were gripping the Coke.

I smiled and took another sip. The soda cut through the mucus in my throat. There was silence as we looked at each other. "Do you think someone can ever really fall in love all the way more than once?"

"What do you mean?"

"I mean make babies with them, pick out cemetery plots together."

"Once is a high number," he said.

"It's not me that changed."

"Isn't that her gripe?" Warren tapped the arm of a waitress as she swished by our table with a tray of empties and asked for two more. He ran his finger around the inside of his glass, then licked the foam off his finger. He tipped his glass up and let a single drop fall into his mouth. "I told you. You gotta' start going out. If you don't get the kids, it'll make it easier to date."

"What a depressing thought."

The waitress returned with Warren's Guinness and my Coke, announced the price, pursed her lips, and smiled. Her eyes were clear, probably the product of good vegetables, and her skin was creamy. Neither one of us reached for our wallet.

"Loser buys," Warren said.

"That was first round." I turned to the waitress and looked at her name tag. *Gwen.* She was blushing, and I couldn't stand to see her suffer. "I'll get it."

"Why would they choose you anyway?" Warren said.

"Excuse me," the waitress said.

"I meant my brother's kids."

"Oh."

"Hey, would you live with this man?"

"Ignore him," I said to the waitress.

"I'm serious," Warren said. "We need an unbiased opinion."

"I'd need more information," she said.

Warren shoved my ten dollar bill toward Gwen.

"You don't have to play this game," I said.

She looked at me as she asked Warren. "Is he rich?"

"He just tipped you six bucks. What do you think?"

Suddenly, something caught in my contact lens, which I only wore for sports because my astigmatism made them ineffective for reading. My right eye was watering up and I blinked to clear it. Gwen bit her lower lip and I thought for a second she was going to reach out and wipe my eyes.

"See, you're making him bawl," Warren said.

"He's probably married," she said.

"What was your clue?"

"I've never seen him in here before."

The contact lens attack subsided and my lid opened and closed again without raking the eyeball. I couldn't tell if Warren was selling me or himself but Gwen seemed to be handling it because her blush faded. She folded the ten in half and stuck it into a deep apron pocket. Hands went up around us as she headed back to the bar.

"What do you think the kids will really do?"

Warren ran a lime around the rim of his glass, tore the pulp off with his teeth, and puckered his face. "Justine's a lot like Jude. She'll want to negotiate a long-term, no-cut contract. When it comes to the voting, gender will prevail, though. She'll stay with Jude."

I snapped the fingernail of my thumb against the underside of the table. "But she and Jude fight all the time."

"She likes fighting. She's Jude's daughter."

"What about Derek?"

"Less predictable, but I think he'd die to be with his dad. No housecleaning, lots of fast food, playing football in the house, sloppy hours. Trouble is he's too much like you. He'll go where the women tell him to."

"God, you've become cynical."

"That's my point. This country's a jungle. Eat or be eaten."

"And I'm being eaten?"

"Big time. No kids, no property, all the bills. You'll need another job just to pay for the divorce."

Warren rambled on with advice to psych me up for the meeting.

The sweet little brother I used to meet at Union Station with Mom and Dad's hard blue Samsonite had suddenly become an expert on divorce. Although he was twenty-eight, he was still the baby in the family. He'd taken the apartment in the U District to keep alive Mom and Dad's impression that he was still in college. I could have sponged off him until he finished a Ph.D. and still not have evened things up between us. Of course, he wasn't going to school. He was arranging bouquets at Johnny's Flowers during the day and playing guitar or seeing his girlfriend Mandy in the evenings.

As Warren talked, I watched the flirtations around the room. There was a Scandinavian woman with soft blonde hair who looked like someone from a shampoo commercial sitting with a guy who stroked strands of his own hair between his thumb and index finger and then smelled his fingers. He looked like someone who would tie up schoolgirls in the basement and torture them with cigarette burns, but she gazed into his eyes with adoration.

As I looked around McCormick's, I felt small-town again and I missed Jude. I missed the patched jeans, the red hobo handkerchief, the scuffed oxfords, and the long-stemmed rose she'd tattooed on her midriff the week after I'd made her go to a firm dinner at the Rainier Club. I missed the looks on the faces of the guys waiting outside the Men's room at service stations when she'd emerge buckling her belt and chewing her toothpick. Jude was my middle finger to the world. I could depend on her to set down all the pretenders.

"I spent my childhood trying to shape myself into one of Mom's Jell-O molds," she'd told me. Now she was ready to take any train out. Trouble was, there was no room for me. I could only hope that her route was a big circle and the sooner she got on the sooner she'd come back and we could work out the details of a new beginning. I'd put her on that train so many times — when she started using her maiden name, when she ditched her ring, when we put Derek in day care so she could volunteer at the ACLU, when we divided cooking nights, when we fifty-fiftied the housecleaning. I always told her everything would be fine and waved until she was out of sight, but inside I was crushed because no matter how we dressed it up, it meant there was something in our life she wanted to get away from.

We were different from each other, yet I'd have fought anyone who said we didn't belong together. I was French's mustard on a bun with a frankfurter; Jude was Poupon and Gouda. My people wore boxer shorts and Weejun loafers; Jude's people wore lacquered-candy earrings, leather clogs, and muslin. Intimacy for Jude was a communal hot tub in the raw; for me, a crowded elevator sufficed. Jude was Voltaire and I was all the czars and dictators of the nineteenth century rolled into a three-piece suit. I was a bean counter, she was the visionary. I memorized the rules like they were the Baltimore Catechism and Jude ripped them up like nasty notes from a jealous friend. I was comfortable in the middle of the pack, and Jude itched for the last spot in the chain when they cracked the whip. I looked at civilization as a cumulative process where the children took the wisdom of their parents, polished it, added modestly to it, and then passed it on joyfully to their own children. "The smart ones," Jude said, "called their ancestors' bluff, tipped over the board, and started their own game."

She'd chosen a hard path for herself. As soon as she'd succeed at something she'd debunk it, saying it was because someone knew her parents, or because she was white, pretty, and harmless. She wanted to be accepted on terms that bore no resemblance to her upbringing. But it was difficult to be a rebel when you lived in a spacious home with a remodeled kitchen and had two small children and a husband who worked in a downtown high-rise.

When I drove up to the house, there was a white Corvette parked in front with a personalized license plate that said *DIVORCE*. I walked up the twenty concrete steps I'd swept and hosed down so many times and reassured myself again that I was smart to be representing myself despite the adage about the lawyer who represents himself having a fool for a client. I rang the doorbell and the familiar two-tone chime sounded. Jude had removed the paper insert in the door knocker that used to say "Stapletons." Male name dominance in the marriage name had bothered her as much as the missionary position. You could still see the scratch marks on the brass from the scissors or screwdriver she'd used to pry out the old label.

"It's Dad," Derek called out as soon as he cracked the door.

I stepped into the hallway and cupped Derek on the shoulder. Jude had cut off her hair; it was so short that it changed the shape of her face. She was drinking from one of the eggshell china cups that were part of the wedding set she'd mothballed in the basement cupboards. I could smell Paris Interlude, something else she'd mothballed.

Charlie Johnson was across the table from her. He'd already doffed his suitcoat and was serving shortbread cookies to the kids. What a fixer this guy was. I wanted to warn them not to touch the cookies. You'll choke on the strings he's tied to them. He was easily six feet four and had huge feet, which were housed in a pair of white bucks that I hadn't seen since Pat Boone. Jude had read me a magazine article once that said male shoe size corresponded with the length of a man's organ.

"Hi, Justine," I said, looking past Charlie.

She looked uncharacteristically self-conscious and I blamed it on the presence of Charlie. Then I realized it was probably her dress.

Jude had also dolled up, in a peasant dress with a laced cummerbund that showed off her figure and a bra that she must have also taken out of storage. "Cy, why don't you get a chair from the dining room?"

"I'll get it for you, Dad." Derek ran into the dining room and returned with a chair that he pushed into the back of my knees. I smelled a rat. They'd already talked it over and Derek was feeling sorry for me.

Jude smiled as I sat down next to her, and I wished again that I'd lobbied the kids when I had them alone, realizing now that they'd probably interpreted my silence as lack of interest. Did I really think that Charlie was going to let the kids decide this? He'd probably choreographed this whole meeting.

"We might as well get started," Charlie said. His eyes fluttered like he'd caught a stray crumb. He reminded me of someone about to do a card trick; no matter which card you picked he'd make it come out his way. Justine had scooted away from Charlie and she was tapping the insides of her shoes together. I'd taught her to take care of herself in Hearts by holding the Queen of Spades, the Dirty Dora, instead of passing it. That way you always knew where trouble was. "I'd like to give everyone an overview of why we're here," he said.

Cyrus, I said to myself, this house is still half yours and so are the kids. You can either sit here on your hands and let this man fancy you out of everything or you can stand up and let the kids know you care. I still wasn't sure why I'd gone into law. There was nothing to suggest that I'd be any good at it. Although I pulled decent grades in school, I was a social bumbler with ears larger than normal that I covered with long hair, an act which some people had confused with rebellion. In my third year of law school, I still blushed when the professor called on me. And, as Jude could verify, I could be cowed in an ordinary kitchen argument. "If you don't mind, Charlie, this is family business."

Derek, who seemed fascinated by the tall counselor in suspenders, jerked his head around in surprise. Justine grinned.

"I just wanted to make sure the kids understood the significance of what we're doing," Charlie said.

"You'd be insulting their intelligence."

"Cyrus," Jude said. "He was just trying to help."

"I think we can handle this without an outsider."

Charlie shot me a dirty look and leaned back into the couch.

If I'd picked up my saucer just then, the cup would have tapped out a tune, I was shaking so much. "I'd like to say something to the kids; then, Jude, you can too." Derek sat cross-legged on the floor like I was going to make up a bedtime story. Justine had finished her shortbread cookies and put her gum back in her mouth. "The hardest thing about the divorce"—I licked my lips and scratched my forehead to distract myself from the precipice I was on the edge of— "the hardest thing is to do this without hurting you two." Instead of looking at the kids, I fixed on Charlie's shoes. "When you get divorced, you have to divide things up, which is easy enough with the furniture. Like your mom might take this couch and maybe I'd take the recliner she never used." Derek chuckled and looked at Jude. "But how do you divide up you?" Derek tried to lighten things up by running a finger from his chin to his belt like an imaginary surgeon's knife. "You need to help us."

"You mean we have to either go with Mom or you?" Justine said.

"Well, that's about it," I said. "We can still work something out for weekends and vacations."

"What about Christmas?" Derek said. "There's only one Christmas."

"You can celebrate twice," Jude said.

"I have a friend," Justine said, "who lives with her mom and her older brother lives with her dad."

"Yeah, who wants me?" Derek said.

"Derek," Justine said, "just listen." She was starting to get serious the way she did when Derek wanted Burger King and she wanted pizza.

"I didn't think you and Derek would want to split up," Jude said.

"Maybe we need a divorce too," Derek said.

The adults laughed politely and shifted in their seats. Even Charlie loosened up at the prospect of another divorce.

"Who gets the house?" Justine asked.

I looked directly at Charlie, "That hasn't been decided yet." I didn't want the Alhambra to be the deciding factor.

"What about Magpie?" Derek asked.

"Don't be stupid," Justine said. "Mom and Dad don't want the dog. She stays with us."

"I have to add one legal point," Charlie said, scooting to the edge of the couch, letting his long arms hang over the coffee table. "The decision by the kids on custody is not binding on the court."

"Just a minute," I said.

"I'm not saying it's input the court won't seriously consider," Charlie said. He was scowling at me.

"I'll support the kids' decision," Jude said. "Right, Charlie?"

Justine stood up and slapped her skirt down where a fold had caught. "Derek and I need our own meeting. This is family business." I was reassured to hear her borrow one of my lines. While the bond between Jude and me had crumbled, the kids' bond with each other had strengthened. Publicly they still fought, but when worse came to worst, they were inseparable. Derek nodded his head and the two of them hurried up the stairs, already arguing with each other. Left in the living room, the rest of us twitched in place, trying to think of something neutral to say.

"The jury's out," Charlie said. "Are there any more of those shortbreads?"

"Sure, the package is in the kitchen," Jude said. "I've also got more coffee."

Charlie followed Jude. I knew he didn't want another shortbread; he wanted to corner Jude in the kitchen and get their signals straight. I guessed that if the kids decided to go with Jude, Charlie would call it a wrap and leave her with the whole package — kids, house, and all the fringe benefits. If the vote went haywire, he'd take it to court. I hoped the kids dropped the Dirty Dora on him.

"What happened to the cookies?" I said, when they returned

from the kitchen.

Charlie and Jude looked at each other and said "Oh" at the same time.

The fact that Jude seemed comfortable with this high-powered divorce lawyer shouldn't have been surprising. Unlike me, she came from a family of considerable public achievement. Her grandfather was a lawyer in Great Falls, Montana who was elected prosecuting attorney five times. Her dad was an investment banker who started work at six a.m. in their den so he could talk to people on the East Coast. He once chaired the Seattle Chamber of Commerce and I'd seen his picture on the wall with the past presidents of the Washington Athletic Club. Although Jude chafed at her family's wealth, she'd been carrying her own Visa card since she was in grade school. Her mother always chided her that she didn't have the drive of her older brother and needed to be realistic about college. "Keep your weight in check," her mother had warned her. "You won't win a man just because you have breasts." Jude always had something to prove.

Our fathers had one thing in common, though: they delegated child-rearing to the mothers. As manager of the Thriftway in Quincy, my dad had to open the doors and give cash to the checkers in the morning and count the take at night. When he took afternoons off, it was to golf for a quarter-a-hole with the owner. In the fall, they'd take a deer hunting trip. Once, they put their names in the draw and won goat hunting permits for the Blue Mountains. When Dad won a trip to Disneyland for the family through a wholesale grocery drawing, he cashed it in and bought a new Winchester rifle with a scope and leather carrying case.

Derek came downstairs with a list of questions in Justine's handwriting, some directed to Jude and some to me. We had to whisper our answers into his ear as he went back and forth across the room. Their questions covered the same areas that troubled me. Who would do the cooking? Would we always live at the Alhambra? Would I ever get married again? I didn't know if they considered remarriage a positive or a negative but I answered honestly. "I doubt it."

I'd never heard of kids going with their dad as long as their mother was alive and not incarcerated, but it felt good to be fighting for them. I wasn't going to be one of those fathers who goes out for a cigarette and never returns. They'd have a father whether I had a marriage or not. As I watched Jude whispering her answers to Derek, I was struck by the thought that she might be a better mother with me out of the way. Justine used to worry because she was developing slowly compared to her girl cousins. For her twelfth birthday, Jude bought her a bra with size C cups she'd have to grow into and made sure she opened it in front of her cousins. The fact that Justine was upstairs directing this investigation was due in no small measure to her mom.

I'd never understood, though, where Jude had developed her combativeness, growing up in a home with more than enough of everything to go around. I'd made the mistake when we married of paying too much attention to her parentage, assuming that the fruit didn't fall that far from the tree. I thought her parents' polished walnut table with leaves to seat ten would someday be ours and when the grandkids came over on holidays we'd set up the game table in the TV room. I pictured Jude patting me on the shoulder to hand me the carving knife and two-pronged fork the way her mother used to do. Jude'd ask me to say grace and I'd add something personal about each of the offspring. While she was doing the dishes, I'd put the table pads into the closet, walk the dog, and smoke a rum-soaked Crook. We'd have a big Liverpool rummy game afterwards and between games I'd find a bag of stale candy kisses and put a bowl at each end of the table like her father used to do.

If her father were alive, he'd blame me for the fact that our kids were upstairs deciding where they'd live. He'd remind me of what I'd said to him in their den when I pulled him aside and asked for Jude's hand. I'd done it that way because that's what I thought he'd probably done and I wanted him to know that I honored those same values. I told him I'd protect Jude and raise kids he'd be proud of.

But Jude didn't need my protection. We didn't have Sunday afternoon roast beef and mashed potato dinners. Every other Sunday was her day off from the kids and dinner was something frozen we ate off aluminum trays. The kids preferred the TV and cassette tapes to conversation. Jude's father would have asked me who was the head of this family anyway, and chased the divorce lawyer out of our living room.

We heard the kids whispering on their way down the stairs. They walked straight over to the coffee table. There was a sobriety about

42

them that made me think that neither Jude or I had passed their rigorous standards and they'd decided to live on their own. Derek stood behind Justine with his lips sealed the way I was sure she'd directed him. This was an announcement the oldest child had to make.

"We've made our decision," she said.

Everyone put down their cups. Charlie tucked in his shirt. Derek poked his sister, telling her to say it, and she brushed his hand away. Her face was grim. She was going to wait until she had everyone's attention. Her feet were together and she stood as prim and straight as the night she came out from behind the curtain in the Seward School gym and announced the name of the Christmas program, "Peace on Earth."

I could tell by the way she began, complimenting me in words that sounded like a Hallmark Father's Day card, how this was going to come out. Judges did the same thing at the end of a trial. Such praise meant one thing.

"We're going to live with Mom," she said.

The instant she said it a pestilence raced through me, weakening my limbs, muting my hearing. I'd never lost one this big. All my hopes of doing it better than my dad were obliterated. I'd been rejected. They apparently saw something safe in Jude they didn't see in me.

Derek started to cry and I wondered if this was really his choice or if Justine had leaned on him. There was so much unfinished business between us. I'd never taken him horseback riding or taught him how to handle a rifle. He always said he wanted to be a pitcher and begged me to teach him the knuckleball and I put him off, saying to wait until his arm matured. I knelt down and he rushed into my arms and squeezed me around the neck, smearing the side of my face with his tears. Through the blur, I watched Justine. She was trying to stand tall the way Jude had worked with her. I couldn't tell if she was still talking or not. I wanted her to let go and come to me. It's not your fault, Justine. I shouldn't have let you do this.

Out of respect, I suppose, Charlie picked up the dishes and disappeared into the kitchen. This was the end of the line, time for a transfer. Jude gave me a crestfallen look as she put her arm around Justine. She'd lost the guy who used to tickle her under the sheets and read Robert Frost to make her sleepy. But she had her kids.

4.

As I sped north up I-5, the wind rushing through the windows drowned out the Bob Dylan tape I'd turned to high volume. I changed lanes without signaling, passed randomly on the left and the right. Drivers blinked their lights at me. If someone boxed me in, I honked and gave them the finger as I passed. Between sixty and sixty-five, the Plymouth shimmied like it was going to throw a wheel. Over seventy, it smoothed out and the ashtray in the dash stopped vibrating. I stuck my head out the window like a dog, trying to open my eyes as far as I could, challenging the wind to rip them out. The air whipped across my face like a high-speed shoe rag taking tears with it. "God dammit!" I yelled in the general direction of Canada. My words probably didn't make it to the rearview mirror.

Past Marysville, traffic was scarce and I could drive any lane I wanted or straddle two of them. When I let go of the wheel, I could pound it with the palms of my hands or slap one hand on the outside of my door and the other one on the seat. "Damn, damn, damn!"

When I was six, Dad had taken my older brother Carl and me tobogganing at Mission Ridge. I remembered how the rain against the windshield had turned to applesauce when we exited the main highway and headed into the mountains. The petroleum smell from the grease Dad had wiped on his logging boots filled the inside of the car. We followed the tracks of another car that had climbed the same hill earlier, bouncing so hard in and out of ruts that I had to sit on the edge of my seat and grip my elbows over the front seat between Dad and Carl. When I told Dad I didn't think we'd make it, he cursed and whacked his hand against the dashboard so hard it made the radio stutter. Carl was ten and slapped the dash with him.

The snow kept falling, the windows fogged up, and we couldn't see the tracks of the other car anymore. The snow tires spun and the rear end fishtailed each time we came out of a turn. Dad started laughing and Carl copied him even though I knew he was as scared as I was. The engine raced and the tires whined like a wounded animal as we crept closer to the top of the rise. When we neared the summit, the car gained momentum as we flattened out and then plunged down again into a blizzard. Dad whooped and hollered and his eyes got bigger as he leaned into the wheel and let the car hurtle forward blindly. Carl pumped his shoulders up and down in rhythm as if to help us go faster.

The next thing I remembered was tumbling against the insides of the car like a tennis shoe in the clothes dryer. There were breaking glass and screams. Suddenly, the car stopped rolling and there was a pure, otherworldly silence. When I opened my eyes, I thought the dust from the seat cushions hovering in the air was the smoke of the afterlife.

I remembered Dad feeding Carl's limp body out the crumpled window opening. There was some shuffling outside, then both of them disappeared and I was alone. Dad had taken Carl and forgotten me. Maybe he thought I was dead. The only sound was the slow gurgle of gasoline like juice escaping from a thermos bottle. It seemed like hours before a state patrol officer arrived and pulled me out. I had to have my arm in a cast that Dad never got around to signing. Nor did he ever apologize for the wreck or explain why he took Carl out and never came back for me.

As I whistled past the sign to Mount Vernon, I decided I was hungry and found a place to make a U-turn in the median. I realized the highways were utterly unsafe if people could act like me, but I welcomed someone pulling me over just for the chance to bitch at them. Now I was sorry I hadn't yelled back at the house. Jude was right; I stored things up. That's probably what Dad had done that day. Mom probably made him take us out so we could use the toboggan they'd given us for Christmas.

In a mall near Bellingham, I bought rum-soaked cigars, a family-size bag of Doritos, squeeze cheese, and a jar of jalapeños that I could spread out on the newspaper in the passenger seat to make nachos. The liquor store had six-packs of airline cocktails and I picked out a pack of margaritas and another one of manhattans. I went back to the Deli for a bag of ice, scooped some off the top, and scattered it across the parking lot. One at a time, I separated the miniature cans from their plastic halter and buried them in the ice on the floor next to me. Then I was back on the road again.

My fear of arrest returned and I held the speedometer to five or six miles over the fifty-five-mile-per-hour limit as I sipped a drink and licked cheese off my fingers. I imagined that the jalapeños were neutralizing the alcohol as I plucked them whole from the stem and flicked the stems and empty cans out the window to destroy the evidence.

When I reached Blaine, the Canadian border, I turned around to avoid Customs and headed south. I finished the margaritas by Everett and opened my first manhattan. I kept thinking of those cultists in Guyana who'd put cyanide in their Kool-Aid and drank themselves to death. At least they weren't alone. Isolation was a form of execution. It shut down all the systems. Jude and the kids were my systems. They're what had justified the deal I'd made with the devil to work my guts out at the law firm. I couldn't imagine quite what the point would be of taking that next step in the morning if Jude and the kids would rather live without me. I felt cheated because the kids didn't even know who I was and now they never would. They'd interpreted my overtime at the office as disinterest. They saw only the remnants of my day, as I hurried to get out the door in the morning and stumbled home spent and grumpy in the evenings.

As I crossed the ship canal, the glow of downtown Seattle swayed and liquefied. The red aviation lights on the Queen Anne transmission towers shimmered like the prongs of an electrified pitchfork. I took the next exit and parked under the freeway where Boylston swerved to connect with Lakeview. Eight lanes of freeway were supported by rows of concrete cylindrical columns on a sloping hillside. The kids and I went down there once and found a camp where transients had left old blankets, cardboard mattresses, Thunderbird bottles, and burned cans with teeth marks on the rim where they'd been opened with wedge keys. We sat there and made up names for each other, pretending we'd just blown into town. Outlaws on the lam. I let them spit and cuss as we sat around a make-believe Sterno fire and cursed our fate. It was the right place for cursing, a kind of Hades where the living roared over your head on the way to ball games and operas, leaving leadened exhaust fumes behind.

I could feel the ground tremble as I unzipped and peed off some of the alcohol. The tires made a rhythmic bump as they sped over the steel expansion joint above me. An ambulance passed with its siren screaming, the beacon light momentarily flaring slices against the

46

high ends of the columns. I zipped up and found a flattened Kotex carton to sit on. Then I placed a dirty corduroy shirt with one arm chewed off and a garbage can lid into the circle to represent the kids. We were going to talk. One of them was going to tell me what went down in Justine's room, why they'd gone with their mom when she was the one who wanted to shitcan them.

I looked at the corduroy shirt. Derek just sat there staring between his knees. "Cat got your tongue?"

There was a manhattan in the pocket of my suitcoat and I popped it open. I didn't even like manhattans. They were Carl's drink. He made them by the pitcher when we went to his house. I could taste the maraschino and wondered why Carl had turned out so different, why he never seemed to mind how sporadic Dad was, why Dad was always his hero. He'd defended Dad's driving. "Anyone else would have gotten us killed," he said. "Dad saved your ass."

I turned to the galvanized garbage can lid with the flattened handle. "Just don't turn out prickly like your mother. You can be such a beauty. And don't be afraid to be wrong sometimes, huh?"

The empty can I threw at the column missed. Through the booziness and cigar nausea, I couldn't help thinking I was a failure. The kid who'd left Quincy to become a big-city lawyer and live in a larger house than his parents had flopped. My parents had hosted my college graduation party at the Grange. Mom's church friends put out trays of wrapped cold cuts, a variety of crackers, and warm miniature meatballs. The mayor and most of the City Council were there as well as some of my high school teachers. The police chief, whose house I'd painted one summer and whose kids were named Jake, Jack, and Jake Jr., made a toast with cheap champagne. "This young man'll graduate from law school and replace Scoop Jackson in the United States Senate," he said. What a joke. I couldn't even keep my marriage together. And worse, I'd turn out to be an absentee father.

It was still dark when I woke up the next morning, and I felt like a boneless chicken breast that had been splatted on a piece of wax paper and left on the drainboard. I was dehydrated and my head throbbed. As I folded a piece of toast around fried Spam with mayonnaise and grape jam to cut the grease, I realized that cooking was one of the reasons the kids had chosen Jude.

I welcomed the distraction of work that morning. The law didn't fuss over my desirability as a father or a husband. One of the senior partners at the firm had been hospitalized with a fluttering heart and I had to help out on his embezzlement case. They thought he might have had a mild stroke. Bob was my assigned mentor when I was an associate, the person who was supposed to mold and inspire me. We went to his house for dinner once and Jude thought he was a howling bore. He was so frugal that he'd shut his car off at red lights and only make long distance calls to his kids after ten p.m. When he got home, he'd shut off the engine, open the garage door, and push his car in the rest of the way by hand. After our dinner, I saw him take his empty milk glass to the kitchen tap, swish a mouthful of water around to get the residue off the sides, and drink it. Bob was the kind of citizen that gave Jude the shivers — Eagle Scout, Symphony Board of Trustees, and Treasurer of the King County Republicans. On the way home, she said, "He probably rinses out and reuses his condoms." We got the giggles.

The day Nixon resigned, Jude called me at the office to play a tape of his goodbye speech to the White House staff. She was giddy. Nixon's troubles had been better than a marriage counselor. After he fired Archibald Cox, even I got suspicious. Nixon had briefly made us allies. After the resignation, I traded my marble-brown plastic frames for gold wire rims and stopped parting my hair. One of my partners joked that I looked like Dagwood but Jude thought it was an encouraging sign.

Our office devoted an entire conference room and two paralegals to the embezzlement documents. One of my jobs was to distill the contents of the stacks of file cartons that circled the table into a persuasive legal brief. At breakfast and lunch meetings, I'd go over testimony with nervous witnesses. Worrying about the embezzlement trial and the kids, my own heart was beginning to flutter.

On the way to work, I'd drive by the house to see what time Jude left in the morning, see if she was taking the kids to school, count the heads in the kitchen nook, see what kind of choice the kids had made. I'd call at odd times during the day and hang up if Jude answered. I was desperate for a scintilla of evidence to prove that they missed me as much as I missed them.

At night, I'd wait until dark and park several houses away, trying to find out if she'd gone out and left the kids alone or invited a strange man to the house. I wrote down the license numbers of cars parked near the house so that I could track them down later through the State Patrol. I slouched in the seat to make my car look unoccupied.

One night after I'd worked late someone in a black VW bug parked in front just as I turned onto the street, walked up the stairs in a hurry, and disappeared into the house before I could get a good look. A light went off in the kitchen and then someone pulled the drapes in the living room. Finally, there was a fly in the trap.

I took the keys from the ignition, got out of the car and closed the door quietly. There was no alley so I figured the best way to approach was from the Sweets' house next door. The Sweets' children had grown up and moved out but Mrs. Sweet still baked cookies and strudel that she shared with us. Every Saturday, Mr. Sweet mowed and edged his lawn, swept the walks and stretched the hose down to the street to wash his car. They loved our kids and sometimes took them to church. We'd stopped organized religion when Bobby Kennedy was assassinated.

I took the Sweets' walkway, which was leafless and clean as washed stones. It rose five or six steps, then ramped parallel to the slope, where there was another set of steps, then a switchback, and finally I was at the top. The grass was damp and slippery under my wingtips as I moved across the lawn toward the flower beds and fence that divided our lots. My shoes sunk into the softness of the peaty soil in the planter strip. Mr. Sweet used to always lean over the fence while I was working on one of the kid's bicycles and volunteer lawn and garden tips. He was a strong advocate of steer manure and turned truckloads of the putrid stuff into his beds every year. That's why his roses exploded and ours looked like stillborn boutonnieres.

I tip-toed along the fence, checking the Sweets' windows for any sign of movement. Their bedroom faced our house and they had a good view into our backyard from the window where their corpulent Siamese cat used to sit. When I stepped onto the lower cross board and lifted my leg over the fence, the pickets stabbed me in the butt. I didn't want to rip my suit but I couldn't touch ground on the other side and tried to estimate the distance. In Quincy, Patty Petty's dad had caught me and Strawberry Nelson in the same position the night we tried to spy on her. When he flipped on the floodlight, he had us sighted between the barrels of a twelve-gauge shotgun.

I finally leapt as high as I could, trying to create enough arc to clear the pickets. Magpie barked from the back bedroom upstairs and I flattened myself against the side of the house. No lights came on. I was at the back wall of the house, just under the kitchen sink, and with my left hand I could feel the outdoor faucet. I reached for the windowsill and, with one foot on the pipe, pulled myself up to look into the kitchen. The stove light illuminated spilled Cheerios and dirty aluminum trays on the counter. I could hear Jude laughing. Maybe she and her caller were having a drink in the dining room to loosen things up. Jude kept a bottle of Stolichnaya in the freezer, something she said her grandma used to do, so she could drink it straight up in a martini glass without ice. The alcohol kept it from freezing, one more of Jude's little secrets that she could now share with the male universe.

I tried to guess who was making her laugh. I would have said Charlie Johnson, except he'd never be caught in a VW. Or maybe she'd followed up on the volleyball player. He'd drive a bug; he loved to cram himself into things that were too tight. More likely it was one of her ACLU friends, who all drove old VWs and Datsuns as a matter of principle.

This was perverse. Jude and I were finished. What was the point of catching her balling some guy? It would disintegrate whatever residue of affection remained between us. Graphic evidence was unforgettable. But if I caught her, I could end this sickening, lingering fascination. Maybe I could make a case for having the kids if their mother was neglecting them in favor of a parade of tomcats sneaking into the house. You were who you slept with.

I lowered myself to the patio. My arms were shaking and there were grooves where the edges of the brick windowsill had dug into my skin. I brushed the grit off the front of me, wondering if I'd have to take the suit to the dry cleaners. Avoiding the rake, wagon, and planter boxes on the patio, I crept along the back of the house. The bottom of the dining room curtain had caught against one of Jude's cactus plants on the sill and left a triangular opening through which I could see two people at the table. They were engaged in an animated discussion, the kind that good first impressions are made of. The only light was the glow from the kitchen so I couldn't make out their faces.

When I reached the street, I tried the door to the VW and it was open. The hedge across the top of the retaining wall hid me from the house. The driver's seat was in a forward position and I had to work to get my knees under the steering column. I could smell the plastic straw in the seat protector and a faint orange blossom perfume. Behind the laminated holder attached to the visor there were some papers that I slid out, looking for the registration. Instead, I found an envelope with phone numbers and dollar calculations on the back. It was addressed to Lillian Epstein.

5.

I went to the Deluxe Bar & Grill for dinner and took a table near the back that had enough light to write by. One of the Group Health therapists had suggested I start keeping a journal to get in touch with myself. I couldn't stand to be home alone anyway. It didn't matter whether I talked to anyone. The clatter of dishes and scraping chairs were company enough. Monday night football played on the TV over the mirror behind the bar.

Jude and I had met once in a noisy tavern like this in Wallace, Idaho when a friend and I were driving home from a spring break ski trip in Kalispell. My friend's girlfriend and Jude had taken the train and we'd agreed to meet at the biggest tavern that had the word silver in the title. In its glory days, Wallace had some of the most productive mines in the west and the most notorious whorehouses. When we walked into the Silver Bucket in our ski parkas, the girls were sitting there in skirts. "You sure look good with color in your face," Jude had said. I don't think she ever blinked that night as we drank pitchers of Pabst Blue Ribbon and she stroked the hair on my arms. On the way back to Quincy, my friend drove while Jude and I necked in the backseat. We were a little tipsy and massaged each other's ears with hand lotion in lieu of other pleasures.

A waitress with dark rings around her eyes, hollowed from lack of sleep, brought my open-face Deluxe steak sandwich. It was medium rare, with juice dripping into the toast, surrounded by thick, hand-made fries. She plunked a bottle of ketchup and A-1 sauce on the table and left. Jude would have gone ballistic; she said I should cut down on red meat and the fries were poison. I wasn't all that hungry and turned the plate the long way to make room for my journal. All I could see was the grease.

I couldn't stop thinking of the kids, how when I came home from school at their age my mom was there. I didn't even own a house key because the door was always unlocked. There was always stuff in the refrigerator to make snacks with. Mom would often have something baked cooling on the breadboard. She'd ask how school went and, if

I was going over to someone's house, what time I'd be home. She always knew where I was.

I tried chewing the matching squares of steak and toast that I'd cut, but the meat was gristly and made my jaw tired so I spit it onto my fork and put it back on the plate. I wrote down things I could do to make up for the black hole I'd created in the kids' lives. More live theater instead of movies, after-dinner conversation, chamber music concerts at Kane Hall instead of the moronic jabber of their rock radio stations. I'd get Justine into girls' soccer. It wasn't too early to have a sex talk with Derek. When I'd filled two pages, I read it over and titled it "The Impossible Dream." How was I going to remake their lives on two weekends a month?

"Writing the great American novel?" someone said.

I looked up and flipped the cover of the tablet closed. It was Lill Epstein. The last thing I wanted was to have my journal entries the subject of next week's women's group. "How are you?"

She nodded at my plate. "Starving for some red meat." I would have expected that she lived off of roots and earth worms. From what Jude had told me, I would have guessed that the only meat in her diet was male testicle.

"Care to join me?" I said, to be polite, while my thumb pushed the chewed remnant of gristle under the fries.

She brightened, actually projecting some inner warmth. "I'd love to. We're practically neighbors, you know." From Jude's Sunday night tales, I'd come to think of Lill as someone in a cloud of steam with fangs and a hook nose. The real Lill was nice-looking, not someone who'd have trouble getting a man. Her hair was the color of fresh rust and her green eyes had a melted quality. The gold cap on one of her incisors gave her a savvy look. We only knew each other from the times she'd come by to take Jude to a women's poetry reading and we'd sit nervously at the dining room table trying to talk about nothing while Jude brushed her teeth or changed. Jude told me that Lill had enlarged her breasts. She'd also told me that Lill and her husband had engaged in some *ménage à trois* before their divorce. The women's group was apparently a way for Lill to dry out sexually. "I live in the Buckley, just down the street from you," she said, her tongue teasing against her upper lip.

Her energy had momentarily shocked me out of my depression but I had my guard up. This small talk was for a purpose. "I thought you had a house."

"Sold it."

I could see the wheels turning. Wouldn't Jude just love to hear how her ex is doing? There was this woe-is-me game that we'd ended up playing, each one of us trying to appear more financially impoverished but emotionally richer than the other. "Let me get you a chair," I said, reaching for the empty one at the table next to us. Here I was practicing chivalry with one of Jude's fellow travelers.

She pulled a tight-fitting brown cowhide jacket off her shoulders. Apparently, animal rights wasn't one of her movements. Without a bra, it was no trick to see the shape of her breast implants through the denim shirt. She hung the jacket on her chair, brushed the hair over her shoulders, and sat down.

"This is a surprise," I said.

"Me being here, or me sitting down with you?" Here came the questions.

"Come on, Lill, when's the last time we were even in the same room together?"

She threw her head back when she laughed and jiggled her hair. "I guess we weren't exactly Sonny and Cher."

Not so fast, I thought. How could she be so facile? "What brings you here?"

"The clatter," she smiled, "and the margaritas."

"I didn't picture you as a festive drinker."

"I like the salt," she said, circling her tongue around the rim of her lips. "How did you picture me?"

I laughed half-heartedly, but better we talk about her than me. "The truth? I'd pictured you into something more husky. Jack Daniels on the rocks. Somebody who likes to kick ass."

She challenged me with her gaze. "A ball buster."

"Amen."

The waitress put down a second place setting for her and asked for her order.

"Give me a Black Label on the rocks," she said, and winked at me. "I didn't want to disappoint you."

"You need a menu?" the waitress said.

"How about a baked potato with cheese and bacon."

The waitress shrugged and left.

"I hope you don't mind the company," Lill said.

"I guess we're all social animals, huh?"

"At least animals," she said, throwing her hair back again. "I'm just kidding. I find it easy to slip into dogma."

"To each his own."

"It can get in the way," she said, letting some wistfulness into her voice. "What's yours, Cyrus?"

"My what?"

"Your dogma," she said.

"Wow. Couldn't we start off with my favorite music or read any good books lately?"

"I'm sorry. Seen any good movies?"

We both laughed.

When her drink came, I ordered a margarita, choosing to blame my last hangover on the manhattans. And then we each had another. This time we clinked our glasses, toasted to dogma, and laughed again. I told her things had been going just great, how the time alone had given me a chance to reflect. The way she watched my eyes, I don't think she was fooled by any of it. Neither one of us had mentioned the only thing that connected us.

"I had a shitty marriage," she said. I glanced around to make sure nobody was listening but we had the privacy of noise. "I could have handled the fact that he didn't do a damned thing around the house. But he stopped talking to me."

I was tempted to ask her whose idea it was to do the *ménage à trois*. "What do you mean?"

"He was inscrutable." She made fists against her chest. "I never knew what he felt . . . or whether. About anything."

"Don't you think he was frustrated by it too?"

"Hah!" She raised the bottom of her empty glass an inch off the table and gaveled it down. "He loved it."

We had our last drink together at the Alhambra. It happened spontaneously as we were walking home. Lill said she'd considered taking a place there herself but had never seen the units so I invited her in for a look. I put on a Simon and Garfunkel tape. The only liquor I had was Scotch so we drank it straight over ice. She took off her shoes and sat cross-legged on the couch, facing me. She said she couldn't see my face in the lamplight so I reached around and turned it off, leaving just the afterglow from the kitchen light. She tilted her head and looked at me with those soft green eyes.

"How are you really?" she said.

It was the question I most didn't want to answer, but the way she said it, devoid of any hint of personal advantage, something gushed inside me like a river suddenly freed of its banks. I covered my face and started crying. I could feel her hands petting my head. The jetsam and flotsam of my marriage rushed through me — pieces of furniture that our parents had given us, bedspreads and pillows with lipstick and drool marks, wooden pull toys with bells and popping balls, *Saturday Evening Posts*, Dr. Suess books, Jude's jump rope. Justine's and Derek's heads were bobbing and sinking, arms waving, with screams on their faces that I couldn't hear over the roar, and Jude was in a dead man's float, face down, beyond my reach. "I'm sorry, Lill."

"That's all right. We all have to blow it out once in a while."

I sniffled and tried to find my handkerchief but I must have left it in my coat. "Wow, where did that come from?"

She raised up on her knees and pulled a Kleenex out of her front pocket. "Something I said?"

I smiled. "As a matter of fact, yeah." My voice was nasal from the swelling of the passages.

She scooted over and put her arms around me. I let my head fall against her. I couldn't remember helplessness feeling so good. The smell of leather from her jacket mixed with the orange blossom in her hair that veiled my face. She painted brushstrokes with her fingers against the back of my neck and I closed my eyes and collapsed into her. Nerve endings were apparently indifferent to ideologies.

When I lifted my head to look at her, she kissed me on the mouth. I slid my hand between her and the couch and pulled us closer together. She rose up on her knees and pushed the weight of her body against me. I tried to move sideways to her but she kept pushing me backward until my head was against the arm of the couch. We scooted down until my head was on the cushions and she flattened herself against me like she was riding a surfboard. Our belt buckles caught against each other as she wriggled between my legs. Her breasts were firm, independent of each other.

She pushed me deeper into the cushions as I tried to reconstruct the events of our evening together, searching for any moral turpitude on my part. I felt contrite because she was Jude's friend, but I couldn't help but want more of her. I cupped her buttocks and encouraged each thrust as they stiffened on the advance and softened on the retreat. I spread my legs and hooked my heels behind her knees. Her breath was coming in shorter and shorter strokes. Jude had always said that males had no corner on sexuality. Some women were so carnal they could fantasize to multiple orgasm. The knock-out orgasm. *Status orgasmus.* I slid my hands up her back, which was warm and sticky.

"No!" She pushed my hands down, but her grinding continued unabated. "We can't."

"But we are."

"We can't . . . do it . . . on Jude." Her voice was strained.

I didn't know if she came or she repented but she finally stopped pushing and fell limp against me, nestling her head under my chin. Simon and Garfunkel harmonized about the bridge over troubled waters. I listened to the sink in the kitchen dripping and waited until her heartbeat slowed.

"Are you okay?"

"I guess I have a soft spot for men who cry," she said. "I'm sorry."

"There's nothing to be sorry about."

"Don't tell Jude."

"We never took our clothes off, right?"

"You must be Catholic," she said, raising up on her forearms against my chest. I expected her to be smiling, but she wasn't. "You're still married, you know. You felt nice."

"Jude and I are separated."

"I know, but it still feels like you're hers." Using her hands to brace against my thighs, she pushed herself up and rested on the back of her heels. Her hair looked wind-blown. She unstuck the front of her shirt from her chest and looked at my crotch. "Not so dogmatic, huh?"

At the door, she hesitated and I hoped she would say something about getting together again. I could see my silhouette in her iris. "I'm sorry to barge in on you like this."

"I could have said no."

Once the door slammed shut, I pressed my forehead and nose against it, and that's when the remorse flooded me. It wasn't for the fact she was Jude's friend: people fell in love with friends of friends all the time, that's who they knew. Jude would probably have done the same thing to me. Her next husband, the stepfather to my kids, would probably be someone we went to school with. I regretted that we'd gone as far as we had. I'd probably already blown it with Lill. She'd peg me as just another guy who wanted to get his hands on her breasts.

The dryer was spinning in the laundry room next to my apartment, with the random clicks of zippers and snaps hitting the sides of the tumbler. Did everyone in this apartment have to do their laundry in the middle of the night? I thought. Were we that far out of sync with each other? I kept thinking of Lill and wondering if it was really Lill I wanted. I turned the tape over, twisted the volume up to cover the sound of the dryer, and hummed along with Simon and Garfunkel.

6.

Jude had the kids for Christmas and I drove home to Quincy with Warren. It was raining in Snoqualmie Pass and I tried to imagine that the raindrops hitting the windshield were snowflakes. The wipers stroked the blur like oars in the water, shuddering on the backstroke.

"Hey," Warren said, "quit moping. Look how great it will be to sit on our butts and watch football without Jude making us help with dinner."

At home, everyone avoided the subject of the pending divorce. Jude's name was never uttered by Mom, Dad, Carl, his wife, or any of their kids. They even tiptoed into conversations involving Justine and Derek for fear that those would lead back to Jude.

"Think of this as a sort of reverse canonization process," Warren said when we were alone. "They're taking her off the pedestal."

"But they don't have to pretend she doesn't exist."

"It's the Stapleton way of grieving."

When I woke up the first morning in Quincy, I was disoriented without the background hum of the freeway. It was the first time I'd been home since the separation and everything in the house reminded me of something I'd done there with Jude and the kids. I mentioned at breakfast how the Plymouth was starting to burn oil, and Dad told me to bring the car into the garage. Warren rode with me on the trip up the driveway as Dad gave us hand signals, cutting us off as soon as the hood was all the way inside.

"What weight oil you using?"

"Beats me."

"You don't know what oil you're burning?"

Warren looked at me, hopeful that I'd come up with a better answer. "I take it to a garage."

"Have you checked the gaps?" I wanted to say what gaps. I hated internal combustion engines. I also hated pheasant hunting, cleaning the leaves out of rain gutters, and diagnosing problems with the toaster, all activities that Dad excelled at. He'd rebuilt several car engines before he was old enough to vote. "Pop the hood."

He flung an extension cord over the rafters, plugged it into the socket above the workbench, and pulled a trouble light down into the engine hole. He pulled the wires off the tops of the sparkplugs and started unscrewing them with a socket wrench. Warren turned over a mop bucket and stood on it so he could get a good view. "When's the last time you had it tuned?"

"In the spring." I was guessing. If he'd asked me the last movie I'd seen, I could have told him who directed, who starred, and maybe who did the screenplay. I didn't watch the mechanics at the garage work. When something acted up, they fixed it and I forgot about it. The only thing on the invoice that interested me was the size of the bill.

"These things are shot," he said, holding the bottom of a dirty plug next to the light. "Look at the buildup." He flicked his thumbnail against the bent prong at the end of the plug. "I just hope you take better care of your clients than you do your car."

"They're why I don't have time to worry about crap like this."

He pulled his head out from under the hood and scowled. "What kind of uppity attitude is that?" He jabbed his greasy finger in the air at me. "Your brother's got an office job but he sure as hell knows what the butt end of a plug's supposed to look like."

He'd done it again. "Dad, don't fix my car. Can you please just put it back the way you found it?"

"Why don't you, hotshot?" he said, dropping the plug in the approximate location of the hole he'd screwed it out of. The sparkplug bounced off the motor, ricocheted against the fan blades, and fell to the cement. Then he stormed out the side door, slamming it behind him.

Without saying a word, Warren climbed off his bucket and dove under the car, reappearing with the sparkplug cradled in both hands like precious metal. "Carl may know how to fix cars, but I bet he can't throw a hanging slider to save his soul. Lighten up, Cy. You make too easy a target for him."

"That's your secret?"

"I use the rope-a-dope. Wear him down from swinging. Once he mellows out, he's a puppy."

The kids and I celebrated Christmas later in the week back in

Seattle. We had two days and one night together. Instead of Quincy snowdrifts, we had puddles that spanned whole intersections where drains had plugged from the downpour. The same haze that hid the sun rising over the Cascades hid it when it set over the Olympics. I'd bought one of those painted silver trees and put it on a card table in the corner of the living room. It was small enough to cover with a single string of lights and a box of red bulbs. The only original element was at the top, where I mounted a stuffed dog that looked like Magpie. It didn't take long for the three of us to open the presents. Derek gave me a Dog Calendar with big stars drawn in for everyone's birthday, including Jude's. Justine bought me a *Lawyer Joke Book* with her own inscription. *Dad, you always said to be prepared for the worst. I thought you better know what they're saying about you.*

I gave them the choice of where they wanted to go for Christmas dinner and they chose the Food Circus at Seattle Center. We walked around the grounds before eating, inspecting the amusement rides that had been dismantled and covered with canvas tarps. Through a fence littered at its base with leaves and candy bar wrappers we studied the rust on the roller coaster rails and dreamed of times past. The booths in the arcade were boarded up, padlocked, and spray-painted with graffiti. A lone American flag drooped from the forest of poles at the flag pavilion. The musical fountain was dry and silent. Derek circled the booths in the Food Circus twice before choosing strawberry waffles and hot chocolate. Justine bought a hickory smoked hot dog and spaghetti which she couldn't finish. Because it was Christmas dinner, I saved her the lecture.

When we got home, we turned the lights on and sat around our stubby little silver tree and talked. Derek told me how Jude dropped him off so early at Seward that he'd started helping Buster, the janitor, until the other kids showed up. Buster had an office in his broom closet where he kept baseball gum for kids who were good. Derek was shooting for the whole American League.

"We sweep the halls in formation, like the Blue Angels."

Justine, on the other hand, hated the early dropoffs. She refused to show up at Garfield until there was a crowd. The ideal was to get to your locker just in time to pick up a book and slide into homeroom while the bell was still ringing. The slightest hint of overpreparedness was poison. High schoolers didn't come from homes; they materialized out of the fog around eight every morning and vaporized again when they wandered to the edge of the school grounds in the late afternoon. I suggested she have Jude drop her at the Seven-Eleven so she could read magazines until it was time for school.

"I'd feel stupid not buying anything. Besides, the manager of the store gives me the creeps."

"Find a friend, then."

"None live close by. And the rain would mess up my hair."

"Carry an umbrella."

She rolled her eyes. "Umbrellas are dorky."

She wanted me to flounder in her helplessness. "You're right, there's no way out."

The kids each had a key to Jude's house and walked home from school on their own. Derek wore his on a neck-chain along with a quarter that had a bullet hole I'd made while target-shooting at the Quincy dump. Derek had spotted it when I was looking for a football needle in the top drawer of my desk and liked the idea that his dad knew how to shoot a rifle.

For old time's sake, I told Derek I'd do a bedtime story. Justine must have heard us because she wandered out to the living room and perched herself on the couch at the foot of his sleeping bag. We agreed to a chain story.

"Something scary," Derek said.

"I can't think of anything that would scare an eight-year-old." The idea was to pretend that the story had really happened and it was just a matter of recall. I lay down on the couch and scooted Derek over far enough so I could have a piece of his pillow. We were head-to-head and I could feel his feet squirming through the bag. "Okay, I remember one," I said. Justine tucked her arms into the sleeves of her nightgown. "When I was little, I had to walk a couple of miles to school. The only way to get there was to pass through Innis Glen. It was the richest neighborhood in town."

"Like Innis Arden," Justine said. She was on to my technique; I'd have to win her over with credible details. "All the houses were mansions that sat behind iron gates with huge sweeping driveways and everyone had chauffeurs and gardeners. You never saw the owners because they traveled in the backseats of long black limousines with shades pulled down over the windows." Derek rubbed his hands together in anticipation. "You know those trees the Sweets have in their backyard?"

"Weeping willows."

"The street where I passed was lined with them, so many that it was always dark. They had to keep the streetlights on during the day." Justine caught my eye and smirked. I reached up and turned off the three-way bulb in the lamp. Derek pulled the sleeping bag up around his chin. "Well, one day when I came by, a kid jumped out from behind a tree with a big stick in his hand. It was the kid I hated most in the whole school. Big Ricky." Derek snapped his head to look me in the eye. His current nemesis was Ricky Sampson, the kid who'd rubbed snot on Buster's baseball cards. "Okay, Justine, you tell us what happened next."

"Does it have to be Ricky?" she said.

"That's who it was," I said.

"Okay, okay. Let's see." She closed her fists and massaged her jaws. "It scared Dad so much he almost wet his pants right there under the willow trees."

Derek giggled.

"Ricky slapped his stick against the trunk of the tree and said, 'I told you not to come through here!' His voice was gruff. He had a big cut on his forehead from a fight he'd been in that day. The blood from the cut had dried up and caked on his face."

"Ugh," Derek said.

"'Why are you coming to school so early?' Ricky said to Dad." Justine had come a long way since the last time we did this. She wasn't going to pass up the chance to get her licks in. "'Only the dinks come early enough to suck up to the teachers.' Ricky whacked his stick against the tree again and the streetlights flickered out. Your turn, Derek."

"No!"

"You can do it," I said softly.

He crammed his eyes shut. "When Ricky looked up to see what happened to the streetlights, Dad ducked into a driveway where someone had left their gate open. Ricky started yelling, 'I'm going to kill you, Stapleton.'" I couldn't help but laugh, and Derek frowned at me. "Dad had one trick that Ricky didn't know about. His uncle was a ventriloquist and he'd taught Dad to throw his voice." Derek cupped his hands, "'I'm over here, you little twerp!'" I guessed that Derek had softened the language for my benefit. "Ricky heard Dad's voice coming out of the hedge across the street and picked up a rock and heaved it at the hedge but it missed and landed on the sidewalk. 'I'm going to bash your brains in, Stapleton!' When Dad heard Ricky whacking his stick against the hedge, he ducked back out of the driveway and ran faster than he'd ever run in his life until he was clear to the other end of the Glen."

"That was good," I said.

"Shh, I'm not done." Derek sat up in his sleeping bag. "When Ricky swung into the hedge, he hit a hornet's nest and a thousand bees came swarming out. Ricky took off down the street with the bees buzz-bombing him. By the time he got to school, Ricky's face was so swollen he looked like Frankenstein. And he never bothered Dad again for the rest of his life."

"Wow," I said.

"I knew Derek would get you out of it," Justine said. "He thinks you can do anything."

I tucked the kids in, turned the hall lights off, and went to my room. When I climbed into bed, the water in the mattress moved like a tidal wave to the other side, bounced off the sideboard, and returned to jostle me. Up, pause, down, pause. Each wave more gentle than the last one. I'd bought the waterbed to show Jude I wasn't such a tight-ass. She thought everyone in big law firms golfed at Broadmoor and slept in a four-poster.

Someday Derek would know the truth about his dad. How he'd kept his waterbed but couldn't keep his wife.

I took the kids to Jude's the next afternoon so they could go ice-skating with friends at the arena. On the way back to the Alhambra, before the postpartum depression set in, I drove by Lill's apartment, a mid-rise with dark brick and a wrought iron gate next to the entryway that opened into a courtyard. On the second pass, I drove to the end of the block and parked. I could taste the squirts of adrenalin beginning to irrigate the inside of my mouth, a flavor remarkably similar to the ginger of Lill's tongue.

The heat of my breath turned to steam as I walked back to her building, stepped into the alcove, and searched for her name next to the intercom. What if she walked out the door just then? Should I lie and say I was looking for someone else? "Epstein, L." was on the fourth floor. My finger circled the rim of her button. She'd probably seen Jude since our evening together and I wondered how much Lill had told her. The sun must have set while I stood there with my finger poised over her buzzer because the alcove and garden lights came on simultaneously. They say you can tell a lot about a person from the way they keep their house. I pictured Lill's furniture draped with the skirts, blouses, and lingerie she stripped off as she returned from her library job.

I backed out onto the sidewalk and looked up to see if I could see her apartment. We hadn't talked about other relationships; maybe she had a harem of guys like me. I crossed the street to get a better angle of the two units on her floor with lights on and watched for someone to walk in front of one of the windows. Nothing.

I returned to the entryway and pushed the buzzer. If it was ringing, I couldn't hear it so I pushed it again and held it for a two-count. I stared at the intercom speaker. Say something to me, Lill. There's no reason we can't just be friends. We can keep the lights bright. I'm not ready for anything serious either. Jude doesn't have to know. I swallowed my juices and took a deep breath.

One more short buzz. No answer.

I got back into the car and debated whether to go home and read *Looking for Mr. Goodbar* or go to Warren's. I decided I didn't have the energy for Warren.

There was a sign taped to my door that said the furnace was out and heat would be restored tomorrow. It was clammy in the apartment and I opened the oven door and turned it to about two hundred and fifty. President Carter had called the energy crisis the moral equivalent of war but I figured I had some heat coming; I hadn't baked anything since I moved in. I'd resume the war when the furnace was fixed.

I'd let the food supply dwindle. There wasn't even any tomato paste to make a pasta sauce with. I found some freezer-burned burritos under the ice cube trays and put them in the oven. I'd make the British thermal units work twice.

While I was changing clothes and putting on wool socks, ski pants, and my bathrobe, Warren called. I warned him there was no heat and no food but he wanted to come anyway. I turned on the tube and half-watched *M*A*S*H* while I opened junk mail and bills and ate my burritos.

Warren sounded like a man being chased when he answered on the intercom. He blew through the door to my apartment without knocking. "Jesus, it's freezing in here."

"Depends if you're dressed for it," I said.

He looked me up and down while he zipped his warm-up jacket to his chin and hugged himself. "You look terrible. Like some shut-in. Are you still going to therapy?"

"Yeah, do you want something to drink?"

"Jesus, we should have met in a food locker. What do you have?"

"There's a Zinfandel open in the cupboard. If you want something warmer, pour a couple of brandies and I'll get you another coat."

When I returned with an overcoat and a scarf, Warren was holding up two socks that were as stiff as fan blades. "What in hell are these?"

I laughed. "That's my laundry. I sometimes do my socks and underwear with the dishes. They must have frozen."

"You wash your underwear with your plates?"

"I do the plates first."

He grabbed the glasses off the table with two fingers of brandy in each. "Here."

We clinked our glasses and downed them.

"What kind of stuff are you doing in therapy?"

"A little of everything, even bioenergetics."

Warren set his glass down and stepped into the middle of the living room with his hands on his hips, leaning backwards. "Come on, men, make your body into a bow," he said, doing a pretty good imitation of the Group Health therapist. "Like you're trying to shoot an arrow right out of your navel. Come on, boys, arch it." He thrust his pubes.

"You got it."

"Give in to the shaking, boys. Tremble with me." And he was.

"I didn't know you knew this stuff."

Warren bent over and let his arms droop like an ape. "Let go now. Open your orifices."

The truth was the bioenergetics had made it easier to talk in the group. Maybe it was my conditioning through team sports. The closest I'd ever felt to other men were those times in the huddle between

66

plays when everyone was panting and bumping shoulder pads and we'd slap each other on the butt as we broke. "We're also doing psychodrama."

Warren popped up and ruffled his hair. Then he ran around the apartment until he found a dishtowel and stuffed it under his shirt to make breasts. He came at me with his hands on his hips and his eyes squinting. "Come on, Cyrus," he said in a falsetto voice. "You think your law job is a meal ticket? I'm supposed to punch your ticket and feed you? I've got news, Bub."

There was a creepy resemblance.

7.

On my twelfth birthday, Dad took his dinner hour from the Thriftway to celebrate with us at home. I remembered him grabbing my new Louisville Slugger bat and Mickey Mantle baseball and taking us to the backyard. He pushed aside a wheelbarrow full of potted plants, pulled a loose shingle off the eave of the garage, and stepped it into the grass.

"This is home plate!" he said, shoving me into the batter's box. Then he paced off to the edge of the holly bushes and spit on the grass to mark the pitcher's mound. I stood there with the bat on my shoulder while Dad loosened his tie and rolled up his pitching sleeve. The first one came at me sidearm.

Slam! The ball exploded into the chalky white siding of the garage behind me and bounced back to Dad. Hidden like a double exposure in the reflection of the garage against the dining room window, I could see Mom and Warren watching us. This was another one of Dad's games where no one explained the rules and there were no practices.

"What's the matter?" he asked, rubbing his palms into the ball.

"I don't . . ."

Slam! The ball crashed into the garage again, this time ricocheting off my leg. I wanted to join the audience and eat Mom's angel food cake with orange frosting.

"One more chance," he said, squinting at an imaginary spot somewhere in the strike zone.

I readjusted my grip on the bat, remembering how you were supposed to line up the knuckles, and looked down to see where my feet were in relation to the shingle.

Slam! The ball flew by before I had a chance to look up.

"You're out!" Dad said gleefully as he walked toward the plate. I didn't know if he was going to start telling stories about his old high school baseball team or slam me into the garage. "See this?" Dad held the ball so close to my face the strings were blurry. "This is life! You stand flat-footed with the bat on your shoulder, it'll go right by."

At twelve, I'd already heard most of his platitudes. The guy who sits on his butt draws flies. Sheep are for eating. Most of them relied on a single theme: do something even if it's wrong. I stared at Dad's eyes, which were dry as marbles, and tried to invent a winning excuse. "I'm only swinging at strikes."

Dad grabbed the bat like he wanted his ups and carried it into the house. He had to go back to work and the rest of us ate angel food cake without him.

Because Justine was at a girlfriend's slumber party, it was just me, Derek, and Magpie at the Alhambra on the last Friday in January. I was beginning to worry that Derek was living under too much female influence, that he'd be the only feminist in his class. I didn't want him to relive the embarrassment he'd felt the day Jude let him wear one of Justine's culottes to school. Derek had gotten into a fight over it in the boy's restroom and needed stitches where someone had pushed his chin against the radiator. I concocted opportunities to let him be a man. At dinner, we agreed to trade places. That meant he had to cook dinner, which consisted of wieners sticky with age that he sliced into the Kraft macaroni and cheese mix.

"Well, son," Derek said in his deepest voice, when we'd sat down to eat, "how are things at the office?"

"Do we always have to talk about the office?"

Derek stabbed two slices of wiener with his fork and looked at me sternly. "Maybe you can explain that last report your boss sent home. That sure wasn't a Stapleton report."

"Geez, my boss has it out for me."

Derek pointed his fork at me and furrowed his brow. "I don't care if your boss is Dracula, I want an explanation."

I wondered if I should play around his question or give him a real answer. "I guess I've been upset by things at home," I said. "My wife and I have separated, you know. It's been hard on us. Most of all, I'm worried about the kids."

He let go of his fake frown and looked down at his plate, where he was pushing a lone piece of macaroni around like it was a shopping cart in the Safeway parking lot. I'd miscalculated.

"You want me to be the kid again, don't you?"

"If it's causing so much trouble"—his voice was on the verge of breaking—"why don't you and Mom get back together?"

I suddenly felt vastly underequipped. Derek stuffed his palms into his eye sockets to stop the tears, his fork pointed aimlessly into the air. With his older sister gone, he could be an eight-year-old again. When I scooted my chair over next to his, he broke into a sob and I pulled him against me. His head was hot against my face. He tried to set his fork next to his plate but it teetered over the edge and fell to the floor.

"I miss Mom when I'm with you."

I patted him on the back, "I miss her too."

He looked up at me, trying his hardest to be big in his rainbow Mork suspenders. His face was puffy and his temples were wet where he'd smeared the tears. "Then when I'm with her, I miss you."

The every-other-weekend-dad thing wasn't working. We had no time to settle in. I was trying to entertain them instead of father them. Anything serious that happened after getting them on Friday night had to be finished by Sunday afternoon when I dropped them at Jude's. I couldn't leave any rough edges that would pique Jude's disapproval.

For an after-dinner treat, Derek and I roasted marshmallows over the oven element. Because I didn't have graham crackers to make s'mores the way you're supposed to, we squeezed the marshmallows and Hershey squares between saltines.

I washed the dishes while Derek went into the living room to do his arithmetic. He'd asked if he could have *Mork and Mindy* on low in the background to keep him company and I let him. As I studied the soup and spaghetti stains on the wall over the sink, I replayed my conversation with him and realized that what satisfied the guys in the men's group wasn't solid enough yet for an eight-year-old.

When I'd called Mom and Dad to tell them about the separation, Mom said it would break the kids' hearts. Dad said he didn't want to tell me what to do and then told me about the friend from high school he'd played baseball with, whose oldest had hanged himself with an extension cord from the banister after their divorce.

Derek had put the burner on too high and the macaroni and cheese had stuck to the inside of the saucepan like crustaceans. I had to scrape it with a table knife to reach metal. For some reason, it made me think of Jude's fantasy of us living in a commune so we could share cooking and child care with other adults. One night we'd actually gone to a planning meeting with friends of hers from the

ACLU. The woman of one of the volunteer attorneys nursed her six-month-old while we talked. When her little girl tired and dropped off, her mother just left her breast hanging out. The executive director rolled a couple of joints and passed them around. Everyone else in the room was convinced of the merits of the enterprise. It felt like they wanted to get me stoned so I'd relent. The director's voice strained as he held onto his hit.

"There comes a time when you have to stop bullshitting yourself," he said.

What a joke. These people didn't have two thousand dollars between them for a down payment. I was their capitalist. The lotus-eaters wanted to parade around in the nude at our little commune in the Elysian Fields and live off my dime. The grass made me anxious and I pictured these two bearded guys hitting on Jude. Share and share alike. I could see them stoned in the garden while I ferried back and forth to the office. At the firm, I was considered liberal because I'd questioned Ford's pardon of Nixon. This group made me feel like J. Edgar Hoover.

Jude could be funny when she got high. She did a parody that night of the executive director arguing in favor of mandatory school uniforms, turning him into Dr. Strangelove. Even the pompous executive director laughed. But her levity turned to vinegar on the way home.

"For once," she said, "consider the possibility that you don't have all the answers."

"I didn't say I had all the answers, I just don't see how a commune is going to solve our problems. I'll have to be away even more. Or doesn't that matter?"

"You had your mind made up before we set foot in that house."

"Not true."

"I could see it in your body language. You didn't uncross your arms the whole night. You practically stabbed my boss with your glares."

"Come on, the guy's a little arrogant, Jude."

"He's brilliant."

"Like tinsel."

"You're jealous."

"I just can't picture myself eating breakfast, lunch, and dinner with him, that's all. Okay, I thought his wife was nice. A little

71

mousy, but nice."

"I thought you liked mousy women."

"Jesus, Jude."

"I noticed you enjoyed the young mom."

"I wasn't supposed to notice her bare breasts? She practically invited us to take turns on her."

"Your fantasy."

"Oh, come on, isn't that what communes are all about?"

"I'm interested in a shared-living arrangement. You're the one that keeps calling it a commune. I want someone to help with the kids."

"Isn't that what I'm for?"

"I mean someone who's available."

"I think the kids are an excuse."

"For what?"

"I don't know."

And I still didn't. My memory had become manic-depressive. I tended to romanticize the good moments and embitter the bad ones. The only accuracy was probably in the emotional punch they still carried. Despite our best intentions, our discussions had often deteriorated into spit and scratch free-for-alls. But the fights made it easier to justify the fact that I was in the Alhambra trying to carve scraps of burnt macaroni into the dishwater and Jude was somewhere else. I decided to let the pan soak and joined Derek in the living room.

"Let's do something outside," I said.

Magpie had wedged herself against Derek and fallen asleep. "It's almost over," he said. *Mork and Mindy* was on Jude's approved list because the characters' sexes were indeterminate. *Laverne and Shirley*, *Maude*, and *The Bionic Woman* were also okay. Shows with traditional families like *The Waltons* were suspect.

"I thought you were doing arithmetic."

He rushed to open the book that was turned pages-down on the floor. Magpie lifted her head to see if what was going on involved her. "It's almost done."

"The show or the math?"

"Both."

A single spotlight lit the green park bench in the center of the courtyard, and four gravel pathways extended like spokes from the bench to the corners of the garden. Even with the windows closed,

72

we could hear TV commercials and clattering dishes. A lady with gray hair in a bun was watering the flowers on her windowsill with an aluminum saucepan. I still felt like a newcomer here even though people I didn't know called me by name when we met at the mail boxes. I didn't consider this place permanent enough that I had to formally introduce myself. It was my idea of a good commune.

"Let's get a popsicle or something, Dad."

"You have any money?"

"Come on, you can spare twenty-five cents."

"I think they're thirty-five."

"Cheep, cheep," he cackled.

We laughed and I dribbled a stream of pebbles onto his shoe.

"How much money do lawyers make, Dad?"

"Wait a minute, how did we get onto that?"

He picked up a handful of the gravel from the path and rained it onto my tennis shoe. "I just want to know. I was thinking of being one."

"So you could buy your kid a popsicle without worrying about the price?"

"I'm not sure I'll have kids."

"Why not?"

He shrugged his shoulders. "I don't have to, do I?"

"No, of course you don't have to. I just thought . . ."

"Then I probably won't."

I studied the back of his head as he formed his initials with pebbles, a perfect *"D S"* on Magpie's ribcage. Derek's naturally curly hair had gradually lost its reddishness and was turning a pleasing bronze more like his mother's. Until told how much Derek disliked it, my dad used to call him "carrot top" and "radish head." Derek would come to blows if someone did that now. The changes inside his head were harder to figure out. He was starting to hold onto secrets.

As he stood, so did the dog and Derek's initials slid back into the path. Magpie shook herself off and Derek rubbed her hard around the ears. "Let's go, girl! Maybe Dad'll buy you a bone."

We left a note for Justine in case she came back while we were at the store. Derek dictated and I wrote:

Dear Rustin' Justin'

Dad just settled a big case and decided to take me to Jaws II, then to Shakey's for pizza, and maybe horseback riding. If we're not

back in time for the Johnny Carson Show, don't worry.
Your dearest brother Derek

Without Derek's permission, I added:

PS. Translation: we're at Safeway to get a popsicle.

We ran into Lill Epstein near the dairy case. She lit up at the sight of us. "Haven't seen you at the Deluxe lately," she said.

I looked at Derek to see if he'd caught it. He politely said hello and then suddenly developed a keen interest in the buttermilk. "We're shopping for popsicles in the middle of winter. How's that for crazy?" I didn't want to talk to her in front of Derek, but the tingle was coming back.

"Look at me." She swished open her trench coat, revealing cutoffs. "I'm dressed for the beach."

We checked out, untied Magpie from the bike stand, and walked home, Derek licking his root beer popsicle and me with a dreamsicle. The apartment buildings faced on the sidewalk and I could smell freshly cooked asparagus, then sauerkraut. Instead of the generous lawns from the old neighborhood, there were narrow planter strips and ivy climbing vertically up brick faces. Winter had stripped the trees of their leaves and dried the branches brittle. The parking lane in the street was piebald with different shades of crankcase oil. Derek's and my closest moments together had happened in silence, playing catch in the backyard or walking the dog, when the only communication came from the slap of the hardball or the jingle of the leash. Jude never understood my silences.

"I didn't know you knew Lill," Derek said.

"She lives around here." If he'd asked, I could have told him the color of her apartment buzzer and mimicked the sound of her breath when she was hot. But he didn't so we just continued walking in silence, my son who'd sworn off children at the age of eight and his father who'd sworn off women but couldn't keep his lips from parching when he saw the leader of the Sunday night women's group in a trench coat. Warren had said I was going to have hot flashes now and then, but I wanted to be more cerebral and less glandular than Warren's model.

Justine was on the couch watching *Three's Company*, with her Afghan wrapped around her shoulders, when we got back. Magpie tried to get her attention for a pet, and returned to me unrewarded.

That's when I remembered I'd forgotten the dog bone.

8.

Every time the kids went back to Jude's I went into a funk and worked late, emerging from the building with my briefcase in the dark, trudging up Capitol Hill toward the Alhambra. I'd started walking to save gas money and avoid the hassle of finding a parking place when I came home. I'd pass groups of kids cruising the sidewalk in torn jeans eating pizza by the slice, couples holding hands, ordinary people in street clothes, and I felt pissed at them because they didn't have to work like me. We'd look each other up and down as we passed and I knew that if anyone grumbled "lawyer" I'd take a swing.

At home, I'd punch the power button on the portable TV and flip channels, watching anything that had a canned laugh track while I ate a Swanson He-Man dinner. I thought of what I hadn't done with the kids when they were with me, like have that talk with Justine to find out if any of her friends were sexually active. I didn't know if Jude had given her the "this is my body, keep your hands off" lecture or the "open marriage" version.

At the office, everyone seemed to have their outings to the Shrine Circus or the magic show at the Moore Theater on the same weekends I didn't have any kids. They'd ask me to join them and then catch themselves. *Oh, that's right, they're not with you.* I could have hung out with the single men in the office but most of them were younger and never-marrieds whose idea of a good time was happy hour at the Top of the Hilton. Occasionally I joined them, eating a dinner's worth of chicken wings, chips, and dips, coming home buzzed enough to do something productive like call Mom and Dad or write a letter.

I wondered some days how I could have the kids for extended periods and still meet the firm's quota of billable hours, which required that I work a night or two each week and some Saturdays. I'd dragged the kids to the office more than once and let them play with the Dictaphone while I drafted a brief or edited an agreement, but that was hardly the stuff that kids' dreams are made of.

But now I had another reason to keep up the pace at work: the negotiations with Jude had deteriorated. Her attorney had introduced the concept of "professional goodwill" to the mix. This was a theory that treated my ability to practice law as another asset of the marital community. In other words, Jude owned half of me. I called Charlie to complain.

"If a garbage truck hit me," I said, "the goodwill would be as worthless as toe jam."

"And if that happens, you can also stop paying child support," he said calmly. "But as long as you're alive and kicking, she wants half."

"What did she do to earn it?"

"It isn't just for her, it's the kids."

"Bull. If she wants my goodwill, she can buy it."

"We're offering to take it in installments," he said.

"You mean I'd be indentured to her."

"I didn't make up the rules, Cy. You married her, you fathered her kids."

I fiddled with a paper clip. "You'd look at this differently if you were married." There was one more approach I hadn't tried. It required me to grovel, but that was better than paying through the nose and feeling resentful of Jude for the rest of my life. "Charlie, someday you could be on the other side of this one. Jude and I are probably history, but you and I will be doing business in this town for a long time. Consider it a personal favor. What goes around comes around. What do you say, good buddy?" The fakery shamed me.

There was a long silence. "You know if I don't fight for everything Jude has coming I'm not doing my job."

"Spare me the sanctimony. Jude's not going to starve. She's got the house and I'm paying support. If she wants more, tell her to go out and get a paying job like everyone else." In the denouement of our marriage, when we'd argued about her volunteer jobs, she'd asked me to pay her for the value of her work as a dietician, food buyer, cook, dishwasher, laundress, seamstress, gardener, and chauffeur using the hourly rates from a Chase Manhattan schedule that ran in *Ms*.

"Can I quote you on that?"

"Goodbye. I've got work to do." And I hung up.

I wanted to take him to court and make him earn his fees. The trouble was, the court would probably make me give Jude half of the goodwill and pay his fees to boot. Unemployed mother versus downtown lawyer-father, the odds said pick the mother. Unless a stroke wiped out the circuits in my head first, I was dead meat in a contested case.

I finally screwed up the courage to call Lill for a movie and she consented. *Revenge of the Pink Panther* was playing at the Lewis & Clark down by the airport. I was still apprehensive about the kids seeing me with someone so I wanted to stay away from Capitol Hill.

Lill looked great in a dark green velvet vest, which she wore unbuttoned, and a blouse with ruffles up the front and on the cuffs. Maybe she was a size smaller when she bought it but the tightness through the chest had a pleasant effect. I always thought Jude had a salty aroma. Lill was definitely dairy, with a hint of butterscotch. I kept glancing at her during the daylight scenes, just to make sure it was her and not Jude.

After the show, we stopped at the Bai Thai, the first restaurant on Pacific Highway that looked like it had some atmosphere. The front door was built into a gigantic bamboo barrel.

"I love foreign food," Lill whispered as an Asian girl led us to a table in the back.

So far, Lill had been a lot easier to please than Jude. Her likes came in broad categories: warm, funny, foreign. There was none of the gender-dueling that I would have expected. I pulled out her chair and took the seat across from her. The waitress dropped the menus and snatched away the other two place settings. Our table was next to the restrooms so there was a constant parade of women in tight pants and patterned nylons going in and out. The ones in leather squeaked like horse saddles as they passed and the spiked heels made even the squat ones look leggy. The waves of cologne that washed over our table made the Pud Thai taste like orchids.

"Everyone's dressed to kill in this place," she said.

"Too much make-up."

Lill quickly glanced at herself in the mirrored tiles on the wall next to our table. Her lashes were heavy with black wax. She had gray eye shadow, emerald green eye liner, and pink lipstick with gloss, although much of that had already come off on the rim of her water glass. "Some of us will stoop to anything."

"I wasn't talking about you."

The prospect of dating had returned all of the old fears about the size of my ears, the plainness of my face, and the shallowness of my imagination, flaws that I'd been largely able to ignore while I was married. Familiarity tended to camouflage physical imperfections and magnify character defects. Struggling for subjects we had in common besides Jude, I talked about Derek's soccer. Throw-ins, slide tackles, and corner kicks. It turned out that Lill loved sports.

"Especially those played in short pants," she said.

"I wish Justine played sports."

"I always closed my eyes when someone threw the ball to me."

"You don't strike me as a blinker," I said. "Did you ever want kids?"

"You're putting me on the spot. Here I am talking to a father who can't mention his kids' names without getting mushy." She rotated her glass to find a clean space on the rim and took another drink of water. As she set it down I inspected it to find the new lip marks. "When other girls played doll house, I played doctor with the boys or shot beebee guns at cars. I was always scared that if I had a kid I'd feed him the wrong food and make him retarded."

"I think everyone has those fears."

"But I had facts to back them up."

"How so?"

"That's another story."

"I thought all little girls dreamed of being a mother."

"Hey, I'm not knocking it. It's a gift. You and Jude got it, I didn't."

The calm introduction of Jude's name into our conversation was actually reassuring. It represented an advancement in our relationship. "I think I dreamed of being a father. I just didn't dream of having kids. Until you see their faces, they don't exist. I couldn't see their faces back then."

The goodnight in front of her apartment was as awkward as I'd feared. What had started out as a roll of the dice had turned into something I wanted to become a keepsake. I let the motor idle while we talked. When she turned to face me and rested her hands on the seat between us, I put one hand on hers. It was a long journey from there to intimacy but I found myself visualizing the steps. The streetlight sparkled off the cap on her front tooth as she talked. Before leaving the restaurant, she'd excused herself to cake up her lips and they looked soft again. We were both leaning on the emergency brake handle, sharing a cane.

Her blouse pooched open where a button had come loose and I wondered if she'd done it on purpose. When I dated in high school, you kissed for months before moving on, but Eisenhower was President then. There'd been a sexual revolution. Lill swayed her back and gave into my kiss, nibbling my lips, and I could taste the cinnamon in her lipstick. She moved closer and I twisted to embrace her more fully, but my hip was trapped under the steering wheel. Her face pushed my glasses against one eye and I let my mouth open wider in response to her. The journey was getting shorter and shorter. I was as erect as the brake handle. She said my name and stroked my face but I was uncomfortable saying hers so I just moaned. In my mind's eye, I could see the spot where her blouse had come unbuttoned. When my hand slid down the front of her and across the ruffles, she made no attempt to withdraw. I rubbed neutral territory between her breasts and wished I had eyes and brains in my fingertips.

At first I thought it was a dream but a man was knocking on the passenger window.

Lill stiffened and pushed my hand down. "Oh God, it's Douglas!"

The man's voice was muffled. "I don't have my key."

We returned to our own sides, ironing our fronts. I pulled out my handkerchief, scrubbed the lipstick off my mouth, and straightened my glasses. When I turned the volume of the radio back up, the news was on. Who was Douglas?

"I better go, Lill." I wasn't ready to duke it out with a man who had a key to her apartment.

"I'm coming," she yelled through the closed window, "hold your horses." There was a matter-of-factness about her tone, like this had happened before. "I'm sorry."

"You didn't do anything."

"About my brother."

"Your brother?"

"He's staying with me while he does interviews."

My heart resumed pumping; the tickle returned to my lips. I shook her hand and she sprang out.

On the way home, I stopped by Dick's on Broadway and ordered fries and a Special. The Thai food had left a hollow spot and I needed protein. The parking lot was full of high school kids with their car doors open and boom boxes playing even though it was March and cold enough to see your breath. People sat on their fenders and sipped milkshakes, bobbing to the music. Watching them made me wonder if the part of me that was young and careless had atrophied, but I yearned for something old-fashioned that would last. Something cast iron instead of plastic.

Warren's phone message said he'd buy me dinner at the J & B Cafe in Pioneer Square, the oldest part of Seattle, which was filled with art galleries, funky restaurants, red brick, stained glass, and soup kitchens for transients. A place where the chic and the shiftless shared the sidewalks. He must have needed another loan, and I momentarily wished that I'd charged him interest on the old ones. With the divorce, this wasn't a good time to be lending more money to my little brother.

The J & B used to be a cardroom—Warren said it stood for "jacks or better"—with a long oak bar that looked like a bowling alley with beer glasses for pins. The regulars on the bar stools eyeballed us as a pale-faced waitress showed us to our table. The place was more bar than restaurant and the menu consisted of corned beef sandwiches, spaghetti, green salad, and garlic bread. Our tabletop still showed the ring marks and catsup and mustard streaks left by previous customers. I wadded up a couple of napkins from the dispenser and wiped the table.

"Before we order, I should let you know I'm tapped out. I'll buy you a beer but I can't play Household Finance this time."

Warren laughed. "What kind of monster have I created? Do you think I'd hit a guy when he's down?" Then he looked over his shoulder and back at me again, all business. "Cyrus," his voice was lowered to a whisper, "Mandy's pregnant."

"Congratulations!" I extended my hand.

"Knock it off, I'm serious."

"This can hardly be a surprise. You've been sleeping together, haven't you?"

"Yeah, and she's been on the pill . . ."

"And she got tired of filling her body with chemicals."

"How'd you know?"

"We went through the same thing after Derek."

"So how come you didn't have another kid?"

"Abstinence." I hadn't told Warren that Jude had her tubes tied. He pushed my arm away. "Get outta' here. No wonder you're getting divorced."

"Why didn't you use a rubber?"

"I hate rubbers. They take away the spontaneity."

The bartender finally came to our table, wiping his hands off on his apron as he spoke, explaining that our waitress had gotten sick. We looked at each other and I was thinking of a dozen places on Broadway where we could have met instead of this sinkhole. Not wanting to contract whatever our waitress had, we ordered our beers by the bottle.

When the bartender returned, he slapped down two long-necked Buds hard enough to make foam ooze out the top. I toasted to Warren and Mandy, and then took the best swig of the bottle, the one that shocked the taste buds. Warren half-heartedly tipped his.

"Now look who's moping? I thought you loved her."

"She's already planning the baby's wardrobe. Can't I make her get an abortion? I'm the father."

"You're just sperm. Once it's in her, it's her choice. If she wants to have the baby, she can have it and there's not a thing you or a warehouse full of lawyers can do about it."

His shoulders drooped and he drew a slow determined breath. Warren had curly chestnut hair, the color of a good acoustic guitar, even though he preferred electric. He looked as angelic as Art Garfunkel, even though he wanted to be demonic like Mick Jagger. He was someone on whom you could see beads and a bandanna whether he was wearing them or not. Although he had a decent build, he'd grown soft. He'd never been interested in contact sports or weights. "I had plans, man. I'm tired of being poor. I wanted to live on a houseboat and do my music." I knew he had no clue as to the contradiction in what he'd just said. The houseboats on Lake Union and Portage Bay were some of the highest rents per square foot in the city—that is, if you were lucky enough to find a vacant one. "I met a guy who wanted our group to cut a demo. I wanted to wait until I had a contract and just drop it on you. Watch your eyes pop out of your head. I could have repaid your loans." He wiped the bottom of his chin with the side of his hand. "If she has the kid, does this mean I'm responsible to pay for it?"

"Only for twenty-one years."

"I won't live that long."

I found myself doing most of the talking during dinner, extolling the virtues of fatherhood, while Warren moped and wound spaghetti noodles onto his fork. I told him about the time the kids begged me to let their dwarf bunnies play in the living room. Jude was away somewhere and I was just trying to read the paper in peace. Pretty soon Derek came in bawling because their bunnies had disappeared into the motor under the refrigerator. Without thinking, I tipped the refrigerator up and the milk, leftover peach halves, and whatever else was in there clattered to one side. But then I couldn't set it down without crushing the bunnies.

"This is supposed to encourage me?" Warren said.

"Justine held a match under there to find them and singed her hair. They rattled dust mop and broom handles off the bottom of the refrigerator. I thought we were going to have to call the fire department. But they finally scampered out and the kids clapped. I dropped the refrigerator back down and we rolled on the kitchen floor laughing. We swore to never tell Jude."

"So you're telling me to get used to living with a little rabbit shit?"

"I'm saying there are built-in consolations. And I remind you that our wills still make you the guardian if Jude and I kick off. The kids think you walk on water." That had been true ever since Warren babysat them on the weekend that Jude and I were in San Francisco for an American Bar Association seminar. He made a one-story high papier-mache´ dinosaur that was tied to the chimney when we came home.

"This ode to children from the mouth of the man who's marriage has just crumbled like a dry sand castle."

Warren seemed uncharacteristically moody and finished two beers for every one of mine as we talked. "I just can't believe she'd do this," he kept mumbling. He grew increasingly resentful each time I sided with Mandy, and I finally decided it was time to go. On the way to the door, he insisted on a nightcap at the bar but there was only one stool free.

"I want to be one of the reg'lars."

82

"Skip it, Warren."

"No, you take the stool. I'll stand. Let's have a shot Rhode Island-style. Short and straight up." His words slurred.

"Then we go."

"Say, fella." Warren was talking to a burly man in overalls on the stool next to me. "Move over and make me a little standin' room."

The guy looked down at Warren with a sneer, then went back to his beer mug.

"That's all right," I said, "we're only going to be here a few minutes."

"Bullshit. My money's good as his." Where the guy's overalls had come unbuttoned on the side, I could see the top of his grungy boxer shorts. He looked like someone who demolished buildings for a living.

"I can move a little more the other way." I stepped off my stool and scooted it over a few inches. Meantime, Warren had squatted down and had a grip on the legs of the other guy's stool, trying to move him over.

"Let go," the man said, "or I'll rip your fucking kidneys out!"

"Come on, Warren!" I couldn't remember seeing him this way. He was the Mahatma Gandhi of the family, the last person I'd expect to pick a fight. "Sir, don't pay any attention to him. My brother's way out of line on this one."

"That bumfuck is your brother?" His breath smelled like a can of tunafish.

"He's dealing with some bad personal stuff. Let me buy you a beer. What are you drinking?"

"Don't give 'em shit," Warren grunted, as he continued to pull against the chrome legs, twisting them so hard that the stool was going to either move or break. Thank God he hadn't lifted weights.

"I don't want your handout," the man said. "Just get his clammy hands off my chair."

"He's had one too many. Just ignore him." I pulled on Warren's shoulders. "Come on, this guy's gonna' clobber you and I'm going to help him." I looked around the bar. Everyone was staring at us. The sick waitress who was supposed to have waited on us peeked out from behind a post.

"Bartender," I said, "can you give me a hand here?" I hadn't wrestled with Warren since he was in grade school. He was an inch taller than me now and twenty pounds heavier.

The bartender wiped off his hands, lifted the gate in the bar, and joined me.

"You get that arm and I'll take this one," I said.

Warren held on like his hands were welded to the stool. We squeezed him between us and inched our grip toward his wrists. The burly guy stayed put, anchoring the stool. When we finally broke Warren's hold, he tried to get away and the bartender put him in a headlock and dragged him toward the exit as the people at the bar cheered. The bartender and Warren burst out of the swinging doors onto the front sidewalk with Warren still cussing into his armpit. The bartender turned him loose and Warren flapped like a rooster, yelling back at they guy inside.

The bartender stood in the doorway. "He comes back, I call the cops."

Warren's hair was flattened against the sides of his head. His face was red, and his eyes were grenades ready to be lobbed back into the J & B. "I can't believe it. They've kicked us outta this cheap place." He looked around and noticed for the first time the small crowd that had gathered on the sidewalk. "I would'n go in there if I were you," he said. "They kicked us out 'cause we're inspectors from the Health Department." He smiled. Whatever switch had flipped on in the bar had just flipped off.

We strolled up Yesler, then down the Occidental promenade past transients on the benches sharing bottles wrapped in brown sacks. Compared to Warren, these guys looked harmless.

"What happened in there?"

"I guess I was feeling a little trapped by the whole Mandy thing." He put an arm around my shoulder and smiled weakly. "Sorry. I forget you have a reputation to protect."

It would have been stupid to get our teeth busted out over six inches of floor space but I was a sucker for Warren's reckless passion. I'd have hit him in the head to protect him. His arm around me made all the brotherly juices well up inside again. "The guy had a good question," I said. "Is that bumfuck my brother?"

A legal messenger delivered a proposed separation agreement to my office on a Tuesday in April despite the fact that I'd asked to have all divorce correspondence sent to my home. There was a half-hearted apology in the cover letter from Charlie Johnson. "Jude was in a rush," it said. "You know Jude." A separation agreement embodied all of the elements of the divorce, and if it was agreed to by the parties it could simplify or avoid the need for a trial. I wanted to sit down and digest it, but I had a trial starting the next day that I wasn't ready for.

Alex Monticello, our client, was the owner of a newly constructed apartment house in Ballard. Like every other construction job I'd seen, it ran over budget and over deadline. The place still leaked like a sieve and Monticello had been unable to rent some of the units. I'd advised my client to withhold final payment, which he did. The contractor sued for payment and we countersued. Now we had to sort through seven thousand pages of documents, twelve change orders, and twenty-one witnesses to decide who owed what. It was a case that should have settled. We were within a hundred thousand dollars of each other in negotiations and it would cost that much to try the case. Surprisingly, I thought, for construction litigation, our opponent was represented by a woman. I was starting to catch on: the female lawyers who'd made the climb up a slope that was still spiked against them were something to be reckoned with.

Litigation was a glutton; the more detail you fed it, the more it demanded. I was working harder to save Alex Monticello's money than my own. I carried the proposed separation agreement to the restroom and came back to it between phone calls with witnesses and the client. The agreement gave Jude the house, child support, medical care until the kids were out of college, and installment payments for her share of the goodwill. I was pleased to see the Smith Barney stocks and the New York Life policy, which had a modest cash value, back under my name. In addition, I got the Plymouth, the furniture I'd already hauled over to the Alhambra, a pine dresser still at Jude's that Dad and Mom had brought us from home when Derek was born, and all the debts. Jude received full custody of the kids, subject to my visitation rights two weekends a month. The stingy visitation schedule hurt, but unless I could prove that she was an unfit mother, my chances of winning custody at trial were nil.

The tabernacle of my goodwill was an office in a high-rise building downtown known as "the black box." My office faced east, toward Fourth Avenue and the freeway, which was where I was the night before the Monticello trial. I got up to stretch and pressed my forehead against the glass, which was cool and smooth. The tail-lights of the cars on I-5 wound south like glowworms toward Tacoma and Portland. I could see the main branch of the Seattle Public Library across the street and the federal courthouse, mostly dark, up on the next block. The only lights on at the courthouse were the floodlights at the entrance and what looked like the table lamp from a window in the law library on the tenth floor. So there were at least two of us fools still working. Looking towards Capitol Hill, I tried to find Lill's apartment. If I signed on to the proposed agreement, maybe Jude and I could stop fighting and Lill and I could proceed unencumbered to wherever it was we were heading. Jude had probably collaborated with her women's group in making the offer. They were probably out there somewhere strategizing her next move.

I'd always believed that Jude and I would somehow settle our differences and get back together, but her proposal in black and white mocked that notion. We seemed fixed on a course that probably represented the biggest mistake of our lives. Gazing into the void at more than thirty stories above the earth, I felt isolated. Who cared if I won the Monticello case? Alex Monticello didn't even know I was getting divorced. When I was on my deathbed, I wouldn't be able to remember his name.

Getting over Jude was like scaling a mountain. I'd reach a summit, thinking I was there, only to discover that it was false and I had farther to go. I'd considered jettisoning the men's group at Group Health, thinking that I could be more honest without an audience. Through my journal entries, I was trying to figure out on my own why the marriage had disintegrated. I always thought there had to be a singular catastrophic event, an explosion you could point to and say, *There, that was it*! My current explanation was the drifting sand theory. The hundreds of single sentences, words, grunts that we'd uttered in frustration at each other. Grains. Sterile, minute, and nearly weightless grains of sand. Without realizing it, the sand had drifted and finally buried us. It was implosion, not explosion.

The kids made it through the school year and, by arrangement with Jude, I had them one week each month during the summer. The time with them was magic. We ate out without the two of them arguing. At the Spaghetti Factory, an elderly couple next to us who the kids had amused during dinner secretly paid for our meal and left a note with the waiter saying the kids reminded them of their own. We were living proof that one coping parent could be more effective than two distracted ones. Not only did Derek play catch with me but Justine joined in. I told her the woman who could do a hookslide and a hookshot couldn't help but love her body. The kids and I wrote up a contract to deal with our most difficult subjects — chores, bedtime hours, TV, bad language, and overnighters. Each time we had another problem, we amended the contract. It was Justine who noticed the absence of legal consideration.

"Dad, this just lists what we have to do."

So we added my obligations: limits on my office hours, reasonable and necessary taxi services, and refraining from saying anything that started with, "When I was your age."

Still, I couldn't help but compare their summer to the way mine used to be. And it depressed me. Summer wasn't just a season between grades; it was the sum and substance of what a kid lived for. In summer, the air was supposed to be filled with the sweetness of alfalfa, carrot seed, oat hay, seed beans, and sugar snap peas, a time when adults faded into the audience and kids took over the stage. We had the run of the town when I was growing up. We organized circuses and carnivals in our yards with magicians and games of skill. At night, we spoke with the dead in the Quincy Cemetery and confessed whom we'd die for. Summer was our sex education, when hot nights emboldened us to ask things we couldn't in school. Summer was a free zone, the chance to shed an old friend and grow a new one, to fall hopelessly in love with a girl at the pool who didn't know your name. I could remember crying on the first morning of school every fall as if summer was a best friend who'd moved away.

For Justine and Derek, summer meant catching the bus at Aloha and Tenth for Country Day School. Although Jude and I billed it as a camp, it was really day care for kids whose parents worked. There was a swimming pool, horses to ride around a turnstile, an archery range, a craft center, an art studio, and a typing room. The kids at Country Day were mostly grade-schoolers and Justine had to put up with spitwads and name-calling on the bus.

"It's humiliating, Dad."

"Next summer you can get a job instead."

Derek had a couple of friends from Seward who went to Country

Day and they turned it into a soccer camp, setting up tournaments with co-ed teams. But I knew that anything scheduled and supervised couldn't really be summer.

Although I tried to share as much of my new life as I could with the kids, the revelation of my budding relationship with Lill was still out of bounds. For all the kids knew, I was a monastic with a downtown law job.

9.

"I'd like to see you, Lill."

"I've got dinner made, why don't you come over? Meet my friend from Germany." She caught herself. "Oh, God, I'm sorry. Isolde's a woman. You'll like her."

The corset in my abdomen loosened. "How did you say her name?"

"Isolde. Like he sold the guitar."

I hung up, changed clothes, and stopped at Safeway to buy a bottle of wine on the way over. The sky was bottomless blue and I wished I had my sunglasses. Finding the shades that you hadn't touched for a year was a ritual in Seattle. There was a pickup basketball game going on in one of the alleys. The people sitting on an old picnic table were drinking beer, smoking, and ignoring the game. I knew it was totally absurd for me to be pursuing Jude's friend, the woman who'd probably convinced her I was the yoke she had to break free of. Was I a masochist or some door-to-door Jehovah's Witness who thought I could convert her? Or maybe I didn't care what she believed as long as I could be with a woman.

Lill rang me into the Buckley and I stepped into the lobby, which was nicely appointed with overstuffed sofas and throne chairs. The crystalline drops in the chandelier shot off rays of blue-green and silver light. The banister curled into a carved ram's head at the base of the stairs. I knocked lightly when I reached her unit. The voices inside stopped and I heard a cupboard door slam, a chair scoot, then the pad of bare feet. Suddenly, the door came unstuck like it had been newly painted and there she was. I offered my hand and she took my sack with the bottle of wine. The room smelled lemony. Her friend gripped me unexpectedly firmly.

"Guten tag."

"Isolde?"

She smiled and Lill said something to her with lots of *ichs* and *meins*.

"I didn't know you spoke German."

"Long story. Enough to get along."

We had halibut that was poached in a white sauce and garnished with pearl onions and button mushrooms. It crumbled as my lips pulled it free of the fork. Isolde and Lill took small pieces of the fish and a green salad serving barely large enough to cover a dollar bill. It was obvious they'd only fixed enough for two. As soon as the first bottle of wine was empty, Lill uncorked the Pinot Gris I'd brought. Isolde dominated the conversation, starting ideas in broken English that ended in German. My jokes got two laughs, one in English and a second one from Isolde after the translation. I plowed through my memory for anything German, mostly memories of my trip through Europe the summer after my junior year of college, one of those three-week wonders with a new city every other day. I remembered lying on a grassy hillside above Heidelberg, floating down the Rhine to Rudesheim, visiting Dachau, vomiting up beer and sausage I'd bought from a street vendor in Munich. I told her about the Adolph Hitler speech I gave in a high school speech contest, but Lill didn't pass that one along.

"They don't talk about that War."

Isolde acted a little drunk and I thought she might be slurring her German as she cross-examined me through Lill. How long was I married? What was Jude like? Why didn't it work out? Were the kids suffering? Was I going to remarry? The language barrier and the Pinot Gris seemed to free her to ask anything she wanted. For all I knew, she was talking about the weather and these were Lill's questions. When it was my turn to be the interrogator, Isolde was ready.

"She's looking for a rich man," Lill said, "and when she finds him, they're going to make a big family." Isolde pushed out her stomach and we all laughed.

To my surprise, Lill made me sit on the couch while they did the dishes, and I wondered if she hadn't duped Jude, preaching doctrines that she didn't practice herself. I pretended to read the *Seattle Times*, but instead read Lill, trying to gauge what kind of effect the divorce might have on her if we finalized it. They talked in German as Lill washed and Isolde dried. I listened for my name to pop up and, not hearing it, decided that Cyrus must be something unrecognizable in German. Lill scraped something into the garbage can and glanced over at me with those eyes. I loved those eyes.

When they finished the dishes they joined me in the living room and Isolde offered me cognac in a clean wineglass, which I accepted. Lill declined. Isolde smoked while we talked about American movies, the major common denominator between our cultures. Isolde thought Dustin Hoffman was too dull, but Robert Redford was a dreamboat she'd make kids with.

"Very Aryan and sexy," Lill said, and we all laughed.

Lill and Isolde finally had an untranslated exchange which ended with Isolde winking at me like Groucho Marx and excusing herself with an ashtray and a book as she headed to the bathroom and drew water for her bath. That left me and Lill sharing the floral peach loveseat, her on one cushion and me on the other. She told me that she and Isolde met while Lill was stationed in the Army in Hamburg.

"I wanted to go to Viet Nam but they wouldn't let us near combat. So instead of fighting the Viet Cong we fought off the advances of our superior officers."

"Why did you do it?"

"I didn't know how to do anything else. The ads said they'd train me for a new career." Each time she furrowed her brow, the high part of the arch in the hairline scar over her right eye blended and disappeared. "My father and grandfather were Army. We were into obedience." She smiled and let her arm climb to the back of the loveseat next to mine.

"Weren't you bothered by the war in Viet Nam?"

"It was just an extension of the obedience thing." She tapped me on the arm. "I'll bet you were a protester."

Her taps felt nice, and I wanted to oblige her fantasy by bragging about some of Jude's anti-war activity and claiming it as my own. "I was too busy worrying about law school and the draft."

"I'll bet you were a hellion as a kid."

"In Quincy, rebellion meant not getting bombed on Friday night. I was afraid to get drunk just like I was afraid to get shot in Viet Nam."

Isolde emerged from the bathroom in a yellow terry cloth bathrobe, with her pocketbook sticking out and her hair wrapped in a turban. Without eye shadow, she looked more wholesome. The huskiness of her hips swished the bathrobe as she walked over to the couch and gave Lill a hug. Then she turned to me.

"Thank you for meeting me."

"*Guten Nacht*, Isolde," I said, using exactly half of my German vocabulary in the process.

When Isolde's bathrobe disappeared down the hallway, I rested two fingers on Lill's wrist. "Was it the Army that turned you into a feminist?"

She smiled. "You make feminist sound like Communist. I don't believe in grand causes. Feminism is good like laughter is good and sex is good. It's great if you have it but I'm not going to rule out everyone who doesn't."

"But I thought . . ."

"I'm not going to give any group that kind of power over me."

Lill called me Saturday morning with an invitation to go with her and Isolde to the coast. She said to pack a change of clothes, a sleeping bag in case we stayed overnight, and a swimsuit. Just before they picked me up, Justine called to ask if I wanted to rent a rowboat with her and Derek at Green Lake. I could hardly say I was going on an overnighter with one of her mom's friends, so I mumbled something about being tied up with work. It just came out, I didn't have to even compose it, and I felt terrible for doing it. Now I wondered what would happen if one of them were hurt and they tried to get hold of me?

Lill and I took turns driving while Isolde sipped white wine in the backseat. At Salem, I jettisoned the freeway in favor of Highway 99, the scenic route. It was a two-lane road that passed big farmhouses with vegetable gardens in the front yards and extra cars in the driveways. There was a string of empty boxcars stored on the track that ran parallel to the highway. The air smelled like pumpkin and straw. It reminded me of Sunday afternoon dinners in Quincy when four or five families brought potluck and the adults drank highballs and square-danced while the kids roamed the fields and played hide-and-seek in the barn.

I slowed down to thirty-five and flipped the tape over to hear "People" again, a song Jude had introduced me to when she thought Barbara Streisand was a prophet and we still needed each other. I couldn't help but think of the trip Jude and I took to the Oregon Coast for our delayed honeymoon, when we stayed in Seaside and played games in the Arcade, shooting air rifles, knocking over lead milk bottles, playing pinball on machines with pictures of bosomy girls and race cars that lit up as the ball caromed off the posts and tripped triggers in the chutes. They let us parlay all of our winnings into a large brown monkey with a pipe in his mouth that Jude chose.

"Carry it on your back," I said.

"With the others." She laughed.

From the bed in our motel room along the promenade, we could see people strolling back and forth, pushing baby buggies, walking poodles. We made love with the curtains open. We were on the same side in those days, us against the world. It felt like we had something that nobody else had, at least until Justine was born and I was still in law school and we were broke and had to mortgage our imaginations.

Lill cussed when we got stuck behind a hay truck with a kid and his sheepdog sitting on top of the load. The hay swayed one way, then the other, as the truck negotiated the curves. Finally, we got a straightaway and Lill gunned us into the other lane, the kid waving at us as we passed. But our freedom was short-lived because around the next bend there was another farmer on a wheel tractor with his lunch box and silver thermos strapped to the driver's seat with black inner tube bands and his blades folded up like the legs of a grasshopper. Lill pointed to Isolde in the backseat as we were coming into Reedsport. She'd dozed off and was snoring with her mouth open.

Our destination was the Oregon Dunes, a vast expanse of sand along the Pacific Ocean about fifty miles long and one to three miles wide. The dunes were formed from the erosion of sandstone that was carried to sea by winter floods and then drifted back to the beaches where it was blown inland in the shape of waves by the prevailing winds. We unloaded in the Honeyman State Park lot which was already active with kids doing bike tricks and bouncing errant frisbees off windshields.

As a kid, I was always afraid of the ocean. When my dad took us to the Oregon Coast, he made me wade out until a wave knocked me over and scraped my face along the bottom while pictures of starfish and clamshells tumbled inside my head. He was laughing when I got up. In the Navy, they threw everyone overboard who couldn't swim. This happened to one of his chess buddies, who survived, but a few days later a loose canvas caught against him in a storm and carried him overboard like a kite. Dad taught lessons about life by telling me stories of people who'd died.

I carried our picnic goods in two shopping bags with paper handles. The surface sand was hot on my bare feet, but as we climbed our steps dug into the cooler sand underneath. By the time we'd crossed over the first row of dunes, we lost the blare of the transistor radios and yelping dogs in the parking lot. Wind patterns were carved into the dunes as if by trowels in the hands of a colossal sculptor. The horizon shimmered from the heat. As Lill gracefully picked her way in a flowing skirt, she looked like the alluring serviceman's bride who lived in the beach house in *Summer of '42*. She'd undone the buttons on her shirt and tied it around her waist so that her midriff was exposed. It was chaste and lithesome. Isolde had changed into a bathing suit with gaudy rhododendrons and wore a faded blue shirt over it. She also kept her socks on to protect the finish on her toenails. When we could see nothing but waves of sand in all directions, we stopped.

"You guys wait here while I scout ahead," Lill said, and she took the shopping bags with her.

Isolde and I tried to patch together another movie conversation, with long silences in between. We were both relieved when Lill's head appeared again on the horizon. Then Lill shooed us along towards her surprise, which was a sand bowl at the top of a dune with three place settings, stemmed wineglasses, a blue-and-white checkered tablecloth, a loaf of french bread, sliced Jarlsberg, pickles, German sausage, and Greek olives in a dish improvised from the cheese wrapper. A bottle of Korbel and a Perrier were resting on the ice bag. The candles were probably superfluous in the seventy-five degree sun but Lill had thought of everything.

Isolde put her hands over her face and looked like she was going to cry, muttering something in German that I figured translated to "Wow!"

Lill showed us how to make chairs by burrowing her butt into the sand, and we copied her, everyone laughing. The champagne cork blew out with a pop that was muffled by the sheer expanse of the dunes. Isolde raised her glass to the sun which was at about two o'clock.

"Prost!"

Only Isolde and I ate the sausage, and I wondered how the two of them had ever hit it off so well. Lill abstained from much of what Isolde craved.

After the meal, Lill scooped some ice cubes out of the bag and chewed on them. Water trickled out of the corners of her mouth and down her chin, the sand absorbing the drops without a trace. Then she uncovered the grocery sacks she'd buried, pulled out a book, and told us to lie back and close our eyes. Once we'd stilled, she read to us in a voice that was tender and full of affection.

Don't grieve. Anything you lose comes round
in another form. The child weaned from mother's milk
now drinks wine and honey mixed.

Isolde jabbed Lill for a translation and Lill motioned for her to wait.

God's joy moves from unmarked box to unmarked box,
from cell to cell. As rainwater, down into flowerbed.
As roses, up from ground.
Now it looks like a plate of rice and fish,
now a cliff covered with vines,
now a horse being saddled.
It hides within these,
till one day it cracks them open.

Lill closed her book and there was silence until Isolde started rummaging through her bag for cigarettes.

"Rumi's a Sufi, one of my confessors."

I listened to the wind swirl over the dunes. Sand as fine as you picked out of the corner of your eyes in the morning coated my face. I smelled the burnt sulphur of Isolde's match, then the weedy smoke of her exhalation. We left each other to our own thoughts. In my fantasy, I was walking barefoot in the dunes with Jude, two ants moving slowly up, then down each mound, but we were lost, and we were looking for Justine and Derek, who were also lost.

Isolde interrupted my daydream. She shaded her eyes from the sun and asked me something in German. In her fantasy, I'd apparently become fluent.

On the loop back to the parking lot, we came over the rise of a very large dune and found a small lake on the other side, a mirage of aquamarine broth ladled into a sand crater.

"Let's go in," Lill said, with the exuberance of a kid who's just found a theater door ajar.

"Do you have your suit?"

"Underneath."

"Mine's in the car."

"So?" She tried to hold back her smile by biting her lip.

Isolde didn't know what was going on, so Lill explained while I turned and stripped down to my boxer shorts. Without a lining, things flopped around a little. Lill's two-piece orange suit was phosphorescent, and she made no attempt to cover herself or cave in her shoulders to hide the natural thrust of her breasts the way some women did. I tried to mimic her self-assurance and resisted the urge to cross my arms and hide my hairless chest. We ran down the dune, not stopping until the water tackled our legs and we toppled over into a lake that was as warm as baby's bath. She came up laughing.

"Now tell me that wasn't worth the drive," she said. Her red hair was plastered against her head except for a wild tuft on the crown that seemed to be laughing with us. I opened my arms and she fell against me, making a gentle slap as skin met skin.

Isolde made us stand for a picture on the shore as I rested my hand on the curve of Lill's hip and joyed to the touch of her fingers playing on my back.

"Cheese," Isolde said.

Lill's tapping resumed as we lay on the floor in our clothes at the Waves Motel. Isolde's rhythmic breathing wheezed from the double bed next to us. She'd dropped off during an Archie Bunker rerun and Lill stripped her down to her underwear and pulled the covers over her. Lill's finger had the same teasing quality as her voice. She found my hand and carried it to the back of her neck, signaling the need for a rub. The smell of Nag Champa incense filled the room. In the candlelight, I could see a trail of ashen snakeskin where the stick of incense had burned itself out on the desktop.

"Thanks to Jude and Isolde, you know my story. What about you?"

"The sordid history of Lillian Roundheels Epstein." She pulled her hand back and let her head droop. I'd touched a sore spot. I should have waited.

"You don't have to."

"People I don't care about anymore know it, so why shouldn't you?"

I let the pads of my fingers brush the flaxen hair on her arms. "Hey, things happen. I didn't think I'd be living in a basement when I was thirty-seven."

"You're right, I do know something about you. You're a pretty straight arrow."

I continued to stroke her arm, combing the hair the way it naturally leaned. If she wanted to tell me, fine. If not, that was all right too. We'd done enough for one weekend.

"I feel like your big sister and you've just asked me how babies are made. I'm a woman with a past, Cyrus." Her voice was serious. "You asked me why I went in the Army. My parents made me. I was out of high school and starting to sleep around. Walla Walla's little tramp. That's when my dad sat me down and introduced me to the alternative of military service. I was thrilled, actually. It was the first non-sexist thing he'd ever done for me. He thought it would make a man out of me. Well, it was more like putting a bumblebee in a cherry orchard. There were twenty hims for every her."

"Wasn't fraternizing against the rules?"

She grabbed her knees and rolled back. "You slay me. We're talking about a batallion of horny men and women. This was after the invention of the backseat and the telephone booth."

"You did it in a telephone booth?"

"And broom closets. You probably believe the pros don't do it on game days."

"It saps your strength, doesn't it?"

"Or doubles it," she said. "I started palling around with this woman from Defiance, Ohio who drank like a fish and had a dirty mouth. We were a great match. Anyway, she started inviting me along on some of her dates"—Lill rested her hand on me—"are you sure you're all right with this?"

It took me years to get over the idea that I wasn't the first man Jude had slept with and she'd avoided the details at my request. But with Lill there was such glory in her voice, like she'd walked on the moon. I signaled her to go ahead.

"We shared her dates, took turns doing her guys. That's how I met my husband. And the rest is history, as they say."

This was a long way from Rumi and should have turned my stomach, but I surprised myself at how protective I felt toward her. "Hey, your dad made you do it."

"I don't believe in all that crap about blaming your parents for everything. Hey, they did their best. One kid's an engineer, the other's a nympho. I could've been a serial killer."

I hoped that she was exaggerating. On the other hand, it was better to know everything about each other now so that we could adjust our expectations. That's what killed relationships, the false expectations. With Lill, there was very little room for that. She came at you in a gallop with her red hair flying.

10.

It was hard to keep a poker face at work when people asked me how things were going. I felt light-headed and wanted to tell them how Lill was drawing me in like a moth to lamplight. Something was alive in me again. I'd even started to wonder how she and the kids would get along and decided they'd think their lives had turned to clover to have someone fun like Lill in the family. But I couldn't rush it. Pace. I had to keep the right pace.

Out of the blue, the Italian contractor whom I'd beaten in the Monticello case called to fix me up with his second cousin. "She's built like Sophia Loren," he said.

In the interests of someday winning him as a client, I played along. "Can she cook a decent parmigiana?"

"She'll cook you all right, counselor," he said, sinking into a sneer that finally erupted into a belly laugh.

"Would I be wrong in saying you're a chauvinist pig?"

He laughed again. "Is the Pope Catholic?"

Lill, deliver me from this bondage.

I called Warren to meet for lunch at Bruno's pizzeria on Pike Street in the middle of the red light district. It was the same place we'd gone with the kids once after a rerun of *West Side Story* when the four of us had marched down the sidewalk on Fifth Avenue afterwards, snapping our fingers in unison like the Jets and Warren danced off the sides of light poles and window sills singing *Maria* at the top of his lungs.

"So tell me more about this trip to Oregon," he said. "I have a feeling I got the version you'd tell Mom." He drummed the table. "You didn't drive five hundred miles just to clean out the valves in the Plymouth. What's she look like?"

"Pretty."

"What kind of build?"

"She speaks German and reads eastern poetry. She's also been a belly dancer and a palm reader."

"A perfect fit. The lawyer and the moonbeam. How's she built?"

"You're so deep, Warren."

"Come on, you're telling me you don't care?"

"She looked great in a swimsuit."

"You went swimming?"

"Wading."

"And? Come on, you're holding out, Cyrus. I invite you into my soul to talk about my love life and have to pry out of you whether you had sex?"

"This is more than sex. I'm nuts about her."

Warren insisted we take the afternoon off and go golfing. We hadn't played golf together since Dad's heart attack three years ago. "The tees will be deserted. We can finish eighteen holes in three hours."

Warren was right. If I didn't sometimes shirk my job, it would own me. "As long as we get home in time for the kids," I said. "This is my weekend."

We swung by the apartment and found my clubs in the storage locker underneath the empty suitcases, skis, and camping gear. Warren's were under his bed, with dustballs clinging to the canvas. "Sheep's wool," he called it.

We put the top down on his Mustang and I turned up a Louis Armstrong song on the radio. "That guy's rasp'll scrub the grime off you," I yelled, as we sailed down the freeway, chiming in whenever we knew the words. Our golf bags stood up in the backseat like a couple of old pals. We were in college again, skipping chem lab. People waved at us.

The pro at Jefferson directed us to the first tee without a wait. By the second nine, the remains of the six-pack we'd stashed in our bags had warmed and the cans foamed over when we opened them on number ten. We stopped keeping score when Warren lost three balls in the ravine on number eleven. Instead of fighting the obstacles, we joined them. If we didn't land in the traps, we'd kick our balls in so we could practice our sand shots. Whoever sprayed the most sand won. We used a one club-length rule, which allowed us to move the other guy's ball behind trees and fenceposts. When I won best rico-chet by playing off a maintenance shed to get back onto the fairway, Warren rolled in the grass like a dog with fleas. By the time we reached the clubhouse, it was dark and my arms felt water-logged from so much swinging and my cheeks rubbery from laughing.

I could hear the tape deck playing in the kids' bedroom as I snuck by on the sidewalk. Jude had dropped them off early. Still a little buzzed from the beer, I crept down the stairs, put my golf clubs back into the locker, rifled through the ball pocket for a piece of Spearmint and tried to think of a good reason why I was wearing jeans instead of a suit. Even though the kids disliked the idea that I worked so much, I couldn't bear to let them know I'd goofed off. It was a transparent ploy for their sympathy. The martyr dad. Derek met me at the door, and looked me up and down as if we'd traded places again.

"Where you been, Dad?"

In situations like this with my own dad, I'd learned that the best way was to say very little and be humble. "How you doing, son?"

Justine joined us with a book in her hand and I hugged them both at once, praying they wouldn't smell the beer. "Where've you been, Dad?"

"With my brother. Warren," I added.

"You've been playing pool or something." She must have smelled the Rum Crooks.

"I had to help him with some stuff." They still looked unconvinced. This was the spot I'd always stumbled on with Dad. I wanted to go to my room, change clothes, and brush my teeth.

When Lill called on Monday to tell me that Isolde was gone, the adrenalin started leaking through the balloon-smooth surface of my glands again. "Just ring the bell, and I'll let you in," she said, and I wondered if it was a Freudian slip.

"Give me twenty minutes."

I stripped off my shirt as I ran for the shower. If it was just talk she wanted, we could have gone to the Deluxe or the bar at Jimmy Woo's. For that matter, we could have done it by phone. This had to be something more. I soaped myself and imagined what it would be like washing her hair. I'd read in *Ms.* that the quantity of hair on a woman was a measure of testosterone and I tried to visual Lill's body hair.

The buzzer in her door latch was still vibrating like an alarm clock as I crossed the foyer; she must have thought I was slow-handed. The interior of the elevator had brass handrails and a see-through glass door the same as the elevators in the Smith Tower. It moved slowly as I peered at the rose carpet on the second floor, more humming and jostling as we passed the third floor. It ran out of steam and bounced a few moments on the fourth floor before the door opened. The air in the hallway was stale, another reason I never wanted to live in a conventional apartment. At least in the basement of the Alhambra, the smells were invigorating ones like laundry soap and Purex.

Lill touched me lightly on the arm as I entered her apartment, an ambiguous gesture, something between a shake and a mistake. I was beginning to love her place. There were plants climbing on poles out of Grecian urns, vines drooping from baskets hanging in the corners, and infant plants in the incubator on the window sill. It was Hammurabi's garden and Lill smelled as fresh as mint.

"You have quite a thing for flora," I said.

"It's my small way of restoring the balance between civilization and the jungle."

"I applaud the maternal urge."

"It's a matter of motivation," she said. "Gender has nothing to do with it." Barefoot and in a full skirt, she looked as if she'd been dancing to the Rolling Stones from the tape deck on the bookshelf. I inspected the hair on the backs of her calves as she went to turn it down.

While she was in the kitchen to get us wine, I checked out her bookshelf, which was a feminist reading list—Sylvia Plath, Doris Lessing, Germaine Greer, Kate Millett—but there were also male authors I'd read—*Tropic of Capricorn, For Whom the Bell Tolls, Summer and Smoke, Cat on a Hot Tin Roof, Lord of the Flies*, and *Leaves of Grass*. Maybe we could find a middle ground. On the notepad next to the phone, spiral doodles emanated like wisps of smoke from the words, "Call Jude."

She returned with two glasses and set them on the coffee table, one on each side of a fishbowl with pink coral. Without saying anything, she pulled a pillow off the couch, dropped it on the floor and lowered herself Indian-style as her skirt billowed like a parachute and settled over her legs.

I took a seat on the couch. "I guess you called this meeting."

She laughed nervously. "We have a problem."

102

I scooted to one side so I didn't have to look at her through the fishbowl.

Lill sipped her wine, eyeing me over the rim. "I happened to mention to Jude how much Isolde liked you and, of course, that led to the trip to the beach. I couldn't lie, Cyrus."

"What else?"

"Well, I didn't tell her I tried to screw you with your pants on, although I think that's what she suspected. She knows me too well."

I looked at the black-iron fire escape that ran diagonally across her living room window. The marmalade sunset made the room glow. "We haven't done anything we have to apologize for."

"I don't want to do a head trip on her, Cyrus. She's a friend."

"What are you saying?"

Her face was a mask bronzed by the sunlight, and it was difficult to tell if this was hurting her as much as it was me. "I don't want to add to her pain."

"I'm supposed to get her clearance to see you?"

"I don't blame you for being pissed."

"What about you? Jude blanches and you retreat?"

"I feel caught in between."

"Can't you tell her to back off?"

She was shaking her head. "We need to cool it for a while until things settle. She needs me."

"I need you too." I was the boatman on the River Styx ready to row her across.

"Jude and I tell each other everything. There would be things I wouldn't want to tell her."

"So don't." She was forcing me to display my capacity for duplicity.

"I care for her. I can't."

"And you and I were just a couple of dogs in heat? Another GI?"

She dropped her head. "That's not fair, Cyrus. I like you. I think you have a lot to offer."

"That's what they always tell the runner-up."

"Let's wait," she said, "that's all I'm saying. The timing is shit."

She gave me a hug at the door, making sure her breasts didn't make contact. It felt more like the embrace of an elderly aunt. I was the last one to let go.

I kicked a beer can ahead of me in the street on the way home until I lost it under a pickup that was loaded with chunks of broken drywall and twisted door frames from some remodeling project. The rain had made pockmarks in the plaster dust. There were a couple of crushed Miller cans and a ripped pair of cotton work gloves tossed into the corner of the load. I tried to imagine a path that stretched from here to my grave and walking it alone.

Jude answered on the second ring. I tried to be as matter-of-fact as I could.

"Maybe you can tell me what you said to Lill."

"About what?" Jude surprised me. This was the kind of confrontation I thought she relished.

"You know about what. About me and her."

"I was just surprised that Lill was seeing you, that's all."

"What's so surprising?"

"You don't seem like her type."

"What is that supposed to mean?"

"Lill is sensitive and earthy."

"And what am I?"

"Cyrus, this is ridiculous."

"If you can't tell, I'm upset. If you want a divorce so bad, why do you care who I see?"

"Lill's my friend. I just wanted to give her a word to the wise about your relationship skills."

"What does that mean?"

"I don't want to talk about this, Cyrus. If you want to know, Derek hit a clothesline pole with his bike and had to have three stitches. He's fine and I've got to go."

"Let me talk to him?"

"He's in bed."

"Tell him I'll call in the morning. And don't lean on Lill. Please."

"Lill has a mind of her own. Goodnight."

I felt like we'd just boxed a round and I needed to jog to cool down. My heart was still racing. It didn't square. Something else was up.

Leo Pescara, the contractor who wanted to set me up with Sophia Loren, called again, this time with a case that was four weeks from trial and red hot. He'd fired the attorney who represented him in the Monticello case, the woman who I thought had put on a heroic case, considering the evidence. Despite my recommendation, he refused to consider a continuance. He said I wouldn't have any trouble; he'd watched me work. Leo Pescara was Napoleon, probably someone who'd been mocked on the playground. He had a long lip and short arms. This time, he'd gotten into a shouting match with the owner's architect over the design of a glass dome in an office building overlooking Elliott Bay. The owner was livid when the city pulled the building permit, blamed Pescara, and sued to recover everything they'd already paid him. It was another playground fight and Leo wasn't going to let anyone push him around.

"You know where the jugular is," Leo said. "A woman lawyer doesn't know her asshole from a blowhole."

It dawned on me that Leo hadn't fired his prior attorney; she'd fired him. As Leo raged, I wondered if he would have hired me if I told him my wife had just flattened me in a single phone call.

I was eating a frozen lasagna dinner out of the aluminum tray and reading a story in *U.S. News* about Hurricane Frederic in the kitchen of the Alhambra when the doorbuzzer rang. The story said the World Meteorological Organization had voted to no longer give only women's names to hurricanes and I wondered how something as macho as a hurricane could have ever been classified as strictly women's business anyway. Then the buzzer jangled like it was stuck.

"I hear you, I hear you!" I ran to the squawk box and pushed the speaker button. "Who is it?"

Several voices crowded into the intercom from the other end. "Dad, it's us! It's us!" They must have been attacked in the Broadway District or someone was chasing them.

I took the stairs two at a time, carrying my fork, my napkin still tucked into my belt. I pictured bloody faces with gravel ground into their skin. When I opened the door, they burst in like a storm, dumping their wet bags and sacks in the hallway. It was pouring outside.

"What's the matter?"

Magpie's shake sent water oscillating like a sprinkler. Justine wrapped her arms around me and Derek wormed his way between us, both of them mumbling incoherently. Hands grabbed at my midsection as I balanced myself in the middle of the baggage. The door was still open and a sheet of water that overflowed the rain gutter blurred the view to the street. A passing car sprayed water wings from his tires.

"We ran away," Derek said.

The rain, tears, and runny nose merged on Justine's face. "Do you know about Mom and Lill?" I suddenly felt chilled. There'd been an accident. "Dad, I'm not going to live there."

"Whoa, what are you talking about?"

"Lill," Derek said, "it's Lill!"

"She's moved in with Mom," Justine said. "They told us they're lovers."

The air in the hallway was suddenly very thin and I started to sweat. I didn't even know what words to use. I called on my best lawyer skills, the ones you used when your witness has just gone south and you had to pretend you knew it was coming. If I'd just let out what was in me, I would have embarrassed myself and frightened the kids. A tangle of limbs and body positions raced through my mind as I tried to separate Jude's, mine, and Lill's. I didn't even know exactly what women did together. Why didn't one of them warn me?

"If anyone at school finds out, I'll die," Justine said. "I don't want to be queer, Dad."

"Let's talk about it downstairs." I reached out to pat her on the shoulder, but by the time my hand got there, she'd bent over to pick up her athletic bag. Pools of water beaded on the rose tile in the entry hall in a complex pattern of lakes and canals. Derek was sullen but not crying. I put the fork in my pocket. "Does your mom know where you are?"

"We just left," Derek said.

I'd never felt them cling to me this way; they always ran to Jude when they were scared. "We can call her later," I said.

"Don't call her, Dad!" Justine said. "She'll make us come home."

"I don't want her calling the police. She'll be worried."

"She doesn't give a damn," Justine said, pushing my door open so hard that it banged against the stereo. "Sorry."

"Change into some dry clothes." I wondered if I sounded like someone had knocked the wind out of me.

I listened to them talking as they headed down the hallway, each one offering the other first choice on beds. This was a change of approach. Apparently they were staying for the night or at least until we figured this thing out. I squatted to pet Magpie and the prongs of the fork jabbed me in the groin. I set it on the footlocker coffee table. Magpie's pant looked like a smile, and I petted her wet forehead skin back over the crown of her head. A crescent of white showed just below the eyelids each time I stroked her.

There was so much I didn't know about what was going on at the old house. I wondered if this had started before Jude and I separated. All those Sunday night women's groups, maybe it was just Jude and Lill. I didn't know if the phlegm in my throat was jealousy of Jude for taking Lill away from me or bitterness at Lill for seducing Jude out of our marriage. I couldn't really believe they were lesbian. Jude was striking out at me and Lill was just playing house with her best friend. They'd read too many books on sexual politics. Men read *Hustler* and turned into predators; women read *Ms.* and turned gay.

While the kids were changing, I turned off the TV and tidied up the living room. Derek emerged in a pair of maroon cotton pajamas with a faded Captain Marvel insignia across the chest and plopped onto the floor next to Magpie. A band of bare leg showed above his wool socks. "What do you think's happening, Derek?"

He squirmed and petted the dog under her collar. "She's been acting different. She does whatever Lill wants and she's bossier than a cow with us."

"She's always been bossy," Justine chimed in.

"I know that," he said, bending his toes back, crushing his knees against his chest.

"I don't care about her bossiness." Justine had put her pink terry cloth robe over her sweats and sat dead center on the couch in her fuzzy slippers. "I just don't like the way they're hugging and putting their hands all over each other."

"They even kiss." Derek made a spit-it-out face.

"What did they say exactly?"

"We had a big meeting," Derek said. "We had to all sit down in a circle and hold hands. I thought she was going to say we had to get rid of Magpie."

The crying seemed to have strengthened Justine. "She said they loved each other like a husband and wife. I know what a lesbian is,

Dad. I know what they do." She shuddered. "Does this mean I'll be a dyke?"

"Where'd you hear that word?"

"Da-ad," she moaned.

"No," I said, very unsure of myself. "It doesn't mean that at all. There's no one else in our family who is." As I said that, Jude's Aunt Harriet flashed across my mind. She'd never married and always took those mysterious car vacations around the country with old friends. In her slides, the friends were always women. I wanted to tell Justine she'd be "normal" but realized that would disparage Jude. It wasn't that I felt any great charity towards Jude, especially just then, but it was a matter of some pride that one of the few vows we'd managed to keep was to refrain from bashing each other in front of the kids.

"If she's lesbian"—Justine looked at Derek as if she wasn't sure she should be saying this in front of him—"how could you and Mom have kids?"

She was getting ahead of me. I'd never paid much attention to homosexuality and passed over articles on the subject the same way I skipped the "Food" section of the newspaper. I wasn't necessarily against it; I just didn't think it was something I had to know. "When your mom and I were together, we were just like any other man and woman."

"Dad," she used her club president's voice, "we have to swear that none of us will ever tell about this." She sounded as if we'd just buried Jude in the basement. "I mean it. This will ruin us if any of our friends find out."

I turned on the TV and went to check the refrigerator. The milk was seven days overdue and fell out of the spout in lumps when I poured it into the sink. I told them I'd go to the store and buy the makings for hot chocolate and toasted white bread with butter lathered all the way to the edges. It's what Mom used to fix us when I came home from a pheasant hunting trip in the rain with Dad. That was back when I thought Dad was weird because he picked wax out of his ears in public with the end of his matches.

I walked south on Broadway past the Taco Time as the rain peppered my umbrella and the gutters washed candy wrappers, cigarette butts, and plastic eating utensils into the drains. I felt responsible for this turn of events. There was something Jude wanted that I never gave her. All those times she'd discouraged us from having sex I thought it was me; maybe it was my maleness. Jude was tired of blunt. She wanted chamois strokes and soft cheeks.

She'd told me about her Uncle Edgar, the way he used to coax her up on his lap while he was sitting in the big chair next to the smoke stand when she was little and move her back and forth in his lap. Sometimes, he'd tuck her in at night and slide his hand under the sheets, and she had to cross her legs and squeeze as hard as she could to keep his dirty fingers out. Now I couldn't remember what I'd ever said to her when she told me these stories. She'd never repeated them and I was afraid to bring them up because of how they obviously upset her.

The Broadway District was supposed to be safe for gays. I looked at the women going by, trying to see who was and who wasn't. How could you tell? I always thought lesbians had hair on their upper lip and butch haircuts. The girl walking ahead of me had jeans that were frayed at the cuffs, where they dragged on the wet sidewalk, and there were patches on the buttocks. Her ponytail was tied with a rubber band and swished back and forth as she walked. She looked like she was trying to be noticed. I watched the eyes of the guys coming in the opposite direction, searching her up and down as they passed. Some of them glanced back to get a look at her from behind. I'd done the same thing when a good-looking girl passed me, a last chance before she disappeared forever from your life. This one had a decent figure and a nice sway.

When she stopped at the flower stand, I slowed down and sidled over to the cans of carnations resting on a bench. I picked up a bunch and put it to my nose, at the same time looking directly at her face.

She was a man.

When the kids were in bed, I called Jude.

"Why didn't you call me sooner? I thought they'd been kidnapped." Jude had her way of putting things. Somehow she was going to make this my fault. Before dialing her, I'd decided to be amicable, but I could already feel my blood vessels contracting.

"Why didn't you tell me about it, Jude?"

"I thought the kids should know first."

"I was devastated. I had no idea."

"I'm sorry. One of us should have said something. Lill feels terrible too." I had the feeling they'd dissected Lill's and my relationship and probably had a good laugh over it.

"Can I ask how long this has been going on?"

"Lill's been staying with us the last two weeks. She's given up her apartment."

"I mean, how long have you known . . ."

"I don't want to go into all that now. I'm worried about the kids."

"Me too."

"I need your support." Her voice was earnest, but not imperative. "Bring them home, Cyrus."

"They're in bed, Jude."

"Don't undermine us."

"Hold on. They've only been here"—I looked at my watch—"two hours and twenty minutes. I didn't steal them. They fled, Jude. They're scared."

"You're projecting."

I could feel her paddle down my throat, churning my insides. "You're out of touch."

"We talked. Everything was fine."

"Like everything was fine with us?"

"I never said it was fine," she said. "You thought it was fine."

"Have you considered postponing this until the kids are at least out of high school?"

"This isn't a trial, Cyrus. We can't just postpone it."

"This is painful. Justine thinks she's inherited it. Can you think for a minute how this might feel to a high school kid who's trying to get a grip on who she is?"

"I wish my mom had told me there were choices."

"Then you could have skipped me and gone direct to Lill. Then you wouldn't have two kids to worry about. So pretend you skipped our marriage and just leave the kids here for a few days."

"I don't want to acquiesce to their schoolyard prejudices."

"Shit," I said, as I held the mouthpiece against my leg.

". . . is a fact of life and if we hide it from them, we're only making it worse." She paused. "Are you still there?"

"Kind of."

"I'll come get them."

"They're due here this weekend anyway, Jude. Let's just lengthen my weekend and let this blow over, okay?"

She didn't answer right away and I could hear her sniffing. She might have even been crying. I had the strange realization she might be as scared as I was, that she didn't really want to be doing this. "Okay, but tell them I want to talk to them on the phone tomorrow. Separately. I think Derek could care less about this. Justine is egging him on."

"Don't be so sure, Jude. Not all men are as dense as me."

"He's only eight."

"Nine, remember. You gave him *Our Bodies,Ourselves.*"

"Oh, yeah."

"Cut them a little slack. You and Lill can see each other when they're with me."

I went back to my lasagna and stuck a finger between the layers. It was cool. I turned the oven to four hundred fifty and stuck it back in. The counter was sprinkled with Nestle's cocoa and toast crumbs. I opened the liquor cabinet in the door over the refrigerator. There was no R&R. I tilted the flat pint of Cutty Sark but there wasn't enough to fill a jigger so I took the cap off and downed it straight out of the bottle. It clawed against the sides of my throat on the way down and seared the nose hairs as I exhaled. I lit the two candles on the kitchen table and watched them flicker in the breeze that blew in from the window over the table, the flames behaving like two dancers who'd never performed together. When he bent over, she stood on her toes and stretched her arms toward the ceiling; when she leaned left, he shrugged right.

It felt like there had just been a head-on collision and I knew the people in both cars. I was confused and didn't know which loss hurt the most or who to blame. I thought of Lill telling me how she'd married in front of a justice-of-the-peace in Lake Tahoe. Their witnesses were another couple waiting in the same line with liquor on their breath, her fourth, his fifth. She said the woman's makeup was so smeared that she looked like a Sunday paper cartoon character. Lill's husband had burned her personal belongings when they separated and fed the rest of them out the window of his car while he was crossing the Utah Salt Flats. Then two years later, on what would have been their anniversary, he sent her a package wrapped in want ads from Bakersfield with her wedding dress. Juices had leaked onto the fabric from the dead robin roosting in the collar of the dress, and in the beak was his wedding band.

Lill's and my courtship was going to be stillborn. It would never feel the lift of an August heat wave or hear the advent of sunrise in birdsong.

Behind a bottle of dry vermouth, there was a peppermint schnapps, something that Jude must have stuck into my box when we divvied up the everyday dishes. Although I couldn't remember ever drinking it, the bottle was two-thirds empty. As I screwed the cap off, dried crystals fell to the counter. It smelled medicinal. I took a mouthful, gargled, and spit it into the sink. My tongue felt sweet enough to suck on.

When the lasagna was hot, I filled a wine glass with the vermouth, lit a candle, and pretended there was something to celebrate.

11.

My take on the news fluctuated with my mood. For what it was worth, I finally had an airtight case to prove that the divorce wasn't my fault. I could stop beating myself up over my awkwardness with intimacy, wondering what I should have done differently. There was, in legal terms, a mutual mistake of fact. We'd formed the marriage contract on the assumption that we were both heterosexual. Now the contract could be rescinded and the parties returned to their original positions. I could finally quash Mom and Dad's glares of suspicion. It wasn't my personality, it was Jude's chemistry. But what was the value of legal certitude if I couldn't exchange it for what I wanted most?

I was still mystified as to how this transformation could have escaped my attention. All those heavy petting sessions in the car when Jude and I were trying to stop ourselves in college, those times she nibbled on my ear lobes and sucked on my tongue, was she faking it? She couldn't have pretended her blood temperature. We'd made children together. And I'd never encountered anyone more heterosexual than Lill. Had I driven both of them to this? Was there something so odious about me that I'd killed the natural attraction between the sexes?

Reluctantly, and only after some serious persuasion by Jude, the kids returned to their mom's, on a trial basis. I think they felt guilty about abandoning her. She'd promised that Lill wouldn't attend parent conferences, plays, or shuttle the kids to practices. Nothing. Lill would be their little secret. I was worried and made a point of calling them every day. I started having flashes of the kids as gay. The mere suggestion of Justine and sex, any kind of sex, made me anxious. I wanted to put Justine in a sexless bubble until she was an adult.

Our first weekend together again, she balked when I told her she couldn't go on an overnighter to Sarah Dukelow's cabin on Whidbey Island. She apparently saw no connection between my caution and her own fears. This wasn't just teenage insubordination; there was bitterness and self-hatred in her tone.

"You're acting like I'm some kind of criminal," she said, sitting side-saddle on the kitchen chair so she could look at the sink instead of me. "Sarah takes friends there all the time. Her parents trust her." She dug her index fingernail into the crack between the plastic seat-cover and the chair frame, making flecks of dried food pop out and fall to the floor.

"Does she take boys along?"

She snapped her head my way. "Who said there were boys?"

"Well, are there?"

The cheek I could see started to pinken as she mined deeper into the seam with her finger. "They're just friends."

This would have been a good time to talk about birth control except that I thought talking about it was tantamount to inviting her to use it. "Are Sarah's parents going?"

"She doesn't have a dad, her mom might go." She rushed her words, the way a person does when they don't want you to put each one under a microscope. There was a burr under her skin.

I'd forgotten. Sarah's mom was the mother I'd met at parents' night in an outrageously short mini-skirt and black net nylons. "Who are the boys?"

She gave a disgusted sigh.

"Probably Ronnie is going," Derek said, looking up from the TV.

"Derek, this is none of your business."

"Who's Ronnie?" I said.

"That's her boyfriend," Derek said. "He's a dude."

Justine shot him poison darts from her eyes.

"Who else?" I said.

She slumped like her spine had crumbled, then mumbled something about never getting to do anything with her friends.

"I'll call Sarah's mom."

"I won't go then," she said. When she lifted her head to look at me, her face was as wet as a fresh finger painting.

I was softening. "It's not you, Justine. I don't trust the situation."

She bolted, pushing the chair over, and ran to the bathroom. I thought she said "shit."

"Good," Derek said, "that means we can go to *Moonraker*! Can I take Ricky?"

"I thought you hated Ricky."

"Not anymore."

"Your timing is terrible."

Justine got stuck in the bathroom when the doorknob came off in her hand and Derek pulled the stem out the other side. I'd left a screwdriver in the bathroom for such emergencies and taught the kids how to stick it in and engage the latch mechanism but one of them had borrowed the screwdriver and not put it back. When I rescued her with a spoon handle, she ran into her room and didn't speak to me the rest of the night. Derek carried the breadboard to her with a cup of instant tomato soup, a burger on toast with catsup and mayonnaise, and chips. The phone cord was long enough to stretch into the kids' room and Justine was either making up excuses to Ron and Sarah or they were plotting my assassination. The only thing left on the plate when it returned were the crusts. She'd even eaten a couple of spoons of soup. A harbinger of better times, I hoped.

While I was watching TV, Justine summoned Derek, who returned with a folded spiral notebook paper.

Can we go to Annie Hall this weekend?

JUSTINE

No *Dear Dad*, no *Love*, no frills. It was a test. I wrote *Yes* under her name and added: *You can come out and watch Eight is Enough. And I won't talk about you-know-what. Love, Dad.*

"What does she want?" Derek said, when the commercial came on.

"We're negotiating a truce. Can you take this back to her?"

"Can I read it?"

"No."

Magpie followed him into the room again, probably thinking that this time Derek really was going to bed.

Partway through the next segment, Justine appeared in a bedspread wrapped around her like a sari. She walked slowly to the end of the couch, with Magpie watching her suspiciously, and fell backwards into it. We finally made eye contact at the commercial.

When the kids were in bed, I took Magpie for a walk. There was so much I could learn from Magpie. She knew how to tune out the static. She could fall asleep on top of a pair of shoes. She lived in the moment. Even though I took her on the same sidewalks, she acted each time like it was a new frontier, prancing along ahead of me with her license and shamrock name tag jingling together. She vacuumed the aromas into her nostrils like so much gossip, finding out which dogs were sick and what medications they were on. She was egalitarian too, spending as much time in the unkept flower beds as the kept ones. Social status didn't impress her. What mattered was the caliber of the odor. When she had to pee, she'd sniff out a used patch, modestly turn her back, and hunker down, leaving something for someone else to read. But she lived for human affection. In Volunteer Park, I'd let her off the leash and she'd saunter shyly up to people sitting on the grass, slowing down as she got closer, waiting for a glance or an attagirl. If nobody acknowledged her, she'd droop her head, gather her tail between her legs, and sidle back to me.

I squatted down and put my arm around her neck. "What should I do, pal?" She just stared at me with those big brown doe eyes that forgave what humans couldn't.

Warren came to the door in his underpants and a T-shirt. His head looked like he'd just taken it out of a suitcase, pressed flat on one side, sagebrush growing out of the other. There were creases and buttonholes in his cheeks. "What are you doing here?"

"It's Saturday, remember? You said you'd help me move the dresser."

"Oh shit," he said, hitting his palm against his forehead. I expected him to invite me in but he guarded the entrance and nodded his head in the direction of somewhere behind the door. "I'm not alone." He looked down at his bare legs.

"Get your pants on," I said, pushing the door open.

"Come on in."

While Warren changed, I looked around. The shades were pulled and I could smell asparagus and garlic, two of the world's outlaw odors. Garlic kidnapped the breath and asparagus infiltrated the urine. There were wine glasses on the coffee table, one of them half full, and an empty pear-shaped Chianti jug with a bamboo wrap on it. A pair of crumpled jeans was crammed into one end of the couch and a red blouse and black brassiere lay on the floor next to a pair of slippers. I picked up the brassiere and puffed out the cups with my fist. They were good nursing breasts. I could hear voices coming from the bedroom, Warren's tenor and playful, Mandy's tender and plaintive. She wanted him to stay.

Warren emerged, the chaos on top of his head covered with a green, paint-spotted beret. "Let's go."

We picked up breakfast at Dunkin' Donuts on the way to get the rental truck. I told him I was buying and Warren ordered six different donuts and a jumbo black coffee.

"I always thought Jude was kind of sexy," he said. I glared at him and his donut broke, where the thumb and index finger pinched it, and crumbled onto the seat. "You know what I mean. In a heterosexual way."

"You don't know jack about what you're talking about."

He was unfazed and brushed the crumbs onto the floor. "Don't you think it's weird that you slept with both of them?" He looked at me for corroboration, but I kept my eyes on the road, and Warren squirmed in his seat. "Well, I can make my own assumptions on that one. I can kind of see women doing it with each other, but men? Jesus!" He spit a piece of orange frosting onto the dashboard and quickly brushed it with his hand, making an orange smear like a comet. "Sorry."

"Trash my car."

"You need to get out of that hole in the basement. Get a place with a fenced yard for the dog, flowers you can pick for a centerpiece on the table. Give the kids their own rooms. Find a new wife. They'd come running back to you in a minute."

We pulled up at a light behind a station wagon stuffed to the ceiling with cardboard boxes, table lamps, blankets, and grocery bags. Pressed flat against the rear window was one of those souvenir plastic ukuleles from Hawaii with a broken string. Someone had used yellow water ski rope to lash a mattress, box springs, and an upside-down kitchen table to the top. Ever since my own separation, I shivered each time I saw a car flattened on its springs with household goods because I knew it meant broken promises. I wanted to see the driver's eyes. If they were beady and riveted, I'd know the anthill had been kicked open and it was everyone for himself. Carry what you can on your back and find cover.

"What's happening with you and Mandy?"

"I'm not the kind of guy to rush a relationship," he said. "And don't give me that biological clock business. I've read the magazines. I'm the kind of guy liberated women seek out. I just don't think a woman should club a man into marriage with her ovaries."

"Are you sure she even wants to marry you?"

"What do you mean?"

"I mean has she said, 'I'm pregnant, will you marry me'?"

"What else would she do?"

"I thought you said you've been reading the magazines. Women are learning to live without men. They're going to sperm banks, they're adopting. Mandy may want to do this without you."

"That'd be a shitty thing to do," he said. "The kid's as much mine as hers."

We stopped at another light and I caught the eye of a panting dog with its head out the window. "I think if she wants to have the kid, you should encourage her."

"Hah, look at you talk! The guy who's crying in his beer over support payments. I don't make a third of what you do, how am I supposed to pay for it?" He rolled the window up and down.

"What happened to less is more?" I'd saved the sermons Warren used to send me from Turkey in a file cabinet with my tax returns.

"My infatuation with poverty." He put his hands up like it was a stick-up. "Live and learn. Hey, I have a new philosophy."

"Why am I not surprised?"

"Parenthood should be a voluntary institution."

"Does that mean you won't charge it on my credit card?"

"You keep reducing everything to money, Cyrus. I'm talking about something spiritual."

"As usual. Money doesn't matter as long as it's someone else's."

"Ouch, my brother the moneylender. Are you pissed because my loan payments fell behind?"

"'Behind' implies they were once current."

"That's another reason why she can't have the kid. I've got to pay you back."

"Oh, no, you don't. You can't blame this one on me. Your girlfriend's going to have a baby. You better start figuring out what that means and come to a meeting of the minds." I was hitting the steering wheel with karate chops as I spoke.

He snapped the cardboard deodorizer tree hanging from the rearview mirror and it spun in a pirouette. "Okay, okay, you don't need to get pissed." He straightened up in his seat and peered out the passenger window for help. "You sound like Dad."

"Dad would have busted you in the chops."

Despite Jude's belief that Warren was a spoiled kid who would someday get his comeuppance, and despite Warren's conviction that Jude had gone over the falls, they embraced on the porch like long-lost siblings. Jude's fist grabbed so much of his shirt that there was skin showing above Warren's belt. She was on her toes and, for a moment, there was airspace between her bare feet and the porch. The kids, who'd stood back in admiration, hand-slapped and hugged Warren on his way into the house. It was the return of the prodigal son.

I peeked into the kitchen on the way by and noticed that the nook table was strewn with dirty dishes and open jars of peanut butter and jelly. Jude offered us coffee in the dining room, where pieces of leftover red and black crepe paper streamers were still connected to the chandelier and the walls. They'd used adhesive tape that I was sure would tear the wallpaper. Instead of the pictures of the four of us that used to hang over the buffet, there was an abstract painting that looked like a vagina with a white lily growing out of it. Also missing was Jude's poster of the first *Ms.* cover with Wonder Woman, in skin-tight red boots, white-starred shorts, and an eagle breastplate, bestriding the earth.

Justine broke the awkwardness. "Before Lill moved in, Mom was letting me practice driving in the Kingdome parking lot," she said. "She used to let me start the car for her."

I felt left out. I'd always pictured the kids' driving as something that was my responsibility.

If I'd been a door-to-door salesman, I would have thought everything was normal here, that Jude and Lill were making a nice home. Then Lill suddenly appeared in the doorway in her artist's smock and I felt a charge surge through me that probably colored my complexion. The kids started fidgeting.

"I have to go to Brian's," Derek said.

"I've got some stuff to do too," Justine said. The two of them exited without saying a word to Lill.

Lill had dyed her hair a flaxen blonde and it was uncombed as if to remind me that she slept there now, but her eyes were soft and full of mercy. None of the gloating I'd expected, and I wished that it was just Lill and me so we could talk about what had happened.

"Hi, Cyrus." A bead of sweat glistened over her upper lip, and she ran her hand inside the neck of her smock to unstick it from her skin. Warren's mouth hung open and his eyes followed her. "You must be here for that chest," she said.

"Yeah. It's a sentimental piece."

She smiled, brushed her hair back and went into the kitchen to join Jude. Warren followed.

I finished my coffee and went upstairs to use the bathroom and scope out the move. Nobody seemed to notice me leave. There was a roll of toilet paper and shampoo on the bottom step waiting to go up and dirty dishes at the top waiting to be hauled down. The sink and the back of the toilet seat were covered with women's things — hair sprays, plastic bottles with white lotion congealed at the spouts, Tampax sticking out of their box like filter cigarettes, a hair dryer with the cord snaking through the basin of the sink, gauze pads, used cotton balls, and tubes of open lipstick. So much for boycotting the cosmetics industry. This had to be Lill's influence, I thought. In a cleansing frenzy one Saturday while we were still living together, Jude had flung her bubblebath, Nair, flimsy nighties, high heels, and Lawrence Welk, Percy Faith, and *Man of La Mancha* records into a garbage can she'd stationed half-way between the bathroom and her closet.

I lifted the seat, flushed someone's unfinished business, and sat down. At first, I couldn't relax but as the seat warmed and I remembered that my support payments still paid the water bill here I was able to loosen up. I swung open the cabinet door to find some reading material and spied a water-stained *How Babies Are Made* that we'd given to Derek. It reminded me of the debate Jude and I had over whether he should be circumcised.

"It's mutilation," she'd said.

"There's no feeling in the outer skin."

"How do you know? Yours was cut off."

"Kids will tease him if we don't."

"I thought guys just worried about length."

"Aesthetics count too. Even a ball-peen hammer has beauty."

When Derek was circumcised I remembered Jude smiling victoriously when the doctor explained that his foreskin circumference put him in the ninetieth percentile.

The master bedroom door was open and I couldn't resist my curiosity to see what changes had been wrought in there. The blankets had slid like a waterfall over one side of the bed. Hardwood floor showed through the legholes of a pair of jeans and panties that someone had stepped out of. But there were no rubber dildos, no tub of Vaseline on the nightstand, no mirrors on the ceilings, and no roach clips. A *Cosmopolitan* on the dresser had a cover story entitled, "Is it Different with a Younger Man?" In the corner, a potted plant was supported from a ceiling hook by Jude's jump rope. There was a faint aroma of incense. I was about to go into the walk-in closet when I heard voices at the bottom of the stairs. I met Jude on the landing where the stairwell turned.

"The downstair's was busy. I hope you don't mind."

She was wearing her brown cobbler's pants and a loose-fitting blouse. She'd lost some weight. "You didn't forget where things were, I hope."

"Somebody left the cap off the toothpaste." I meant it to be funny but it came out critical.

Jude smiled politely. "Some things never change, I guess."

I tapped my hands on the railing. "Sorry I jumped on you the other night about Lill."

"Your reception was a standing ovation compared to my mother's."

"Martha knows?"

"She came by here on the way to somewhere and, you know me, I thought it would be a good opportunity to get it out on the table, so we took a ride to Nordstrom's together."

"What happened?"

"She flipped. Slapped me in the face and carried on about how sick it was. Her daughter shaming her dead father's name and all that." There was a tremor in Jude's voice. She was one step below me and I stepped down so she didn't have to crane her neck. "I told her I'd rather boff a woman than sneak into bedrooms and finger-fuck little girls like her brother did."

"Jesus."

"I made her stop the car and walked home."

I almost put my arms around her, something I probably should have done the first time she'd mentioned her Uncle Edgar. But I was more afraid now than I was then that she would rebuff me because I was a man and, therefore, partially responsible. "Your dad wouldn't have let her do that to you, Jude."

She turned and hurried up the stairs.

12.

I was cross-examining the owner's structural engineer when my secretary came into the courtroom. She had a frightened look like she'd been running from someone, and she was choking a pink slip in her hand. It was completely out of context—she'd never come to court—but everyone in the courtroom noticed her. By the third day of trial you knew who was connected to whom and Paula was a stranger.

"Your honor, may I have a moment, please?"

"We can take the afternoon recess now, counsel."

I checked the clock behind the judge's bench. We were twenty minutes ahead of the usual three o'clock break, and I didn't want to use up any of my chits if I didn't have to. "That won't be necessary, your honor."

As she came closer, I could see she'd been crying. "It's Justine," she whispered. "She's at Virginia Mason. They found her in the garage with the motor running." It was as if she'd pulled one of those big levers in the service box. I was suddenly shivering. She shoved the pink slip into my hand. "The doctor's phone number."

When I turned, I felt dizzy. Pasty white faces hung in the room like paper lanterns I wanted to swat away so I could get to Justine. I heard my client calling me from the distance. I didn't want to even utter Justine's name in this room, which had suddenly been reduced to a pit of vipers hissing over money. "I have to go, your honor."

I must have communicated something dreadful by my demeanor because, without a single question, the judge slammed his gavel down in his most decisive ruling of the day. "This case is recessed until nine-thirty tomorrow morning."

I left my secretary to make the explanation to my client and pack up my briefcase while I ran out the door. It was like there'd been an evacuation order and I was the only one who'd heard it. The elevator stopped on every floor. Men stepped back to let ladies enter first. A woman with one baby in a sling and another in the stroller got on at the third floor, where the district courts heard traffic tickets and

123

domestic harassment cases. With my back, I pushed a heavyset man against the wall to make room. The door caught on the handles of the stroller and automatically re-opened. The woman was as oblivious to the door as she was to her baby fussing in the sling. I wedged my heel into the rubber bumper and pulled the stroller all the way into the car.

At the Fourth Avenue entrance, I stood in the street and hailed a Far West taxi. My heart was bumping and heaving. Taxi drivers knew what a fire was. He grunted something in Indian or Pakistani and made a diagonal from one side of the street to the other, crossing four lanes as I looked out the back window with him. We raced up James. When the yellow light at Sixth changed to red, he held his horn and blasted through the intersection. As he pulled into the ambulance entrance to the Emergency Room, the meter said two dollars and sixty cents. I dropped a five over the back of the front seat and bolted.

Justine was in a glass and steel hyperbaric chamber that looked like an iron lung. The nurse said they were saturating her with oxygen, trying to loosen the carbon monoxide that had attached to the hemoglobin in her blood and been absorbed by her tissue. She was unconscious when the ambulance brought her in, with a carboxyhemoglobin level of forty-seven percent. They let me stand next to the chamber. Her face was a cadaverous white and she was stock-still. Children were supposed to bury their parents, not the reverse.

"Are you sure she's breathing?"

An Asian nurse in a green gown pointed to a gauge on top of the chamber where a black needle stuttered between the green and yellow zones. Each time it fell into the yellow I thought it was going to plummet to zero. There was another gauge which measured atmospheric pressure.

"We have her at sixty-six feet below sea level," she said.

I hadn't even noticed Jude in the flock of green gowns working the room. She was pale and bit her lip as she spoke. Her voice was on the edge of crumbling.

"When I went down to leave . . . the car was running. She must have taken the keys from my purse."

I put my arm around her and she leaned into me, like the first time we'd commiserated over Justine when the car backed onto her port-a-bed. I shuddered, picturing Justine in the darkness of our garage, which was a concrete tomb burrowed into the hillside below the house.

"Was there a note or anything?"

"I don't know. I came straight here in the ambulance."

With my arm still around Jude's shoulder, we watched our Justine swimming for her life under sixty-six feet of water. They said there was no way to know how much had been absorbed by her tissue. The nervous system and heart had the highest metabolic rate and were the most susceptible to carbon monoxide poisoning. The sheet that covered her had been tucked under at the sides and made her look like a mummy. I prayed an *Our Father* and asked forgiveness for the divorce and for being so blind as to have not seen this coming. The needle kept losing power. *Stay in the green, Justine. I'll be a better parent. We'll talk about it. You don't have to resort to blackness.*

After the second hyperbaric treatment, they transported her in a gurney with a lumpy wheel that bumped as we followed her through the hallways to her room. Once in her bed, she crept out of unconsciousness long enough to see us standing over her. She didn't say anything but her eyes moved from me to Jude and back again. Her eyelids opened and closed slowly, like she was pulling a weighted theater curtain up and down. Her eyes locked on mine with an openness I'd never felt between us before. If there was any shame for what she'd done, the purity of the oxygen had diluted it. Then she dropped off again.

Jude's mother, Martha, came by later in a red evening gown with a fox pelt over the shoulders and her face tanned from a Caribbean cruise. Her gentleman friend in a white tux carried his hat in his hand. They looked like they were on the way to a charity auction, where everyone got boozed up and bid for weekend trips to San Francisco and Acapulco. Her hibiscus perfume dueled with his lemon after-shave bracer. Martha broke into tears when she saw Justine, and her friend helped her into the chair next to the bed.

"I'm sorry, Pudding. You don't need your grandmother doing this on you." Justine hated to be called pudding.

Jude disappeared for her dinner break in the hospital cafeteria as soon as her mom showed up, so I had to make my own conversation with her. I hadn't seen Martha since the separation, an event that was already a defining milestone in my life. Justine's attempt on her life in the driver's seat of Jude's car would be another.

"You're looking pretty chipper, kid," Martha's beau said, as he stepped up to the bed and rested his hat on the bedding somewhere over Justine's left knee. I didn't even know if he'd met her before.

Martha stopped sniveling and escorted me by the elbow over to the doorway and into the bright hollowness of the hallway. Her fingers dug into the flesh on the inside of my elbow joint. "This is Jude's fault, you know."

"I don't think . . . ."

"I'm against the whole divorce idea." She snapped her head as she said it. "Leaving someone with a good job for a woman?" The implication was that if it had been a man it might have made sense. "Now she's neglecting the kids."

"They aren't neglected, Martha."

She looked mystified.

I nodded toward Justine. "She's a complex kid. There's millions of pent-up fears in someone her age. Any one of them could have set this off."

"You're being soft on Jude," she said. "You were always too soft on her."

"The world's changing, Martha. We can't bully and bark our way to the top anymore." I remembered all the times Jude had complained of her mom's bitching about her weight, and Jude telling her she didn't want to look like a model, and she wasn't going to starve herself for someone else's stereotype. Of course, Jude burned more calories worrying about her mom than she ever could have lost with a diet.

"Bosh!" Martha almost spit on me. "Women's lib is bunk. Don't you see that?" She looked past me to Justine and her friend at the bedside. "It's just bunk."

Jude and I stayed with Justine at the hospital that night, and Lill stayed with Derek. I called Derek to tell him what was going on.

"Justine's going to make it, pal, but the doctor wants to keep her under observation and take some more tests to make sure her levels stay down. How are you doing?"

"Magpie and I want to sleep in her bedroom."

"That's a good idea."

Jude and I took turns sleeping in the second bed in Justine's room, which had a thin mattress and a button to raise and lower the pillow end. Justine woke up in the middle of my shift and seemed to be free of the weariness that had possessed her earlier. The last time I'd tended to her at bedside she was seven and they'd taken out her tonsils.

"I'm sorry, Dad," she whispered, her lips too dry to stretch. She gripped my hand. Then she looked over to see if her mom was listening, but Jude's breathing was slow and rhythmic. She clamped her eyes shut. "I've been feeling so ugly." Her lips quivered and her chin tightened into a knuckle. "Someone at school said I was sexless."

"Jesus, Justine." Her accuser's words resonated with my own guilt; I'd periodically thought the same thing of Jude.

"I couldn't go back to class, so I just left school and wandered around. I knew he was right. Because of Mom."

I knelt down next to the bed so that my head was near hers and wrapped both hands over her fists like they were a warm stone. "Justine, daughters don't always turn out like their mothers. Look at your mom and Martha."

She smiled and squeezed my hand. "Don't tell Derek about this. He'll be freaked out."

"Don't worry about him. Just you get better."

I knelt next to the bed until she dropped off and her breathing became audible. Then I sat in the chair, rested the back of my head against the wall, and closed my eyes.

When Justine was five, we dressed her in a bunny costume and took her to Volunteer Park for the public egg hunt. It was a madhouse with all of the kids crowding around the man in the microphone who was dressed in a padded rabbit suit. His little helpers in fairy suits with transparent wings stood inside the rope barrier to keep kids from hunting until the gun went off. It was a children's version of the street demonstrations at the '68 Democratic Convention. Justine wanted to go home, but we made her stay and helped work her closer to the rope. Most of the kids were uncostumed, including a gang of boys next to Justine with pillowcases and plastic bags tucked into their belts who whistled and shouted at the bunny to shoot his gun. Besides marshmallow eggs and chocolate bunnies, the fairies had hidden plastic eggs with quarters in them and golden eggs with tickets to the Poncho Theater.

When the gun fired, someone knocked Justine over and her headpiece twisted down over one of her eyes. We lifted her up and urged her on, watching as she shuffled across the grass with her bamboo-weave Easter basket. Every bush and tree she looked behind had already been picked clean. Older kids flashed by her like skyrockets, showing off eggs and candies to their parents behind the rope. When the whistle blew to stop the hunt, Justine had an empty basket that she dropped at our feet. She was crying. I scurried around until I found one of the boys with a pillowcase and paid him a dollar for a handful of candy that I put into her basket.

I could hear the sound of voices at the nursing station and the pad of tennis shoes passing the open door to Justine's room. Jude and Justine were both snoring and, I thought, they did sound a lot alike. Justine had inherited so many traits from her mother that I wondered if sexual perplexity was one of them.

The first night Justine was out of the hospital and the kids stayed with me I found a half-smoked joint in the cigar box from my dresser amid the campaign pins, contact lens case, mood ring, Canadian coins, spare keys, football needles, and other miniature paraphernalia. It was dry and hard and the paper was bumpy where it molded around the crumpled grass. One end of it tapered to a smoking hole the size of pencil lead and the other end was blunt and ashen where it had been tamped out, the leftovers from one of our nights with the Baldwins, when they'd bring their kid over for a potluck dinner and a jug of Gallo Burgundy. Their girl was the same age as Derek and we'd have Justine play out in the yard or the basement with them while we passed a joint in the kitchen for an appetizer. After dinner, we'd put the kids to bed, pass another joint, and turn on the Moody Blues. Then we'd get ravenous and vandalize the kitchen for strawberry shortcake makings. We figured Justine was too young to know the difference between cigarettes and pot.

Jerry Baldwin worked on the UW campus and had access to all the dope he wanted. I was scared of getting caught and losing my bar membership so I never kept a lid in the house. We bartered sandwich baggies with a little dope in the bottom in exchange for our babysitting their girl. I only smoked when we had company. For me, the laughter was the turn-on; for Jude, it was the idea of my breaking the law. I used to worry when we made love after smoking pot that she was fantasizing I was one of her ACLU buddies. The first time Jude let me come down on her we'd had some of the Baldwins' grass. Maybe that was the start of her transformation.

I rolled the little butt from my cigar box between my fingers, closed the lid, and put the box back into the sock drawer. When Justine turned twelve, we stopped doing the grass. I hadn't even thought of the stuff for years. But with the kids in bed, I thought, why not close the door, open the window, and finish this one off? It was better than having them find it. Besides, I needed an escape from the stories of adolescent suicide that had begun to jump out at me from the newspapers and I also needed relief from watching Justine for the least hint of depression.

I lit a candle and dripped wax onto a saucer to create a base. Then I turned off the light, climbed into the center of the bed, and put the saucer on the bedspread. The joint crackled when I lit it off the candle flame. Seeds. I was surprised at how easily I was able to open my throat and draw down the first drag. I held my breath and let the dope find its way into the bloodstream where it created a rush of parental euphoria. It felt so reassuring to be under the same roof with the kids, even if it was only for the weekend. Justine's incident had made me treasure our limited time together even more. We were surviving the pandemonium.

The first exhalation left me light-headed as I sat there motionless. A wisp of smoke trailed off the end of the joint, making it look like it had died. Against the cement wall of the bedroom, I could see my shadow. The torso that rose out of the mattress fluttered and swayed like a genie coming out of its bottle as the candle flame flickered next to me.

I lay back, closed my eyes, and took another toke that went straight to the groin, microdots of cannabis leaking into my scrotum. Lill floated into the room, unwrapping herself as she moved. Her clothes were translucent and fell off her pale skin like silk sliding from marble as she walked toward me, her pubic hair the color of port wine. Go ahead, Lill, I thought, unzip me. She swept the air with her free hand like a blind woman trying to find the edge of the bed, and I tried to imagine the orange blossom scent of her hair and the pad of my thumb brushing over her scar.

Then the hot cone from the joint dropped onto my bare stomach and I jumped up and brushed it to the floor. I thought I heard something from Justine's room and put my ear next to the crack. What if one of the kids walked in on me? I held the roach up to my eye and there was no sign of heat. It was dead. I thought of flushing it down the toilet but I didn't want to leave the bedroom with it so I pinched it off the hairpin, threw it to the back of my throat, and swallowed it the way Jerry had taught me. It lodged partway down like a spitwad, and I tried to make saliva but the insides of my mouth were juiceless. I opened the window and waved the smoke out with a pillow. Then I wondered if the probation officer upstairs with the pug face would smell it and call the cops. The window accidentally banged shut when I unhooked the chain and I clenched my teeth, sure that I had aroused either the kids or the pug.

With my clothes still on, I slid under the covers and pulled them up to my chin. This was the other reason I'd stopped smoking this stuff: it made me paranoid. But this time the paranoia was warranted. I felt horrible for even thinking of Lill, especially with the kids here. I kept thinking of Justine bringing home a girlfriend in overalls and a pocket protector, of Derek loitering around rest rooms in the park to pick up men, of some zealot like Dan White who gunned down Harvey Milk in the San Francisco City Hall coming after them.

In my dream that night, I took a woman to the Greyhound bus station who slipped off her ring and stuck it into my pants pocket as we stood in the breezeway next to an idling bus, the diesel fumes making me nauseous. She turned, handed her ticket to the mustached driver standing at the door, and bolted up the steps. Once she reached her seat, she whispered something to me through the tinted windows, and I answered her with voiceless words that moved my lips.

Derek was at a friend's house that Saturday, so I had to think of something to do with Justine. I asked her if she wanted to have someone over. Negative. Or go bicycling. Negative. Or take Magpie on a hike.

"You can go without me," she said.

There was no way I was going to leave her home alone. And I couldn't imagine just the two of us sitting home without talking about it. I needed distraction. I wanted cheerful. She finally agreed

130

to go to Longacres.

In order to save two bucks, I used general parking, which was distant from the entry way but free, and took the shuttle train, which looked like a series of coupled golf carts. I thought she'd get a kick out of the open-air ride, but she seemed glum. I wanted sunshine, but the sun was behind a cloud formation resembling a pile of poker chips. Justine dragged behind as I led us to a bench close to the finish line.

"Look at that infield," I said. "It's landscaped like Buckingham Palace."

"The people seem just ordinary."

She was right on that one. They called it the sport of kings, but the stands were filled with paupers and pretenders, a melting field of races where every tongue could utter win, place, show. She hung her hooded sweatshirt over the back of the bench and I folded my Scotch-plaid sportcoat, a Christmas gift from Mom, into a square on the seat next to me. I taught her how to read the racing form—date and length of race, track condition, position at each call, jockey weight, speed rating. She seemed to be coming alive and started studying the form, circling and ranking her top three horses the same as I did, but our choices seldom matched. During the parade to the post, she'd go over to the rail and watch the jockeys canter their horses by.

"Don't just go with the prettiest silks," I told her.

She scoffed. "I'm more interested in their rump muscle."

In the fifth race, with quinella wagering, she put her two dollars on Indian Justice and Suicide Sue. I almost said something—the doctors said it was healthy to talk about what had happened—but I didn't want to put a damper on things. I put five bucks on Shindig across the board on the basis that she was coming down in class, had a five-pound weight advantage, and had recently been claimed by the leading trainer. Justine's two horses thundered past in a photo finish for first, and she whipped me with her form and laughed as Shindig limped over the line second from last. She was so excited she knocked her coke off the bench.

"My horse must've pulled a rump muscle." I didn't care who won. I just wanted her to smile, to put some experiential distance between the incident and the rest of her life. I just wanted her and Derek to stay with me, to start doing all the stuff we still hadn't done.

I was glad for the distraction of the two black gentlemen who sat on the bench behind us and chattered constantly. From their conversation, I gathered they were machinists at Boeing. They'd bet at the window, and then bet against each other from their seats. The guy in the checkered shirt tapped Justine on the shoulder after she won the quinella.

"Ma'am, do you mind telling me who you're on in the next race?"

Justine was taken aback and looked at me as if to see if it was okay. "I'm on Momma's Boy," she said. "His jockey's already won two today." Justine may not have been gleeful, but she was still a quick study. She'd already picked up on the importance of propensities, including gender. The jockey she liked was a her.

"Say, I hadn't noticed that," the man said, looking down at his program. Then he laughed and nudged his friend, "Whad I tell you?"

We made our bets and squeezed out a place against the cement railing for the last race, watching the wheel-tractor drag a rake-frame around the track to erase the footprints from the last race. Erasure was one of the things I liked about the track. Each race was a new start, independent of whatever confusion and bad luck had preceded it. After the tractor passed, it looked like someone had combed the ground, leaving narrow peaked rows of nutrient-rich topsoil that birds lit on searching for angle worms.

Our friends were still there when we went back to the bench to get my coat and Justine's sweatshirt. The man with the baseball cap, who'd bet against Justine's horses earlier, extended his hand. "Say, young lady, you wouldn't mind telling me where you'll be sitting tomorrow?" Then he broke into a belly laugh and swatted his buddy.

Justine smiled. She was better, but it seemed temporary. What would she feel like on Monday, in school, in her room? On the way home I tallied up in my head how much I'd spent for the day's entertainment, including pretzels, roast beef sandwiches, ice cream, drinks, admission, and bets. It was less than the cost of the eighteen block ride Justine had taken in the Shepard ambulance.

I tried but I couldn't get the image of Justine's pallid face in the hyperbaric chamber out of my mind when they went back to their mom's. I was measuring my life by the number of days it had been since the incident, hoping that each additional day would blur some of the detail in my memory. You didn't have to be a psychiatrist to know that Jude's situation was eating at Justine. She spent a lot more time in her room; she wasn't eating well. She didn't even get on Derek's case as often. Maybe we could excuse the first incident as a surprise, but if it happened again, it would be because of negligence. I needed Jude's help.

I didn't recognize the person who answered the phone at Jude's and thought I might have dialed the wrong number. There was a cackle of voices in the background. Not sure if it was the right house, I asked if Jude Martin was there. I still wasn't used to calling her Martin.

"It's me, Jude."

"We're having women's group, can I call you back?"

I was still miffed that she hadn't called me back when I'd left a message at her office. "I've been doing some more thinking about our situation." As I said it, I realized that it sounded like the preface to a request for reconciliation. There was no interruption; she was still on the line. I closed my eyes and just said it. "I think you need to break it off with Lill, Jude. At least, don't live together."

"Lill's moved in. She doesn't even have a place."

"That isn't an insurmountable obstacle."

"It isn't just a matter of leases and legal arrangements." Her voice sounded tired. "We have a relationship. What have they been saying to you?"

"Nobody's trashing you."

"They pick up on your silence, Cyrus."

"Am I supposed to spend my weekends extolling the virtues of this arrangement?"

"You're homophobic."

"Jude."

"I need her. I'm not going to let another relationship die." It was the closest she'd ever come to saying she regretted what had happened to us.

"This isn't a matter of blame."

"You make it sound criminal."

"Jude, I think the kids are afraid of you."

"This doesn't have anything to do with you and Lill, does it?"

The glass panels of the Safeway phone booth, which I'd chosen so the kids wouldn't eavesdrop, were steamed up. The proverb written in ballpoint pen on the aluminum just over the coin slot said: *Marriage is prostitution with one man.* I wiped my elbow against the glass and noticed a little girl standing outside clutching a quarter in her fingers. Her mom had probably told her to call after she'd seen what kind of fish was fresh. The things mothers made their kids do. "What are you going to do, Jude?"

"I'll spend some more one-on-one time with them away from the house. I'm as concerned about them as you are."

It was a start but it wasn't enough. On the walk back to the apartment, I went over the conversation the way I'd reexamine the argument in a motion I'd lost. I decided that I was the wrong person to carry the message; there was too much clutter between us. We always ragged on each other. She didn't have it in her constitution to give in and I took too much glee in seeing her squirm. We needed someone she trusted. Maybe Warren. She always liked Warren. She said he had inherited all the virtue in my family. But he'd still be perceived as mine. I needed someone who was hers.

13.

Lill agreed to meet me at Volunteer Park on the benches by the cylindrical brick water tower, which looked like an English fortress. From the top of the tower on a clear day, you could move from barred window to barred window and take in a different postcard view of Seattle: sailboats tacking in Lake Washington, the snow-capped Cascades, the site of the 1962 World's Fair, Queen Anne hill, the Olympics. Because I was early, I walked the pathway around the park and gawked at someone throwing a tennis ball to his dog, a man practicing chip shots, and a woman on a camping stool doing a watercolor painting of the greenhouse. In the city, the park served as the surrogate for the deserted roads and coulees that were so plentiful in places like Quincy.

Jude had taken me to Volunteer Park to watch a meteor shower the night we made Justine. She had a blanket in her trunk that her dad made her carry for emergencies, and we laid it on the grass next to the reservoir and talked about the black holes in the universe that sucked light into them like magnets. She unbuttoned her shirt and I tickled her with a long, tasseled weed. When it got cold, we rolled ourselves up like a rug in her blanket.

The crows were making a horrible racket, arguing with each other in the top of a pine tree by the path, as I watched Lill cross the meadow toward my bench. She was wearing a cossack blouse that was gathered at the wrists and hung loose outside her jeans. Her hair caught the gold in the autumn sunset as she moved across the grass with the lightness of a ballet dancer, rising up on her toes with each step. My pulse quickened and I had to remind myself that this was strictly a matter of diplomacy. When she crossed under the pine trees, she shielded her eyes and looked up to see where the noise was coming from.

"Thanks for coming," I said, and there was that bumbling moment of silence when your mind is all thumbs and you don't know who the two of you are to each other anymore. Then Lill lifted her arms and I rushed in. The strength of our grip obliterated the necessity for footnotes. "How are you doing?"

"Idle pleasantries or the truth?" Her voice was next to my ear and she gave me a last quick compression that signaled the end of our hug. "I'm worried about Jude. She'd never admit it to you, but she's beginning to wonder if we've bitten off more than we can chew." Lill sat down on the bench, kicked off her shoes, and wrapped her arms around her knees. "Has she told you any of the crap that's been going on?"

I shook my head.

"Remember your next door neighbors, the Sweets?"

"Sure, they used to bake for us. Treated us like we didn't own an oven."

"Jude thinks he's the one who's been making the phone calls. She recognizes his voice."

"What phone calls?"

"His standard line is something about Sodom and Gomorrah. He'll call in the middle of the night. Last time he called, she blew a bike horn into the receiver and hung up. She won't call the police. Two weeks ago someone put a dead cat on our porch with a Tampax sticking out its ass." The fists she made with her toes squeezed the blood out of the knuckles. "I keep expecting rocks through the windows."

"No wonder the kids are freaked out."

"We've kept most of it from them. Not a very good advertisement for living with their mother, is it?"

"How are you handling it?"

"Better than Jude. Something in my checkered past must have calloused me to this kind of crap. But it's been ages since we were intimate."

"Whoa. That's more than I need to know."

"She acts like I've been seeing someone on the side." Maybe that was the genesis of Jude's question to me on the phone about Lill. "I've been canned goods. Honest. She found a wine glass on the nightstand and thought it was suspicious. I told her it was poltergeist."

I cut her off. "Lill, I think the kids should live with me. I don't want another suicide attempt."

"You must think I'm a witch. First I eat your wife, now I screw up your kids. Cyrus, if she loses one of the kids, our relationship is history."

"Just talk to her, okay?"

"What makes you think she'll listen?"

"Make it sound like a way to get back at me."

Lill shook her head. "It's like you two had never met. You're not exactly Attila the Hun. You're actually fairly well evolved. Considering." She squinted into the sun. "I'll talk to her." She shook her head and started to water up. "Dammit, I don't want anything to happen to the kids either." She shook her hair and sniffed to clear away the sentiment. "God, look at me."

There was one more thing I was dying to ask her and something told me she'd be willing to talk. "How did it happen, Lill?"

She knew exactly what I meant. "Jude and me?"

"Yeah."

She cupped my hands together, then cracked them slightly open. "Whitman said sexuality is like the clef of a symphony. A signature."

I stared at the gap between my two thumbs. "That's it? Just sex?"

She smiled. "Don't ever say just sex. You can't separate sexuality from humanity." She said it softly and squeezed my hands back together. "Personally, I've always considered it an extension of our appetite for intimacy."

"Did it have anything to do with her Uncle Edgar?"

"I doubt it," she said. "If every little girl who got molested turned gay, we'd outnumber the Democrats."

"So how could you two . . . have husbands?"

"There's no big line in the sand, Cyrus. We all have the capacity to be intimate with the right person." She rubbed my hands. "You remember Isolde?"

"Sure, your German friend."

"She said it was a matter of not being able to read the music. When I married, I was still trying to figure out the music. Still am."

"But Jude . . ."

"Relax." The lilliputian laugh lines running from the corners of her eyes and mouth disappeared. "Think of yourself as a midwife. You helped deliver Jude into the place where she belongs."

"Its a nice thought, but I feel cheated at the thought that our marriage was just some rite of passage. If that's what it was, we shouldn't have brought kids into it."

"Life toys with us," she said.

As Lill and I walked out together, I puzzled over the idea of Jude as a prisoner. She must have been miserable pretending to be the good heterosexual mate, attending firm socials, talking wife-to-wife with my mom on family visits, trying to generate the affection in bed she knew was expected. I was tempted to take Lill's hand. It had been so long since I felt the softness of someone else's palm, and each time I saw her she seemed less the idealogue and more the pulsing, stumbling human being. The noise intensified as we came closer to the birds. There were crows in the two tallest trees taking turns swooping into the middle tree, going as deep as the trunk, then emerging into the open air and attacking again.

"My God, there's an owl up there." I stood behind her and pointed with her arm. "See him?"

She moved her head against mine and I could smell cream soda in her hair. "Why are they doing that?"

"The owl is the predator."

"But she's minding her own business."

"They want her out of the park."

Derek was supposed to be at the main entrance of Seward after the last bell for a show and dinner with Jude, but he never showed. It was part of her campaign for more one-on-one time with the kids. She told me she waited a half hour, walked the hallways, then went home and started calling his friends. Finally, she called the Seward principal, who summoned me and Jude to his office.

Mr. Washington stood about six foot three, spoke in a deep plantation-owner voice, and had the physique of the linebacker he used to be when he played for the Huskies. I wondered why the School District would waste such brawn in an elementary school where the kids still queued for lunch and fire drills. He'd already loosened his tie and collar.

"Shouldn't we be calling the police, Mrs. Stapleton?"

Jude wisely let the mistaken title pass. There was no sense confusing the school district with the intricacies of our domestic situation. "I think he'll show up. There'll be some simple explanation."

"You're the lawyer, Mr. Stapleton, what's the standard operating procedure here?"

I imagined Jude bristling the way she used to when my dad

directed political questions to me. She was chewing the insides of her cheeks. Derek had seemed fine last time we talked on the phone. We'd joked about Jim Zorn, the pass-crazy quarterback of the Seahawks. Derek said he was afraid they were going to lose to the Raiders on Sunday. Pessimistic but not suicidal. "I think we should report him missing."

Mr. Washington sat on the edge of his desk. "That all right with you, Ma'am?"

"Sure."

"Use my phone," he said, tugging on his tie. "I've already left word with his teacher in case she hears anything. She said he's been a little quiet lately. I understand he's usually quite the come-dian."

Jude gave me a knowing look, and I wondered if we should have mentioned what happened with Justine. We'd been faithful, at Justine's request, in keeping it a secret. Mr. Washington stepped out of the office while Jude called nine-one-one. She gave her home phone number and mine. The emergency operator probably figured another broken home, no wonder the kid was missing.

"Why don't we do some looking around on our own, Jude? Maybe he's back home by now."

Mr. Washington re-entered the office with a short stack of file folders. "I'll be here a while. Give me a call when you hear some-thing."

"We really appreciate your help," I said.

"You attorneys must get cases like this all the time," he said.

We shook hands. His felt as big as a baseball glove.

I stopped by to pick up Justine and Magpie at the house and we drove the Seward neighborhood, determined to do every alley and street between I-5 and Lake Union. Jude took the Roanoke Park area. I tried to visualize all the possible harmless explanations for his disappearance, but Justine's anxiety was contagious. As we crept down bumpy alleys between garbage cans and heaps of grass clip-pings and hedge trimmings, I kept expecting to find him slumped against someone's garage door, crippled from a hit-and-run.

"I knew he was upset," Justine said.

"How do you mean?"

"The way he's just shut down. He used to defend Mom. Now

he's given up."

Justine had my full attention. She knew about giving up. I watched her as she rubbed her thumbs hard against her index fingers and rotated her head trying to see both sides of the street. Derek was always so positive. Maybe I hadn't given him enough credit, ignoring the possibility that he'd inherited my own ability to dissemble and rationalize. We passed sailboats drydocked on blocks along the waterfront with extension cords and tarps draped over the gunnels and guys with face masks sanding keels that rested inches off the ground. We drove every street between Seward School and the Alhambra, and then I called the desk officer to see if the police had found him. No luck.

Justine and Magpie came back with me to the Alhambra. Neither Justine or I were hungry, so we fed Magpie and then just lay on the floor petting her, waiting for the phone to ring. At a few minutes after nine, there were footsteps coming down the stairs. *Ka, bum. Ka, bum.* It was the syncopation of dejection. We herded to the door and swung it open.

"Where have you been? The police have been looking all over for you." Now that he was apparently safe, Justine reverted to her role of Derek's guardian.

Derek just stood there in the doorway, shivering in his short-sleeve shirt, his pants wet half-way up the calves, and his tennis shoes caked with clay. There were blotches of grime around his eyes where he'd been rubbing them. He ignored Justine.

"We've been worried about you, partner." His school book with the Rolling Stones cover dropped open-faced onto the floor, spilling note papers. Magpie sniffed the mud on his pants.

"Are you going to ground him, Dad?"

"I need to find out what happened first."

"It looks like he's been goofing off in some swamp."

I wished Justine could back off and show her little brother a portion of the compassion I knew was inside her. I patted him on the shoulder and stroked his hair the same way I used to when he woke up with a bad dream and crawled into the waterbed with Jude and me. It always mystified me what a three-year-old had to worry about.

"I wasn't goofing around." Derek's words were muffled by my stomach.

"Then what were you doing?"

I frowned at Justine. "Get some dry clothes on," I said. "Then we can talk." The kids kept spare clothes at the Alhambra so they wouldn't have so much to carry back and forth.

Magpie, the most non-judgmental member of the household, followed Derek into the bedroom.

"You better call the police," Justine said, unable to resist organizing me.

I called Jude to tell her that Derek was safe and that the kids were going to stay with me overnight. The Alhambra had become the kids' half-way house, the place they came to when things flared up at their mom's.

While we ate toast and sipped hot chocolate at the kitchen table, Derek, in his print guitar and harmonica pajamas, told us how he'd left school and hiked through Interlaken, a steep, forested ravine that cut pie-shaped wedges into the north end of Capitol Hill, and then into the Arboretum. He pulled up his sleeves and showed us the rash from the nettles he'd encountered while hiding under the 520 bridge. Once it got dark, he heard two men shouting at each other.

"One of them kept saying he'd cut the other guy's balls off." His story sounded like one of his childhood nightmares.

"Why didn't you just come home?" Justine asked.

His cheeks bulged with a bite of toast. "Didn't feel like it."

"Are you still pissed at Mom?"

"Justine, watch your language."

Derek gulped a lump down his throat and answered. "Yeah, kind of."

That seemed to satisfy Justine because she got up, took a spoon out of the drawer, and reached into the bottom of the Nestle's carton. Her spoon tapped the metal bottom, scraped against the sides, and emerged with a heaping scoop of cocoa crystals that she dumped onto a saucer. She rejoined us at the table and begin dipping her licked finger into the chocolate.

After they'd brushed their teeth, I tucked Justine into the hide-a-bed in the living room. Even though it was for only one night, she'd made the room look like an estate sale, with clothes draped on the furniture and hangers suspended from the candelabra in the floor lamp. She also stationed two folding chairs next to the bed for her lotions, Kleenex, brushes, and magazines.

"I'm glad he's home, Dad, but you have to talk to him about

Mom's thing." Alone with me, she was soft and worried again.

Derek was under the covers flat on his back and his eyes wide open when I came into his room. He'd made a bed on the floor out of pillows and blankets for Magpie, who lay there gazing adoringly at Derek. I took a seat on the edge of the bed and wedged my cold toes under Magpie's belly.

"Okay, why'd you skip out on your mom?"

He twisted his head sideways and pulled his knees up as if to protect his balls and mumbled something.

"What?"

"I didn't want anyone to see her."

"Why not?"

"They'd know I lied."

"About what?"

He forced his eyes shut so tight they made creases like cat whiskers from the corners. "I told everyone she was dead."

I waited for him to elaborate, but he was more comfortable taking questions. Magpie, whose back legs scissor-kicked in little jerks, had already fallen asleep and was in her first dream. Derek leaned off the bed and put his hand on her side until she stopped kicking.

"Did you consider telling them the truth?"

"They'd think she's a freak."

"What do you think?"

"I know she's not normal."

It would have been easier for me to argue Derek's side of the allegation, but I knew he wanted to be proven wrong. I remembered when I was young my grandpa on Mom's side making me read G. K. Chesterton's *The Defendant*, which had essays on the defense of nonsense, the defense of rash vows, and the defense of ugly things. Reading that book was as much as anything else I could point to the reason I became a lawyer. "Mediocre people are normal," I said. "You know Albert Einstein?"

"Yeah."

"He wasn't normal. He invented the theory of relativity and helped develop the atomic bomb even though he was a pacifist. Einstein was a genius."

Derek stared at the ceiling. "Name someone else."

I had to think for a minute. "Stevie Wonder."

"He's blind."

"Has to read with his ears. What's normal about that?"

"Who else?"

I was on a roll. "Did your mom ever tell you about the time she and Justine camped out on the federal courthouse lawn?"

"No."

"Justine was seven. She and your mom chanted and waved banners protesting the war in Viet Nam and slept overnight in Army tents with a bunch of strangers."

"Really?"

"You were there too, inside your mom. She was eight months pregnant. Does that sound normal?"

He raised up on his elbows. "I know Viet Nam was bad."

"Everyone says that now, but not the night your mom slept downtown."

"Why didn't you go with us?"

That was the same thing Jude had asked me, but there was no way I was going to join a bunch of street protestors when I was in my first job in a downtown law firm and hoping to someday make partner. "I was embarrassed someone I knew would see me," I said.

His eyebrows registered surprise. "You mean Mom had more guts than you did?"

"Pretty bad, huh? Let me tell you something else about your mom. I think she's in love." His blink popped his stare like a soap bubble. "That's normal as water. Parents love kids even when they screw up. You love Magpie when she chews up your hardball. Your mom loves Lill." Derek fell back and wrapped his hands underneath the pillow, sifting it all to make sure there weren't any clinkers. I put my hand on his head. The pulse of a million nine-year-old molecules warmed my palm.

"Why do people call them queers?"

"The same people said Columbus would sail off the edge of the earth."

"That's how I felt under the freeway. Like I'd fallen off the edge of the earth."

14.

Rush hour traffic on Interstate 90 was bumper-to-bumper across the floating bridge, but I let people cut in front of me with a wave of my hand. Warren and I were on the way to Quincy, and I was hoping homecooking and twenty laps around the track at the high school would help me get my bearings. At Factoria, the logjam loosened and pavement started to reappear between cars like a murky river as the aggressive ones blinkered their way into the passing lane. We gassed at the Shell station in North Bend and bought snacks at the mini-mart. With each odd mile on the odometer we earned a stale pretzel ring. On the even ones we got to swig from the Gatorade wedged between my gym bag and the back of the passenger seat.

Lill's first diplomatic foray had met resistance. Jude told her they'd work through it with the kids and made an appointment with a family counselor for the four of them. She was convinced that it was still fallout from the divorce and the kids were bound to act up regardless of the sex of her new partner. I found myself pulling for a *coup d'etat*. The next time the kids ran to me, I wasn't going to let them go back. I'd hold them hostage until Jude and Lill cleaned up their act. A State Patrol car appeared in the rearview mirror with the blue light flashing. I was sure something had happened to one of the kids and they'd come to find me, but it whizzed past.

"You know," Warren said out of the blur of tire tread and wind, "that Lill is a charmer. You think lesbians ever cheat on each other?"

"Never thought much about it."

"What do you think Jude would do if some stud seduced Lill?"

"Is this a knock-knock joke?"

"She'd flip out."

"At least that."

Crossing Snoqualmie Pass, the car sputtered even though the fuel gauge showed half full. We made it as far as the turnoff to the Hyak ski area when we lost all power and had to work our way onto the shoulder. The driver behind us honked, then gunned his engine and passed us with his middle finger pressed against the passenger window. So much for the good karma I'd earned in the traffic jam. I pounded the top of the steering wheel with my palms. Dammit. If it hadn't been for the separation, we would have traded the Plymouth in by now for something with a warranty. I put on my right turn blinker and both of us slid out the passenger side. I took a business card out of my wallet, found a dull golf pencil in the glove compartment, and wrote a note to leave on the dashboard. "Best offer accepted."

With our bags slung over our shoulders, we started hoofing it back to the general store at the summit. The gravel crunched underfoot. Each car let out a windy guffaw as its headlights blew by me. Forget it. I wouldn't stop for you either. This was the kind of situation where I would have called Warren, except that he was with me. The AAA membership was in Jude's name.

"Let's call Dad," Warren said.

I grimaced. "He's still a hundred miles away." The prospect of explaining to Dad how I had let the car run down like this was simply too daunting. "I'd rather hitchhike home and call a towing company in the morning."

Warren shrugged. "*C'est la vie.* But let's get a drink first."

Next to the general store there was a bar and truck café. *Me and Bobby McGee* was playing on the jukebox. In my jeans, a pair of broken-down loafers, and a Gatorade stain down the throat of my shirt, I'd hardly be mistaken for a member of the Washington State Bar. I was more believable as the guy who'd just been released from the Walla Walla penitentiary with twenty bucks in his pocket.

After a few drinks, Warren befriended the barmaid and she found us a ride back to Seattle with a lanky fellow in Levi's with holes in the knees and a crumpled button-down cotton shirt. I suddenly felt overdressed again as we followed him to the parking lot. The back of his jeans drooped like an empty mailbag as his feet shuffled along the asphalt. A cigarette dangled from two fingers in his right hand. His Chevy station wagon leaned right. Through the dusty windows, I could see a set of drums in the back amidst a clutter of sleeping bags, rolls of toilet paper, cans of pop, and sundry articles of clothing. The flap on the carton of Pennzoil where I sat was ripped open and there were three cans missing.

"Shove that shit into the back," he said.

"Needs a ring job, huh?" Warren said.

"This fucker needs a heart transplant," he said, as he pumped the gas pedal in bursts and puffed a cigarette that seemed glued to the only thick part on him, his lower lip. The starter labored against the flywheel, which turned so slowly that I could count the revolutions. "Come on you cocksucker," he said. House plants, Jude used to say, picked up on the conversation in the room. If you wanted to say one was dying, she made you go outside the room. If the same were true for cars, we weren't leaving the parking lot. But then it backfired, shuddered, and started humming. Carney, our driver, smiled through the smoke bush that had grown out of his cigarette.

The car chattered once we were in the passing lane, where he drove exclusively. Warren tapped me on the shoulder and we exchanged glances. I was sure the steering mechanism was going to snap and wished that I'd changed my will. Everything still went to Jude; I wanted it to go to the kids, with Warren as trustee. The mustiness in the air was the same as the mold from the orange someone had left in my glove compartment one winter when the latch got stuck. Wind whistled through the bullet hole in the window by my ear.

"Car came with it," Carney said.

"Kind of unusual."

"Yeah, you'd expect it to be on the driver's side. Want one?" He extended his pack to me with unfiltered Camels sticking out like stairsteps.

"No thanks."

Warren, who didn't smoke, took one and gave me a dirty look, which I knew meant that he thought I was standing in judgment on our driver.

"I appreciate the lift," I said. "Our car died coming out of the pass."

The lighter on the dash popped and he put the flare against the tip of his cigarette. The glow made his lower lip look like a piece of salmon sushi. Then he extended the lighter over his shoulder and into the backseat for Warren. Carney took a long drag, held it a few moments, then blew it into the ceiling upholstery.

"You from out of state?" he said, as if that might explain the cultural gulf between us.

"We're Seattle. Where you from?"

"Eugene. Home of the duck fucks." Obviously not a University

146

of Oregon alum.

"I noticed your drums," Warren said. "You do gigs up here?" He had to yell to be heard over the collision of the car against the night air.

I thought Carney said, "Wherever." He didn't elaborate and Warren didn't follow up. The thought occurred to me that this guy could be Derek in twenty years.

I studied the controls on the dashboard. Although they weren't lit, the heater controls were on *Off*. "You mind putting the heater on for a bit?"

"Busted. Have to use a blanket." He tipped his head toward the back end of the station wagon. Getting a blanket seemed like a lot of trouble and would only widen the gulf between us. He didn't seem to mind the chill but, of course, he kept a string of cigarettes going.

Warren pulled a quilt out of the back and wrapped it around himself. "Can't beat home cooking," he yelled into my ear.

Carney drummed out tunes that were apparently playing in his head, slapping and tapping his knee, the dash, the wheel, anything within reach. His neck undulated like a snake charmer to the rhythms he created. He leaned his head back and yelled at Warren.

"So what's waitin' for you back home, cowboy?"

"My woman, who else?"

The driver shook his head. "Sounds like you're pussy-whipped." I hadn't heard that expression since college and wondered if it was sexist or ardently feminist.

"Ther're worse fates," Warren said.

"Worse what?"

"Fates," I yelled.

Carney gave me a quizzical look.

"Worse ways to die."

He laughed, then punched the lighter and reached for the pack in his shirt pocket all in one celebratory swing of his arm. "Women play games with your head." Carney tapped his pack against the steering wheel until he could get his lips around the tip of another cigarette. Warren turned him down this time. The lighter popped and he took a long philosophical drag. We were going to learn how the man on the street was handling women's lib. He blew a piece of tobacco off his tongue. "I had one like that once. Bitch," he muttered, and I momentarily wondered if I had a moral obligation to

147

straighten him out. Jude had taught me to speak out, but this guy was a ride, not my brother. "She was into all that equal pay and fucking on top shit. She had one problem though."

Warren leaned over the seat to hear him better. "What was that?"

"Couldn't keep her cunt in her pants."

I chuckled along with Carney and Warren.

"She cuckolded you?" I said.

"She what?"

"Cuckold," I said, as he leaned his head my way. "It's related to the cuckoo bird. They lay their eggs in someone else's nest."

"I like that," Carney said. "Cuck-old. Rhymes with fuck-old?"

"You got it."

"You a professor or something?"

I didn't want to break the illusion. We were just starting to communicate. On the other hand, here was a chance to convert a skeptic. "I'm a lawyer."

"Fuck me! No way!" He took his eyes off the road and looked me up and down like he'd just noticed there was someone in the cockpit with him.

"No shit. Official member of the bar."

"You probably got a pretty wife with long tan legs and a couple of kids in private school."

"Used to," Warren piped in.

"God bless you, man. What happened?"

I told him an abridged version of my story, leaving out any mention of the lesbian twist. Carney nodded his head knowingly as I spoke. Every time I gave Jude a compliment, Warren qualified it.

"That Jude's some pistol," is all he said when I finished. Then he seemed to drift into his own reverie for a while. I could feel the car pulling to the right, but Carney kept both hands on the left side of the steering wheel to keep us moving in a straight line. "I stopped once for this woman," he said. "She had a chest that was flatter than her tire." He fumbled for his Camels again and punched the lighter. "But she had the face of an angel. Made me smile just looking at her. When I was done with her tire, guess what she said?"

"No idea."

"You helped me, I feel like I should let you sleep with me."

"No shit, she said that?" Warren asked. His elbows were locked over the frontseat and he'd pulled the quilt up around his neck.

Carney lit up again and his skinny chest swelled as he sucked down that first drag. "So what would you do with that, counselor?"

"That's remarkable. I wouldn't know what to say."

"'Ma'am, that won't be necessary,' I told her. Can you believe that? Must've been my good upbringing." He laughed mid-drag and started coughing.

"What did she say?" Warren asked.

"She gave me a big watermelon. I cut it open and we sat right there on the shoulder each having a slice. Spittin' seeds between our legs and our hands drippin' with watermelon juice like a couple of farm kids. All the time she's looking at me with that angel smile. I could've shot my wad." Warren was tight against the front seat like we were riding a toboggan together. "The truck drivers in India say they have to have sex to release the engine heat that fills their bodies. I should have told her that."

Carney was shocked when he dropped us at the Alhambra and Warren told him I lived in the basement. We traded business cards. He fished his out of the glove box and turned the domelight on, the only thing electrical besides the lighter that worked. There was a blue snare drum in the center of the card with yellow atoms in orbit around it. *Carney Browner and the Lasers.* With a pen from the visor, he scratched out the phone number on the card and wrote a new one.

"Call me if you get in trouble," he said.

My marriage officially ended with a wimper when Charlie Johnson sent me the findings, conclusions of law, and the decree for my review and approval. I still wasn't entirely comfortable with Jude getting custody of the kids and me being relegated to visitation two weekends a month, but Justine was showing no signs of depression and seemed to be over her incident. Derek and his mom were still duking it out but I had become convinced from talking to the Group Health professionals that he was waging a valiant fight for Jude and me to stay together. Our little Man of La Mancha. What wasn't happening said more than anything. They weren't running to me to save them from the turmoil at the house Lill had described. They were sticking with the decision to live with their mother that they'd announced last fall in the living room.

While I held my pen poised over the signature block, a thin voice in me waged a half-hearted battle to stay my hand. But a louder, more commanding voice said it's over, it can't be fixed, move on. Whoever it was I wanted, I knew it couldn't be Jude. End this state of ambivalence. *Sorry, Derek.* I waived notice of presentation, returned the papers to Jude's attorney by messenger, and he entered them *ex parte* the same day.

A page came over the speaker for me while we were discussing new partner admissions in the large conference room, and I excused myself to take the call in my office. I hated those meetings anyway. The unspoken premise was always money. The more partners, the thinner the wedge each of us took from the pie. Someone always brought up the associate/partner ratio. The higher the better. Just when an associate became profitable, we made him (there had only been one her) a partner and cut him in on the profit. It was enough to make me a socialist. Maybe I was still just in mourning over the divorce.

Mr. Washington, the principal of Seward Elementary, was on the line, and had Derek in his office.

When I arrived, Derek was slumped in a chair next to the principal's desk. At least he didn't look hurt. Mr. Washington quickly ushered me by the elbow to the hallway and the hydraulic closer on the door exhaled behind us. The big clock over the door said 2:10 p.m.

"What's the matter?"

He spoke in hushed tones. "We found him on school property smoking marijuana."

"Shit!"

"There were two of them but the other kid ran. Derek won't say who it was. The janitor found them under a tarp that covers the rider-mower."

"You're sure it wasn't just cigarettes?"

"It wasn't cigarettes," he scolded.

"I believe you, I'm just stupefied."

"I have to ask you, sir, do you have reason to believe your son is the supplier?"

I blanched. "Supplier?"

"Where could he have gotten it?" I started to answer and he held his hand up to caution me. "I'm not naive, I know some people think it should be legalized. I just need to know what's going on here."

"Mr. Washington, I can assure you he didn't get this at my house, if that's what you're implying."

"I've been principal here for eight years and I'm rather proud of my record." Then he clenched his fist and pounded his index finger like a tack hammer into the cork bulletin board next to us. "I've never . . . had a single . . . case . . . of drugs . . . in my school." He was an imposing advocate. His voice dredged only double bass notes. He looked up and down the corridor, then leaned into me. "What is your family situation these days?"

His question twisted me like a sponge, squeezing beads of perspiration to the surface. My suitcoat suddenly felt too heavy. Mr. Washington was the personification of all my self-doubts. "We're divorced, you knew that?"

"I gathered from the dual addresses. What else is going on?"

"What did Derek say?"

"He's being evasive. That's why I'm asking you. His blowing a weed under the tarp is a symptom of something else. I think he wanted to get caught."

"They're living with their mom," I said. "I get them a couple of weekends a month and we split holidays. Everyone's still adjusting."

He scratched his spine against the door frame and shook his head as I talked. "Sounds like something's out of torque."

"Believe me, everything's fine."

He pointed toward his office. "With all due respect, sir, you may want to reconsider that statement. If my son were the fourth-grader getting high, I'd say things couldn't get much worse. Something bad's going down here and I suggest we check it out."

He was right. Mr. Washington was an ally, someone who could help me get to the bottom of this. I should be welcoming some professional energy. "You're right, Mr. Washington. Tell me what I can do and let's get on with it."

Mr. Washington agreed to not involve the police in return for my commitment to cooperate in letting the school district's counselors make an informal investigation, spend some time with Derek, interview me and his mother. Frankly, I was a bit surprised at his interest. Everyone said the Seattle public schools were going into the toilet. White flight. The best students were heading for the suburbs and transferring to private schools while the teachers who remained were punching the clock, cooing for the public once a year at parents' night, and dogging it the rest of the time. Like a samurai warrior, Mr.

Washington had leapt front and center to fight anyone who would threaten his chalk and blackboard empire.

I was furious at Derek and told him so when I got him to the car. "I don't get it, Derek. You're smart, you get along with people. This kind of crap is dead-end."

Derek kept looking out the window. I didn't know where to take him so I pulled over in front of Don's Grocery and let the engine idle. "How many times have you done this?"

He mumbled something.

"What?"

"A couple," he shouted into the dashboard. That's the same thing he'd told Mr. Washington.

"Where'd you get it?"

"A friend."

"Where'd he get it?"

"Dunno."

"Whoever this kid is, he's no friend of yours and I'm going to call everyone in your class until I find him."

Derek bunched his fists into his eye sockets and leaned into the passenger door, his forehead resting on the window sill. "Don't call."

I put my hand on the shoulder of his jacket. "I'm trying to help you, Derek. The way to get your friend in trouble is to ignore this. The next time it'll involve the police. I can tell you this: if it happens again, the police will be the least of your worries."

I felt like a truant officer marching him up the stairs to the old house. Before opening the door, I brushed my hand through his hair to make him look less disheveled. He gave me a tentative smile, but he still looked like a chastised dog. I stayed with him until Jude came home, explained the situation to her and then left.

I descended the twenty stairs slowly, my heart coiling and uncoiling like a slinky. I didn't feel right leaving Derek there. I felt so inept. I didn't know how to be a parent. The kids needed more than self-reliance. I needed to show them an emotional intricacy that I'd never developed. They needed to trust me with their pain. Whatever was bothering them, they were willing to risk it with a mother they were embarrassed to be seen with in public. Maybe they didn't know how much I wanted them.

15.

While Derek prepared his sauerkraut and wieners for our Friday night dinner, Justine and I walked Magpie by the mansions in the historic district on Belmont. The bushes were trimmed like poodles, bare in the legs and torso and puffy at the extremities. Real poodles stared at us through leaded glass windows from cavernous dining rooms with chandeliers that glowed like upside-down wedding cakes. There were brass emblems on marble columns at the entrances to the driveways. At a house with railed balconies and flower boxes outside each of the upstairs windows, a man in rubber boots hosed mud off a driveway that curved under the portico.

"If you and Mom had stayed married, could we afford to live in one of these?"

"You mean after all my lectures on the difference between happiness and net assets, you want to throw it over for a thirty-room house with servants' quarters?"

Justine jiggled Magpie's leash to distract her from the base of a stone wall which held the secrets of the canine universe. Magpie braced her feet, disconnected her voice command center, and sniffed up and down the wall like an anteater. "I don't even know what net assets are," she said.

"It's something your parents tell you after puberty."

"You've never told me about that either."

"Didn't your mother?"

"Kind of," she said. Fortunately, she didn't pursue it as we sat on someone's curb and petted Magpie.

"What's going on at home, Justine?"

"Everything's about the same."

"How's Derek doing?"

"He was bitchy during the week. Pulled practically everything he owned out of the closet and spread it around his room."

"Sounds normal." Magpie had meantime left a big dump on a parking strip that was manicured like the felt on a pool table. I'd forgotten to bring along plastic bags, and tried to jostle it with a stick toward the tree circle.

"Ick. Just leave it, Dad. One of their servants can pick it up."

"It's no worse than changing your diapers."

"I thought Mom did all that."

The kids went back to their mom's on Sunday night and I hoped that Justine would call to give me a report on things at the house. Maybe she and her mom had had their talk. The only person who called on Monday was a carpet cleaner who said he'd be in the neighborhood with a special.

Downtown Seattle felt like a pile of highrise office buildings in a wasteland of pissed-on sidewalks and clogged arterials again. I came home before dark and walked to Safeway for something to cook or, more accurately, heat up. Even on Capitol Hill, the air was smoky with exhaust and cluttered with noise as I followed a parochial school girl in a Navy blue uniform dress and knee socks, walking hand in hand with her father. She bumped against his side, taking direction from the swing of his arm and the nudge of his hip, showing unconditional trust in his guidance.

In the men's therapy group, we'd done some father work which I'd thought at the time was pretty far removed from what was bothering me. My dad was a good provider and generally urged me forward, but I couldn't remember him ever actually listening to me. His vision of me was independent of anything he really knew about me. By default, I'd usually done what he wanted. He complained that he'd missed college to fight in the war, married early, and ended up working for wages most of his life. Although I'd married early too because Jude was pregnant, I was obedient in the rest of his regrets, running scared as a jackrabbit straight from kindergarten to law school and becoming a partner in the minimum six years.

"A man's only as good as his job," he'd told me. Whenever I'd tried to broach the subject of my problems with Jude, he'd brushed it aside and asked instead about my work, and when I started to tell him about my work he'd talk about his even though he was already retired. I'd sworn that I'd listen to my kids if I ever had any.

Jude and I had always scheduled a Christmas trip with the kids. The last year we were together we rented a condo at White Pass and skied. There was a heated outdoor pool where the adults brought

154

their drinks and planted them in snowdrifts next to the Jacuzzi while the kids threw snowballs at each other and watched them melt in the pool like sugar cubes. This year Jude was meeting her brother and his family at Whistler, where he'd rented a place large enough for both families. I knew she had to be doing this strictly for the kids because, as Jude was fond of saying, her brother could be a pain in the ass. And she'd gone without Lill.

Most lawyers in the firm took off the week between Christmas and New Year's. Those of us left felt like we were doing time, and I needed to break out. I was worried about the kids but there was nothing I could do when they were with their mom. Hopefully, they were having the time of their life skiing. Seeing them only on occasional weekends, I was learning to stuff my parenting into a bag when they weren't there. Denial was one of the skills I'd developed as a lawyer. There were simply too many crappy things happening that you couldn't change.

On the day before New Year's Eve, I called Dana Dukelow, the mother of one of the girls in Justine's class. I found her number in Justine's school folders. She was the single mother I'd seen at parents' nights in the miniskirts and patterned nylons, the one who let her daughter Sarah take friends to their cabin on Whidbey Island unchaperoned. I asked her to go roller-skating New Year's Eve. I hadn't roller-skated since senior prom when our class rented the rink at Soap Lake and people wheeled around in suits and evening gowns.

After we'd picked out our skates, Dana disappeared into the ladies' locker room and changed into Spandex tights, a flared green skirt, a white ruffled blouse, and a matching green ribbon for her hair. The rink had tied balloons to the lights and taped an "Auld Lang Syne" poster over the refreshment stand. As we skated around the floor to the sounds of Linda Ronstadt and Barry Manilow from the cluster of boxed speakers laden with mistletoe that hung over the center of the floor, Dana seemed oblivious to the fact that most people were wearing jeans and sweatshirts. On a couples-only number, she took my hand.

"Come on, I won't bite you."

Fortunately, many of the roller-skaters there probably hadn't been born the last time I skated so there was little risk I'd run into anyone who knew me. Besides, lawyers didn't skate. I envied her the way she could close her eyes and let her head float back on the straightaways, careless as to who saw us or what they thought.

She invited me in when I dropped her off at her house. "We can turn on the tube and watch the year end."

"I hate that countdown with the ball thing."

"I hate being alone when everyone else is having fun," she said.

I looked around the living room while she went into the kitchen to fix us a Harvey's Bristol Cream, which didn't sound all that good after the spiked eggnogs at the rink. Everything was neat as a pin. Magazines and sections of the morning newspaper were fanned across the coffee table. I lifted the lid off a giant glass apple and found it filled with jelly beans. The purple ballpoint pen in the holder next to the phone was lilac-scented. There was a pillow carefully positioned in each corner of the couch. I slid my hand between the seat cushions and fished out a pair of dirty sweat socks, and felt a pang of discomfort for being there. I should have at least asked Justine if it was okay to go out with the mother of one of her friends. When Dana returned, I quickly stuffed the socks back into the sofa.

"It's so quiet here when Sarah's at my mother's." She stopped at the bookshelves, shoved in an eight-track cassette, and turned down the lights. "Morning Has Broken." I loved Cat Stevens. We had the same initials.

She handed me my drink in a crystal glass and then took a seat so close to me that her bottom brushed my arm on the way down. "They were my grandma's," she said. "We have a set of eight."

I must have had a puzzled look.

"What?" She laughed and leaned her shoulder into mine. "What did you think I was talking about?"

"I guess I was spaced out."

"He has a sexy voice," she said.

"But how many words a minute can he type?"

No reaction.

She went back to the kitchen for a second round, this time returning with the bottle and using one of the magazines for a coaster. Things were getting more homey and I slid down next to her on the floor.

"I used to be a pretty good skater," she said. "My boyfriend would tie a ski rope to the back of his bike and pull me around the neighborhood."

"We used to line up people on the grass and build bike ramps to see how many we could jump over."

She sipped her Bristol Cream and studied me. "It's okay to tell the kids about this, isn't it? I tell Sarah everything."

I shrugged. "Sure."

Dana was a bit of a talker, or else she'd been starved for an adult audience. She told me her story, how she loved being a travel agent, how her husband had cheated on her, where she went to church, how proud she was of her Sarah. Her voice grew velvety. "If you'd been the one who pulled me on my skates, do you think we would have, you know, done something about it?" She giggled and nudged me.

This was where I should have turned on the Times Square rally and sobered up. She was just trying to be nice and I was letting myself slide back into a state of self-delusion, forgetting everything I'd learned. I stretched my arm out and drooped it over her shoulder. With my eyes closed, I stroked the back of her neck and imagined her floating with her arms thrust behind her the way she did at the skating rink. She leaned over to set her glass on the coffee table and, on the way back, I greeted her with a slow kiss. There was no flexing of her lips; she let me do all the moving. She whispered something into my mouth and I guided her to the floor in the space between the coffee table and the couch, making a perfunctory effort to sort out the consequences of this.

"Is this okay?" I asked.

I slipped my hand between the rug and her back, trying to feel the knobs of her vertebrae. She arched to give me more space. Then I noticed the rag doll sitting on a throne of floor pillows in the corner, watching us with her button eyes and thready smile. She looked like the doll Justine had slept with until the face rubbed off and Derek amputated its legs with a pair of scissors. I couldn't think of the kids and do this. Starting to feel very Catholic, I rolled onto my side, away from her.

She slid her hand down my ribs, stopping at my groin. Then she lifted her head and looked at me. "I don't usually have this effect on people."

"It's not you." Something was holding me back that I didn't have the heart to even bring up. A good body and a puckered mouth weren't enough. We needed roots and we didn't have any. In their own mushy dialect, my insides were speaking to me with the profundity of Churchill.

"This way, you can still like me in the morning," she said.

She mussed my hair and gave me a kiss on the cheek at her door when we parted.

I drove down Broadway on the way home. Usually, I would have stopped at Dick's for a cheeseburger but my stomach felt queasy. A couple of people were trying to do one of the dance steps that were embedded in bronze on the sidewalk. Punks with purple hair, bicycle chains, and handcuffs hanging from their belts leaned against parking meters smoking and gawking at passersby. Girls with blue lips and frizzy hair strutted their stuff. The Hari Krishnas and Moonies had gone home to bed. Everyone left was on the make.

There were no parking places at the Alhambra and the streets were full so I used a rounded corner that nobody had taken. Walking back to the apartment, I pushed on my stomach trying to find the source of the pain I felt in the intestines. My forehead felt sweaty and I held onto several deep breaths to force oxygen into my brain. I looked up to find stars, wanting something expansive, but a dull fogginess hovered just beyond the tops of the buildings, reflecting back the lights of the city. The only noises were the buzz of streetlights and accelerating car engines. I would have fallen on my knees and prayed to the chirp of a cricket, the cackle of a chicken, anything living.

As I descended the stairs to the basement and fumbled for the key, the nausea in my stomach swelled like a bladder that knows it's close to a bathroom. I pushed open the door, left my key in the lock, raced down the hallway, snapped the switch on, lifted the seat, and knelt with my hands on the rim of the bowl. The first heave turned my belly over but nothing came out. I detested the thought of cream sherry and vowed never again to drink it. The next movement forced my mouth open and expelled another dry, gagging heave. My face felt as clammy as the porcelain. I thought of the beatnik Jesus from therapy who'd fooled around with his wife's sister and realized we were cut from the same plain male cloth. I hadn't made any progress.

The water in the bottom of the toilet bowl shimmered from the leak in the tank that the landlord had never fixed and it reminded me of the sunken battleship *Arizona* that I'd seen at Pearl Harbor, the way water distorted things that didn't belong. I studied the rusty brown stain under the circumference of the rim and the hairs between the bolts that hinged the back of the seat. Another dry heave, more violent than the first, left a twice-cooked taste of Harvey's that burned my throat. I fixed my brain on the image of wormy duck meat and the vomit finally sprayed out of my mouth, spoiling the water a chunky orange. Saliva dripped from my lips and I knew that the disfigured face looking up at me from that pool was my own.

16.

In January, I left for work in the dark and came home in the dark. Sometimes, I'd drop my clothes on the bed as I undressed, get under the covers in my stocking feet and underpants, and listen to the water gushing down the drainpipe as people flushed their toilets or unplugged their bathtubs. The gutter emptied onto the sidewalk next to my window and, when the rain slowed, the drips echoed as they hit the galvanized elbow at the bottom. Occasionally, the woman with the cat in the unit above me had overnight company and I had to listen to her bed creaking and thumping. One night at about three a.m., I heard her giggling outside the door to my apartment and bumping the walls like she was trying to get away from her fellow. One of them hit my door and rattled the latch. Then I heard the gushing of hot water into the washer, which meant I'd later hear the tumbling of the dryer. The excesses of love.

One night, I sat on the edge of the bed in my shorts and studied the black and white pictures of the kids on the dresser. Derek was about four years old with long, curly hair, wearing those quilted pants that had burned up on a camping trip when I tried to dry them out over the fire with a marshmallow stick. He sat on the top step of the porch at the old house with an arm over the dog and one leg tucked under his bottom. His foot barely touched the next lower step. Without the distraction of motion or color, my imagination breathed its own life into the picture. I could feel the heat of the red-painted cement rise from the porch and hear the whap-whap of the sprinkler from the Sweet's lawn next door. If Derek had stood up, I would have held my arms in front of him like a gate in case he stumbled.

Justine was flying down the slide at Roanoke Park in her corduroy brown parka, with her knees rising over the hump in the middle of the slide and her hands gripping the railings to slow herself down. The gulping smile of a controlled fall. When she hit bottom, I remembered how she knocked me over and ran back up the make-believe rocketship to do it again. I also remembered how Justine cried once when I tucked her into bed because the Martin cousins were coming the next day. She said they made her feel stupid because they all played musical instruments and did sports. Jude's brother used to chatter constantly about what his kids had done at scout camp, how many candy bars they'd sold for the school raffle, and what they were going to be when they grew up. I secretly hoped that one of them would serve time.

Jude's brother was a card-carrying Republican, who'd led Freedom Fighter discussion groups in college with Herb Philbrick tapes that described how the Communists had infiltrated the State Department and were systematically giving away the third world to the Reds.

"The only time he ever cried in his life," Jude said, "was when Goldwater lost the election."

Jude's brother knew all of her buttons and never hesitated to push them when his family stayed with us. For those brief interludes, there was someone in the house with less consciousness than me.

"Kids who go to daycare are fifty percent more likely to have eating disorders," he said.

"But their socialization skills will be higher," Jude said. "They'll tap dance on the graves of the kids who don't go."

"Where is the women's movement on families?" he said.

"We're taking fertility pills to outbirth the silent majority," she said.

These were the discussions we had on obligatory holiday dinners while I stacked the dishwasher, Jude covered the leftovers, her brother's wife swept up crumbs in the dining room, and her brother fingered an unlit Jamaican cigar that Jude made him smoke outside. In his own house, her brother had a paneled den with stand-up ashtrays and a portrait of Douglas MacArthur over the fireplace.

It was with trepidation that I accepted Jude's invitation for lunch. We hadn't seen each other face-to-face since the divorce was finalized. We agreed to meet at the Athenian, a restaurant in the Pike Place Market just off the produce aisle, with swinging saloon doors and a counter for the regulars who came in for coffee and loaded it with sugar and non-dairy creamer. The handmade sign over the grill said "No Loitering."

When I arrived, Jude was in one of the narrow two-person booths next to the windows that overlooked Elliot Bay and the ferry terminal. She looked good in a gray blazer and pants and, despite the exhaust grime on the windows, the sun gave her hair a pleasant glow.

"I thought it would be handy to your office," she said.

My antennae were twitching while we talked about whether Iowa City, Iowa's first female firefighter would be allowed to breast-feed her baby at the firehouse, a subject I'd brought up.

"How are the kids?" I finally asked.

"It hasn't exactly been Ozzie and Harriet."

I fiddled with the plastic-laminated menu. "They're getting along with Lill?"

"Lill's been wonderful. She gives them lots of space." I pictured the kids sitting alone in those big upstairs bedrooms, listening through the heat registers to Jude and Lill giggling in the kitchen while they cooked. "It'll take a while. How's it going with you?"

The waitress saved me, asking if we wanted anything from the bar. If anyone still ordered double-martini lunches, it was here.

"What do you have on tap?" Jude asked.

"Rainier, Miller, Heineken, Bud," she said, without moving either her lips or the pencil in her hand. She returned to chewing on her cud while Jude deliberated.

"I'll have a bottle of Mickey's," Jude said, nodding to me to order.

"I'll have the Athenian steak sandwich, medium, and more water."

The waitress studied the top of Jude's head while she flipped through the plastic pages of the menu. Jude wasn't my responsibility anymore; she could take as long as she wanted. I looked down on the Alaska Way Viaduct and watched the cars on the top tier heading north. It was a concrete monstrosity built before the days of environmental consciousness, when people just wanted to get there. Puddles of water spotted the tar roofs of the warehouses and industrial buildings below us.

"I'll have the Manhattan clam chowder and a slice of garlic bread."

The waitress stabbed the pencil tip into the pad and ripped the menus out of our hands. Jude gave me a smile like someone had just said cheese. Tap, tap. The butt of my knife continued to rap through the napkin to the table.

"This isn't about money," she said, "in case that's what you're worried about. As far as I'm concerned, the decree put all that to rest." That left her relationship with Lill. I laughed nervously but my eyes were on her fingers, which were pressed together so tight that the blood darkened the skin under her nails. "I'm worried about Justine. She's been distant again. Coming home late from school. Missing dinners. She won't say where she's been or who she's with. I got suspicious and went through her drawers." One of Jude's feet accidentally kicked me under the table. Her lips quivered. She reached into the pocket of her blazer and set three condoms on the table in our booth.

I felt like someone had kneed me in the groin. I thought we'd passed through Justine's hell. "She's only fifteen."

"A fifteen-year-old has all the equipment."

"I know but . . ."

"At least she's using protection," Jude said.

"There's something so calculated about these things." I flipped one over with my index finger. The ring shape showed through the foiled label that read *Stimula* and *Vibra-Ribs*. "How long do you think . . .?"

"It's post-separation, probably post-Lill."

"You've talked about sex with her?"

"I told her it was overrated, but obviously she isn't taking my word for it. Any suggestions?" I stole a glance at the Alaska Way viaduct where the cars were now swimming upstream like sperm. "Maybe you should talk to her. I can't even tell her what to eat so I doubt I'm going to be able to tell her what she can put in her vagina."

"Jesus, Jude. Don't be so crude."

"I'm sorry, I'm just worried. Mad I guess. I didn't want to surprise you again."

I picked up the check but Jude insisted on paying the tip, with a short stack of Susan B. Anthony dollars. We parted in front of a fishmonger, where a monkfish lay sideways in a bed of ice with its mouth gaping at us as Jude surprised me with a hug.

The finalization of the divorce had re-opened the old wound of whether I knew anything at all about what it took to make a relationship work. Between a husband and wife or between a parent and a child. I realized I'd been hiding behind Jude's zaniness and pretty much blaming her sexual identity crisis for what had happened

163

between us. Maybe it was something else. It was as if we'd success-fully assembled a complicated machine from a set of plans and found a place for every part but, when we plugged it in, it sputtered and died. I had earned a good living, went to the kids' recitals and games, and helped around the house. But I was never very good at all the little moments, when Jude and I were sitting alone in the kitchen nook eating leftovers on a Saturday afternoon and I had nothing to say. Or when the reading light was snapped off in the bed-room and we were sliding down under the covers and there was that awkward silence, wondering whether if I stroked her hair she'd think I wanted something, but afraid to say anything for fear that it would start a discussion that would make sleep impossible.

Jude had crossed lines that I hadn't and when I tried to pull her back onto the safe side she fought me and we found ourselves in a tug-of-war. If I'd let myself see her in all of her passion the way other people saw her, I feared that she wouldn't have been mine any-more, so I tried to possess her the way a kid clutches a favorite blan-ket and sucks on it and pulls on it and eventually tears it to shreds.

The school district's counselor called me for an appointment, saying that she and the social worker from Child Protective Services wanted to meet at the Alhambra. The night before the meeting I mopped the floors with PineSol, cleaned the oven, sponge-washed the fruit and vegetable bins in the refrigerator, and scrubbed out the rug stains. I didn't want to take a chance they'd find a causal con-nection between the dustballs under the bed and Derek's dope smok-ing. I recognized the competitive element in this. They'd also be interviewing Jude in her four-bedroom Capitol Hill home with a peekaboo view of Lake Union and a yard. If all I had was a base-ment, at least it would be a proud basement. I didn't want me or my home to be the reason for Derek's behavior.

The woman from CPS, Mrs. Leonard, had a gray bouffant hair-do and could have been a classmate of my parents. I knew those val-ues and they didn't include divorce. "Do you mind if we look around?" she asked, clutching a clipboard with a pen holder.

They snuck in and out of rooms, their heads bobbing and whis-pering as they went, and I thought of my college poetry and Prufrock. *The women come and go talking of Michelangelo.* Mrs. Perryvan, the counselor from the school district, had wide nostrils and I worried she'd smell traces of the dried-up joint I'd finished off in the bedroom a few months ago.

"Both kids sleep in there?" one of them asked, nodding with her forehead toward the second bedroom.

"They rotate," I said. "This is transitional. As soon as things level out, I'm moving back into a house." I'd promised myself not to apologize—it red-flagged the holes in your case—but I knew that the single-family home was the benchmark of respectability, a place where everyone had space to be alone. Truthfully, I'd grown to enjoy the inventiveness of living in the Alhambra, where a dining room chair had to also serve as a nightstand, where we had to check each other's plans so we wouldn't all end up in the bathroom at the same time. Mrs. Leonard seemed confused. "One of them uses the couch and the other takes the bedroom," I said. She lengthened her face and stared once more through the bedroom door.

Mrs. Perryvan opened the refrigerator. I'd beat her to the punch and stopped at Safeway for lots of leafy green vegetables and fresh fruit, as well as milk, yogurt, and cottage cheese, items which I knew without the kids to eat them would grow mold before I could finish them. She inspected the canned foods and cold cereal shelves and the liquor cabinet over the refrigerator, which I'd slimmed down to a single, respectable bottle of Cutty Sark. The total absence of vice would draw suspicion. When the visual inspection was complete, we convened at the coffee table, with the ladies on the couch and me in the chair I pulled up across from them.

"Well, what's the verdict?"

They looked at each other, neither cracking a smile. Mrs. Perryvan pursed her lips and I noticed a tic in the right side of her face. "We won't be making the final decision on this, Mr. Stapleton. As I'm sure you know, there's a process. We'll just be making a recommendation."

I looked at Mrs. Leonard, hoping that her colleague had exaggerated the seriousness of this. "I'm not sure I know what you mean by process."

"We're getting a little ahead of ourselves," Mrs. Perryvan said. Despite the twitching, her voice was steady and somber. "Maybe the easiest way to get at this is to tell you what we know and give you a chance to comment."

I was beginning to wonder if they'd come to the wrong house.

"This is about my son Derek?"

"We know about Derek."

Mrs. Perryvan modestly squeezed her knees together so that the runs in her nylons were parallel. "We also know about your daughter's attempt on her life."

"And your wife's homosexuality," Mrs. Leonard added.

Mrs. Perryvan's tic was contagious. It felt like my whole face was jumping. "How did you find this out? Our medical records are confidential."

"Our only interest is the welfare of your children," Mrs. Perryvan said. "The medical information came from Virginia Mason. You signed the consent." She fingered some documents in a flat leather pouch leaning against the couch skirt. "This."

At the bottom of the page was my new signature. Since I couldn't change my name, I'd decided to change the shape of my signature. The old one was too straightforward. In the new version, the first and second name ran together and ended with a kind of lightning bolt that underlined the signature. The page she held out to me had the lightning bolt. I vaguely remembered signing a form after skimming it in Mr. Washington's office. For the first time, I read it carefully. It authorized the school district to make Derek's as well as Justine's records available to agencies and consultants employed by the district and authorized the release to the district of their medical records.

"I didn't realize you were going to get Justine's records too." I remembered the pallor of her face through the hyperbaric chamber and felt like a traitor.

"We thought we better check on both kids," Mrs. Perryvan said. "We're required by law to report any evidence of abuse."

"Abuse?" I said.

Mrs. Perryvan treated my question as rhetorical. "As far as your wife's . . . situation is concerned, we interviewed her and her woman friend. They were quite open about it all."

Mrs. Leonard patted her bouffant. "I would even call it proud. You did know about it, Mr. Stapleton?" There was a tragic undertone to her voice.

"Where are we going with all this?" I said.

Mrs. Perryvan, straight-backed, using only the front six inches of the chair cushion, folded her hands prayerfully on the clipboard in her lap. "Our review is not complete, but I don't think I'm stepping out of line"—she glanced at Mrs. Leonard who was nodding her concurrence—"in saying that your children are suffering. We believe that your ex-wife's sexual conduct is the potential root cause of the childrens' problems."

"Mr. Stapleton, let me add something here." Mrs. Leonard's legs were crossed so that one of her granny heels rubbed against the edge of the table. "I've done some research into the effects of parental homosexuality. Not surprisingly, it's quite deleterious, especially on adolescents. It's a trying age at best. Your wife's, excuse me, ex-wife's behavior is undermining their sense of self-worth."

"Neither Mrs. Leonard nor I have any bias against homosexuality *per se*, but where children are concerned, it's a different matter."

"Don't you think the kids' problems could just be the result of the divorce? The kids feeling at sea and all."

"We see lots of divorces," Mrs. Perryvan said. "There's something else going on here."

"Derek sent us a signal," Mrs. Leonard said. "Fortunately, we might be in time to do something about it."

"Like what?"

She leaned toward me. "Do you have any objection to the children living with you, Mr. Stapleton?"

"Of course not, but what about Jude?"

"Are you willing to do whatever is necessary to give the children a proper home?"

"Of course, but if you're talking about taking the kids away from Jude she's going to consider that a little drastic."

"Suicide's a little drastic," Mrs. Perryvan said.

I'd already decided to get a second opinion. These two women seemed a tad outdated. I didn't know how much of their conclusion was science and how much narrow-mindedness. Mrs. Leonard had a gaudy diamond on her ring finger; her husband was probably in real estate sales. Mrs. Perryvan didn't have things quite as easy. I guessed that hers was the primary income and her husband was physically disabled. With people less hidebound, I could have explained away Derek's incident as something I'd done myself as a kid, only it would have been a cigarette. But Justine's behavior was something else.

"We'll be talking to each of the children."

167

"Don't . . ."

"Don't worry, we won't be as candid as we've been with you," Mrs. Perryvan said.

"By the way, we think your apartment is very cozy," Mrs. Leonard said as she stood up, bracing herself with one hand on the coffee table. "It would make an adequate home for the children. In fact, it's lovely. My husband would die of clutter if he had to keep his own place. I know your law firm too. They've represented the district." God knows who she'd talked to. The thought occurred to me that she might just enjoy spreading this story around with her friends downtown.

"This is strictly confidential," I said, as we walked the four steps to my entry door.

"Of course," Mrs. Perryvan said, extending her hand. "You'll be hearing from us, I'm sure."

They turned their wide backsides to me and trudged up the stairs, each of them gripping the wooden railing to facilitate the climb.

I dug through my wallet and found the phone number for Dr. Tony Brava on the back of a business card where I'd listed my blood type, Social Security number, and the 800 number for my car insurance carrier. He was the psychiatrist at Group Health who co-led the men's therapy group.

"I've dealt with gay parents," he said. At least his vocabulary was contemporary. "More men than women." As he spoke, I pictured Tony's chest hairs in the open neck of his shirt. "This kind of trauma goes to the kids' bottom line. I'm not saying it's just her being lesbian. You could have the same reaction if she was a screaming alcoholic or physically abusive."

"That bad?"

He applauded the school district for getting off their butts and praised Mr. Washington. "There's a guy that operates one hundred percent for his kids. Not a bad guy to have on your side. Washington had a younger brother who fell through the cracks and died with a needle in his arm. He'll make this a crusade."

Tony's comments disturbed me. We were well past the who-does-the-dishes and should-mom-shave-under-her-arms stage. This wasn't a case of marking an X for McGovern/Shriver and feeling

168

good about yourself even though your candidates won only seventeen electoral votes. We couldn't afford to piss this one away. I had to have the crusader mentality of a Mr. Washington. My only friends in this deal were my kids.

17.

I stayed late at the office to bone up on child custody laws. I was surprised to learn that in the mid-nineteenth century children in Washington were still considered the father's property and the father would normally be awarded custody in the event of a divorce. Jude would flip if she knew that. It wasn't until the Industrial Revolution when men started working long hours in the factory that the pendulum swung in the other direction and the courts developed the "tender years" doctrine to justify a preference for awarding custody to the mother. It was hard to think of a girl with condoms in her drawers as still being in her tender years, but Derek was another matter. The current test was the "best interests of the child" and the court examined any conduct by the parent that affected the child's welfare.

Out of habit, I jotted notes on my yellow legal pad as I plowed through the stack of books on the table, putting a bold five-pointed star in the margin for any points which helped me. None of the reported cases involved lesbian mothers or gay fathers. If they did, such facts certainly weren't discussed in the reported opinions. For the mother to lose custody, she practically had to be a substance abuser, child abuser, or prostitute. If only our situation were that cut and dried. Still, I knew from what was happening to our kids that Jude's relationship with Lill was just as deleterious. This wasn't a moral judgment, it was parental. If I gave a damn about my kids, I had to wake up and do something. I couldn't wait for them to do it for me.

I probably made my decision while I was futzing with the coffeemaker in the firm's kitchen, trying to measure out enough coffee granules from the package to make a single cup. That's always when true wisdom came, when the brain was in idle, when I wasn't trying to cram something in, when I just let it do its own search. It felt right. Like a new key, it moved all the tumblers.

I called Mr. Washington to ask for his help. He'd given me his home number and that's where I reached him. "I've decided to amend the divorce decree to take custody of the kids away from Jude."

170

"Now you're talking, counselor." I could hear the television news in the background. "I'll tell you this. If you didn't do something, the school district was ready to file an action for parental deprivation against your ex. You can still use the district's reports to hang her." He gave me the name of an attorney who used to do parental deprivation hearings for the Attorney General's office. Someone who knew the in's and the out's of these kinds of cases.

Then I called Jude.

"I thought we'd salvaged enough respect that at least we wouldn't stab each other in the back."

"If I didn't do this, the school district would have tried something worse."

"Tell the school district to go screw itself."

If there was any doubt in my mind as to the wisdom of taking this course of action, Jude's belligerence quickly dissolved it. "You left a pretty good trail. All their people had to do was follow your droppings. What did you expect?"

"Why don't they blame you for this? You're as divorced as I am."

"I'm not having sex with a live-in man, Jude. The social workers said you flaunted it."

"What did you want me to do, lie? This is a witch hunt"—her phone must have hit the wall and I pulled my ear away from the receiver—"and why did you let them get into Justine's medical records? That was none of their damn Nazi business."

I didn't want to get diverted. "The point is the kids, Jude."

"Quit blaming it on the kids."

"Look, I'm as distressed as you. Strike that. I don't know how distressed you are, but I'm very distressed. And I'm simply not convinced the kids' living with you is good for them." I could hear her cussing under her breath. "I'm willing to help work something out so we don't have to go to court."

"Fuck your good intentions. I'm not going to stand by and watch you cut my heart out. I'll fight it every step of the way."

"How much checking have you done, Jude? Have you talked to any professionals?"

There was a pause, a silence that sometimes followed the spewing of the venom. Maybe she was just reloading. "God, this is so overwhelming, Cyrus. I'm not trying to scar them. Honest. But I can't stand the idea of our kids living in a world where this kind of shit goes on."

We were back to dogma and I was tired of dogma. I wanted to get past that. "I don't have anything more to say, do you?"

"As a matter of fact I do. I think you should stop hitting on the mothers of Justine's school friends."

We hung up and I flopped out on the couch, wondering whether I could get back into the book the Group Health doctor had recommended, but I was too stirred up. Jude had a way of making all of my ideas seem like leftovers from a medieval banquet. She was always the one fighting for enlightenment.

I put on a jacket and headed out for a walk. Talks with Jude were like pot; they made me paranoid and restless. I was starving for a walk on Broadway, to see punks with greasy hair, Hari Krishna chanters with red and green paint on their faces, scatological messages on the tile at the Safeway. People who had nothing to do with me or Jude.

Through a reliable source in the bar, I found out that Charlie Johnson had refused to represent Jude. "Bad for business to represent a lesbo," he'd told a friend, who told my friend. Charlie apparently preferred the more predictable and slack waters of heterosexual adultery. Instead, Jude had hired Gloria Monroe, the lawyer who'd previously represented my construction contractor client, Leo Pescara. My overall assessment: Gloria could deliver the goods. I'd have hired her myself.

The family decision-making machinery had broken down with the filing of my petition to amend the divorce decree. Jude wouldn't speak to me. As far as she was concerned, a faceless reaper was working his way up her row with his scythe.

It wasn't that I didn't trust the adversarial process. I'd lived off it, I'd defended it against detractors. It was a system that allowed each side to throw its best stuff and let the crucible of twelve good people or one learned judge sort the wheat from the chaff. The truth would win out. But being an advocate for someone else's cause was qualitatively different than choosing sides in a family fight. I had to use conscience instead of rhetoric and live with the results afterward. Our dirty little family secrets were threatening to break out the bottom of the bag I'd been carrying on my back.

A senior partner in the firm was nibbling on a carrot stick when he stopped by my office one day. "I ran into a mutual friend of ours." His smug look made me wary. "Ben Washington."

I stopped taking breaks in the coffee room for fear that the people who knew what was going on would ask me about it. The Pescara appeal had been taken away from me without explanation and I suspected it had something to do with client relations. Leo must have found out my ex was a lesbian.

I fully expected Jude to cancel my regular weekend with the kids, but she made a point of calling me to say that the kids were expecting me to pick them up on Friday afternoon. "I'm not going to stoop to other people's level," she said. I surmised that her attorney had probably advised her not to pull any shenanigans, especially now with the hearing coming up. I decided to surprise the kids and take them to the ocean for the weekend. Derek had soccer Saturday morning, so we agreed to leave after his practice.

Iron Springs Resort was a series of cottages perched on a bluff overlooking Copalis Beach. A wooden stairway zigged and zagged down a steep draw, from one landing to another, until it hit bottom. The beach had a collection of monster driftwood pieces: whole trees with giant root balls scrubbed clean by the tide and sections of washed-out piers worn smooth and bleached bone white, like the site of a prehistoric Armageddon.

After unpacking, we played frisbee on the beach. The pressure of the sand massaged my arches and created space between my toes. The wind played tricks, sometimes lifting the frisbee with an updraft just as you reached for it and sailing it over your head. Magpie chased every throw with her teeth bared, enjoying the power she must have felt at making the earth move with each push of her paws. When she caught it, all three of us had to chase her down as she teased and dodged us. Derek dove for catches, not bothering to brush off the sand that coated his cheeks and his pants. I was surprised at how adept Justine was. Most beginners didn't know how to keep the edge down, which allowed the frisbee to rise and slice like a golf ball. She also caught it close to her body without flinching.

"Let's see how many we can catch in a row," she said. "No goofing around, Derek." There wasn't a game made that Justine couldn't turn into a test. In the old days, I would have said she was extreme-

173

ly competitive for a girl.

Magpie became bored when we stopped dropping the frisbee as much and parked herself in the middle of our triangle. We made a big deal of each consecutive catch that matched one of our ages. Justine caught number nine for Derek and fifteen for herself. I strained a hamstring catching twenty-nine for Warren and the kids clapped. When I caught thirty-six, Justine yelled "Jude," which seemed oddly distant and I chided myself for reading too much into everything.

"Dad's next," Justine said. "Don't wreck it, Derek."

"Hit me deep, Dad," he said, taking off on a run.

"Don't," Justine said. "You'll mess up."

Derek darted left one step, then right, then left, throwing his arms into space and shouting with each lurch. Magpie perked up. She had an eye for waggishness and wanted in on it. Derek pirouetted in the sand and broke toward the ocean with Magpie trotting to catch him. Taking into account the breeze coming off the water, I brought my arm behind my back and swung with all my strength. The frisbee swished by my hip and into the glare of the setting sun. Its intended pathway was the hypotenuse of a triangle that Derek had to close with his churning, nine-year-old feet that were kicking up divots as he ran.

Justine moaned as we lost sight of it in the brightness.

Derek's eyes were trained skyward as he looked back over his shoulder. From my vantage point, the frisbee was one of those dark spots that floated across your vision after someone popped a flashbulb. Magpie was running stride for stride at Derek's heels. As the frisbee dropped low enough to be seen again, the wind slowed it, Derek let up, but Magpie kept coming. Dog and boy collided, rolling like tumbleweeds across the sand, Magpie's white chest then Derek's carrot hair and plum shorts visible. As they came to a stop, the frisbee hovered in the air just beyond them, then settled to the sand, gyrated like a bottle cap on a countertop, and stilled.

When Justine and I caught up with them, Derek had his arm around Magpie's neck and was patting her. His mouth was so caked with sand it looked like a squirrel hole. Justine knelt and brushed Magpie with one hand and Derek's shirt with the other.

Derek looked at her. "Aren't you mad I missed it?"

"It wasn't your fault. Dad's just one year too old for this game."

I dropped to the sand and wrapped my arms in a huddle around the three of them. Derek spit sand through his grin.

We walked into town to eat dinner at a café with a gas pump out front and a general merchandise store that stocked chips and pop, clam-digging shovels, dusty souvenir ashtrays, and ceramic starfish. Derek ordered a bacon-burger with fries and Justine chose the salad bar. She'd already succumbed to the image of the models in the supermarket teen magazines and started to worry about her weight, a social expectation I would have loved to relieve her of.

There was a silence after we'd placed our orders while Derek fiddled with his belt buckle and Justine ironed the edges of her paper napkin against the placemat. Neither of them had brought up the custody issue, and I didn't know if Jude had even discussed it with them, although I guessed that she had. The bell on the door jingled each time someone came in to pay for gas. In the kitchen a radio played that we could only hear when the waitress pushed through the swinging door and let Willie Nelson or Maria Muldaur out. Gradually, the swings of the door shortened and muffled the music like a mute on a trumpet.

"What's going to happen to us?" Derek asked, his eyes in his lap.

"What do you want to happen?"

He twisted his neck one way, then the other, trying to form a sentence. "I don't even know what it's about."

"You know what it's about," Justine said.

I waited for her to continue but she rolled her lips and stared in the direction of the cash register. Derek's fork made a tap-tap sound against the table. Public places usually made it easier to talk about this kind of stuff, kept it from getting so dark, but we were strangers waiting for an introduction. "What about you, Justine?"

"I don't know." She looked around as if measuring the strength of her voice against the distance from us to the people two tables away. "I did *not* like those two ladies from the school district or wherever. I practically had to take them through my laundry basket. They wanted to know if there was any nudity in the house. Like I showered in my pajamas." I wondered if Jude still jump-roped in the raw and whether that had been another sign that I'd missed. "Mom's no fun anymore. She's not eating. Her and Lill are fighting. She just seems tired of it all."

"What's wrong with Mom?" Derek asked. "And why did you

guys even marry?"

The kids and I had never discussed why we'd gotten married. I'd never thought of it as something that was any of their business, but I wasn't sure I could give Derek a fair answer to his question, partly because I wasn't entirely sure why we'd divorced. The one should have been counterpoint to the other. I still wasn't convinced that Jude would have chosen a new path for herself if we'd managed a better marriage. "We liked each other a lot. Then, gradually, I guess we just forgot why."

"This is so crappy." Justine's face cracked and she started to cry. "Sometimes I just wish you'd left me in the garage."

"Come on, don't say that." I scooted my chair over and put my arm around her. She grabbed her napkin, spilling her knife and spoon onto the table. I slid my hand under the hood of her sweatshirt and tried to rub her neck, but she turned away to hide the crying. My eyes were a little blurry but I could see Derek across the table standing lookout, checking to make sure no one was watching.

Back at the cottage, we put a match to the kindling tepee in the fireplace and played Hearts and then O Pshaw. The kids bickered during every hand. Justine wanted to toast a marshmallow and Derek teased her that it was a kid thing. They started a pillow fight with each other and I tried to distract them with my grumpy man imitation, where I squinted my eyes, hunched my back, and came at them in a hoarse voice with a limp like one leg was a stump. They used to run out of the kitchen screaming when I did that in the old house, but I couldn't get them to move this time.

Afterward, Derek threw sticks to Magpie on the beach while Justine and I sat on a tilted remnant of a pier that had washed ashore. I told her that I knew about the condoms, which suddenly made me feel sweaty and sticky underneath my polypropylene windbreaker. She looked downbeach toward Derek and Magpie as I talked.

"I don't want to put some big parental judgment on this, but that worries me."

"It's nothing," she mumbled, as she tore a splinter off the pier.

"My mother told me that sex enhanced you with someone you loved but cheapened you with anyone else. I didn't know what she meant for a long time. Partly, I guess, because she never actually used the word sex." Justine just played with her splinter of wood as I talked. "Are you still there?"

"I'm not a tramp."

"Meaning?"

"Meaning I'm just mad."

"What did your mom say about it?"

"Just make sure your partner is using one."

"That's all she said?"

I wanted to explain to Justine how that kind of flip attitude was partly why her mom and I were in this mess, but I knew that Justine would feel she had to report back to her mother, and I didn't want to make her the courier of my anger.

In the middle of the night, Derek crawled into bed with me, something he hadn't done for a while. We watched the branches of the maple tree swish back and forth in front of the floodlight outside our unit, creating a series of inkblots in motion against the wall.

"This is the best time I've had all year," he said.

I wanted to weep at the thought of what could have been, at what we'd missed living in this craziness. But as I listened to the dull roar of the waves and the wind whistling under the eaves, I still felt a warm glow inside me, the kind of high a marathon runner is supposed to get. The same yawing ocean I'd feared as a kid seemed safe. I was feeling very much a father and I didn't want to go home.

Mr. Washington's voice on the phone was as gruff as an opposing counsel's. "This Monroe woman is fighting back. She's hired a male and female psychiatrist. Smart, huh?" I was on auto-pilot. "I'm sure I don't need to tell you about your own business, but you're going to have to score some points for us."

So many times I'd been on the other end of this conversation, encouraging a reluctant witness. "Mr. Washington, I don't want this to become personal."

"I don't mean anything dirty, just the facts. You're not getting cold feet, are you?"

From the weekend at the ocean, I was more convinced than ever that it would be healthy to have the kids with me. Once they were with me and things settled down, I could work out a visitation schedule with Jude. There was a satisfaction in knowing I could finally make a lie out of her complaint that I was a spectator parent. "I'll do everything I can," I told him, "but you can understand my feelings. I lived with Jude for over sixteen years. We've known each other

177

half our lives."

He cleared his throat. "You sound like Hamlet. The picture couldn't be any clearer. If the kids stay with her, you're going to lose 'em." He paused to let the weight of his words sink in and I envied his certitude. "I'm not anti-feminist, Stapleton. Don't worry, my wife wouldn't let me be. But homosexuality is a whole 'nother kind of poison."

I hated overstatement in anything other than a closing argument in the courtroom, but I didn't have a convincing rebuttal. "This is a private conversation, Mr. Washington. That's why we can talk like this. Trust me. When I take the stand, I'll speak with a clear voice."

"Good. Ms. Monroe is going to stub her pretty toes on this one."

"Do you want to testify, Mr. Washington?"

"Couldn't keep me away."

"Then don't say her toes are pretty."

His laugh rumbled into the receiver. "Thanks, counselor."

The phone woke me about two in the morning. Warren was in police custody.

I put on a pair of cords and dug a dress shirt out of the laundry basket. Not knowing what kind of trouble it was, I threw on a sport coat and stuck in my checkbook in case I had to kite a check for bail until I could borrow some money. A robust officer with a wad of chew in his cheek was sitting at the night desk, reading a shopworn copy of *Slapstick*. I hadn't been in the County Jail since taking a tour there with the Bar Association when I first became a lawyer.

"I'm Warren Stapleton's brother," I said, and he shoved a clipboard at me with a sign-up sheet.

I waited in what was the lobby for further instructions from the officer. "Three Times a Lady" was playing on a fuzzy transistor radio under his desk. Finally, they let me into the visitor's room. Warren was on the other side of a grimy plate of glass, slumped over with his forehead on his arms. When I tapped on the glass, he looked up.

"What's going on?" I asked.

Warren rubbed the sides of his hands against his face. He looked like he hadn't slept in days. "Mandy broke up with me and I got a little wasted."

"I thought you wanted to break up."

He shook his head. " I rear-ended somebody and they did my breath."

"Dammit, Warren, that's just stupid. I've got enough to worry about without this kind of crap."

Warren had that same pissed-off look he had the night in the J & B when he took on the guy at the bar stool, but he bit his tongue and held it until after the desk officer accepted my bail and we walked out of the County Jail together at about three in the morning. There wasn't a car in sight in either direction on Fifth Avenue and we turned and headed up the hill to the public lot next to the freeway entrance. Neither of us said anything. I figured he was looking for me to throw my arm over his shoulder and laugh the whole thing off, but I was still miffed at him, not just for the wreck but for his seeming lack of contrition.

He muttered into the pavement as we jaywalked Jefferson. "I told you I could help get the kids back but you won't let me in on it."

I'd told him he didn't have any personal knowledge that would be useful in the custody dispute. His contacts with Jude had been minimal since the separation and his knowledge of Lill was purely anecdotal. Mainly, I didn't want to drag him into it and enlarge the damage between Jude's family and ours. "There's nothing you can do, Warren."

"You don't show some moxie, you're going to lose 'em." He kicked a flattened pop can up the hill. "I'm ready to fight this thing with you and you're parsing the evidence. Let me in on it."

"It's my fight, pal."

As we drove in silence to the Alhambra, I wondered when Warren would experience the sting and bliss of his own parenthood. It was a transformation that began without your knowledge in a dark room full of whispers and joyful spasms and culminated in a birthing process that produced a chemical change in the mother, flushing undivided loyalty and candlelight romance out with the placenta. Forever after, love had to be shared and the husband and wife became partners. And like partners, they fought over the profits and losses. When things went bad, they hired lawyers to partition the remainders. And what was once a whisper in the dark became a roar in the light.

179

18.

I'd checked out the attorney that Mr. Washington had recommended in Martindale-Hubbell. Larry Delacord was Order of the Coif at UW Law School and had practiced with the King County prosecuting attorney as well as the attorney general's domestic unit before going into his current five-person practice in the Hoge Building. Divorces and domestic relations were the mainstay of his firm's business. Nobody in my office knew the first thing about domestic relations, an ignorance that was typical of the larger law firms in town. I couldn't have used my own firm anyway, because the canons prevented it from participating in a case where one of its own attorneys was a party.

The first time we met, Larry greeted me in his waiting room, which Jude would have loved. No brass, no glass sculptures, no cut flowers, no pretense. Just the morning newspaper dumped on top of a cluttered wooden table. Larry was a stuttering, flat-footed lawyer that I would have guessed to be in his early forties. On first blush, I was skeptical of Mr. Washington's choice, but there was a kindness in his thick handshake and a sincerity in his voice. A litigator didn't have to be slick, I knew that; it was more important that he be believable. He was wearing a white shirt with sweat stains around the collar and a narrow deacon's tie. His desk was hidden behind a maze of grey, steel filing cabinets that filled his windowless office and spilled out into the hallway. On a Farmer's Insurance calendar taped to the side of one of his filing cabinets, there was a picture of foxhounds milling around a group of horses with riders in red jackets and high boots. The hunting imagery resonated with me. I also noticed how many case names had been penned onto the calendar, a prolific workload. Another good sign.

While he was with the Prosecutor, Larry told me he'd handled civil commitments at Harborview Hospital where it was his job to commit people alleged to be dangerous to themselves or others. "It was called the cuh . . . crazies calendar," he said. "I turned out to be guh . . . good at it." When he got stuck, he closed his eyes and concentrated until the words burst forth like gunshots. "No sur . . . prise. My . . . fav . . . rite course was ab . . . abnormal psych." He smiled the same pleasant smile that I saw in the framed picture on his desk with his wife and six kids. The pace of his delivery allowed me time to look around between comments. "Cuh . . . couldn't get into med school."

Larry told me he'd represented the Seattle School District in a parental deprivation case, where he had to prove sufficient abuse and neglect to permanently and irrevocably sever the parental relationship. "That's wha . . . what Mr. Wa . . . Washington wanted here. If he had his way. But don't . . . don't take custody fights lightly. We . . . we've still got an uphill battle. She's the mom."

The second time we met I reviewed a report that had been prepared by one of Jude's experts, who'd separately interviewed Jude, Lill, and the kids. The case had already turned into a contest between social workers and psychiatrists. I blushed as I read her report, then became sweaty and, by the end, I was irate. It was full of half-truths and innuendo. I'd been "sleeping around" since the divorce. I'd disappeared on "secret trips" and "lied to the children" about my whereabouts. I'd taken them "gambling at the race track." I had a "history of drug use." Maybe Warren was right; I was a candy ass. Jude's team was using nuclear weapons while I was aiming high with my Winchester, giving warning shots.

As Larry explained, I was also on trial and the entire parental history, Jude's and mine, would be under consideration. If I was a whoremonger, there was more reason to leave the kids with Jude. Larry took scrupulous notes — there was no stutter in his penmanship — while I gushed out my side of the story. Knowing he'd heard crazier stories made it easier.

"You . . . slept with Lill Epstein?" His eyes were open windows.

"Not since she moved in with Jude. I didn't really sleep with her. I'm not saying the thought didn't occur to me. And fibbing about that overnighter to the dunes was just so there'd be one less thing for the kids to worry about."

"Wha . . . what about the drugs?"

"Since leaving Jude, none. I take that back. I may have smoked a leftover joint or two." He wrote furiously and stroked the oil out of his hair. Here I was living out my old nightmare of confessing to the prosecutor.

181

"Were . . . were you a user?"

Maybe I'd said too much already. There had to be a statute of limitations on this. "Jude and I used to keep some in the house. We'd smoke socially with friends, mostly hers." I waited until he'd stopped writing. "Larry, it's not an issue, is it?"

"Too small . . . potatoes."

The longer we talked, the more his stutter seemed to subside and, by the time we were done, I hardly noticed it. He had a religious zeal about his work, and I could tell that he enjoyed saving people from the predicaments they'd created for themselves. Jude and I were your regular sinners. He didn't despise anyone; he'd already absolved us. Now he just had to administer the penance, and I was confident he'd do it as compassionately as he committed the crazies to their fourteen-day stays at Western State.

Jude's mother surprised me with a long-distance call from Palm Springs a few days before the hearing to find out what was going on. I heard the clinking of dishes in the background as she explained that they'd just finished nine holes and were cooling off in the clubhouse.

"That woman from the school district had a lot of questions," she said.

"What did you tell her?"

"Well, I told her the truth. Jude was born with a silver spoon in her mouth. She had a privileged upbringing. This whole business is as surprising and revolting to me as it is for everyone else."

"Did they ask you to testify?"

"They mentioned it."

"Against Jude?"

"I prefer to think of it as in favor of sanity." She whispered a drink order to someone, with no ice. "You know my attitude on this. I think it's a fad. Jude's always been susceptible to fads. When she was in college, she wore her hair like Jackie Kennedy. She'll pass through it and, when she does, she can have the kids again."

"Have you talked to her?"

"I tried, but she won't talk to me. That's why I called you." She was slurring her words and in a hurry. "Are they blaming me for this, Cyrus?"

"For what?"

"Her sexual deviancy."

"I hadn't heard that, Martha. Should they?"

She laughed. "You know better than that. I'm hetero' to the core."

Her parting words were Martha's version of encouragement. "I'm sorry you married a lemon, Cyrus. I'm ready to fly in if you need me."

My mother's voice was thin, like someone had put it through a strainer, when she called the next night to tell me about Dad's heart attack.

"This is worse than the first one," she said. "He should have had the bypass." Since Dad's hospitalization for a myocardial infarction three years ago, he'd been on nitroglycerin and digitalis.

"How do you think he's taking it?"

"You know your father. He thinks he'll live forever." My parents knew I was divorced, but I hadn't told them about the custody petition. Like everything else, I thought I'd wait until there was an outcome, and I didn't want to worry Dad in his condition. "You don't have to come over."

"I'm coming over, Mom. But I'll have to be back for something with the kids."

"I don't want you to miss anything with the kids."

I considered flying but the schedule into Ellensburg was limited. I didn't trust my Plymouth on a trip over the pass, so I rented a two-year old Ford Pinto with twenty-eight thousand miles from Rent-a-Wreck.

I'd come to look forward to going home less and less. It reminded me of everything I'd done wrong in my life. My brain switched to a lower gear when I was around my parents, especially Dad. I couldn't form coherent thoughts. I had to work hard just to contribute to the simplest conversations. It was as if I'd been lobotomized, with everything that I'd done since leaving home surgically removed. Vocabulary that I used in my work became jumbled in the face of Dad's skepticism. Words popped out that I didn't even know the meaning of. I couldn't muster an opinion on anything that mattered to Dad. I had the vocabulary of an adult but the experiences and syntax of a child. My ego dried up and blew away in his presence. I couldn't manufacture a sincere statement about who I was or what I did. So instead, we talked about what everyone else was doing or about what we did twenty and thirty years ago when I still lived at home. None of us could generate an interest in the man who'd grown up and married and made his own family in Seattle. I vowed from my cockpit in the little Pinto that things would be different this time over. There might not be another chance.

I asked directions for the hospital from a checker at a grocery store in Ellensburg, which in its size and ambience reminded me of the Thriftway that Dad had managed in Quincy. There was a big freezer in front of the store with ice, block and cubes. You could trust the customers to tell the checker if they were going to pick up a bag. On either side of the freezer, there were sagging racks with potted pansies, daisies, geraniums, and bags of bark, fertilizer, and charcoal briquets.

The hospital was a modest two-story building, about the size of the elementary school my brothers and I had attended. When I told them who I was at the desk, the nurses gave each other knowing smiles.

"So you're the son," the one with the blood donor button on her cap said.

"One of them. There's three of us."

"I'm going up," the Asian nurse said. "I can show you his room."

We took the elevator, which was deep enough for a stretcher and smelled like someone had spilled a bottle of rubbing alcohol in it. As I watched the nurse, I imagined my dad bawling her out the way he used to bawl out waiters who didn't bring him crackers with his soup or sugar substitute for his coffee.

"I take it my dad's been a pain in the ass."

Her hands rushed to cover her mouth as if she'd been the one to say something offensive. "Oh, no, he's the patient. It's all part of our job."

Dad was in a private room with the shades pulled and the television going. The bed was tilted up and he had one of those tubes clipped to his nose. Mom was sitting in a straight-back chair next to the bed.

"Lee," she said, "it's Cyrus. Cyrus is here to see you."

His face and the bald space on his head were sweaty. The tube in his nose curved down like a plastic mustache. When he used to work seven days a week, he shaved every morning before I ever saw

184

him, but now his cheeks were covered with grey stubble.

"What's the matter, they fire you?"

"Lee," Mom said.

"Mom said you were sick."

"Hell, I'm not sick. My arteries are clogged. You'd look like this too if you couldn't pump any blood through your heart." The exertion strained him, and he closed his eyes to regain his breath.

Purely out of duty and the knowledge that this was what you did at the bedside of your ill father, I moved closer. Mom stepped back to let me pass. The truth was, I was scared to get near for fear he might slug me. "Take it easy, Dad."

"They're starving me up here. Everything's soft and gooey like baby food. It's making me gassy."

"He's supposed to take another pill," Mom said.

"I want a cigarette, that's what I want. Audrey won't give me a measly cigarette. Get me a cigarette, Audrey!"

"Dad."

"Get me a god damned cigarette."

"Dad, quit yelling."

"Butt out. This is between me and your mom. Audrey!" Mom was backed against the wall with her hands over her face.

"Don't yell at her," I said. "For God's sake, you're sick. She's trying to get you better."

"I can yell at my own wife. Maybe if you'd yelled, you'd still have one." He was wheezing and stopped to stock up on the oxygen that was coursing through the plastic tube.

I knew this was neither the time nor the place to be arguing with him. But when would it be? We always got to this point and then I slunk off into the kitchen or, when I was young, went outside and hid in a tree. "You think that's why Mom's stayed with you? Because you've bossed her around like some drudge? Fetch my cigarettes? Jesus, Dad." His eyes were wide open and he was glaring at me the way he always did, but he was too weak to do anything but listen. "No, I didn't yell and prod Jude the way you've done to Mom. In fact, I've tried to do everything the opposite of you."

Mom was tugging at my arm. "That's enough, Cyrus. He's too tired."

"Let someone help you for a change, Dad. Get down on your knees and thank her for putting up with all your bluster. You're running out of chances." I'd gone way out on a limb, and the oxygen was getting thin. I could feel Mom's arm around me.

"Get out!" he said. "Both of you, get out and let me die in peace. If I wanted a lecture, I would have called the chaplain."

"He didn't mean any harm, Lee. I'll get you your silly cigarette."

"No, Mom, don't."

I wrapped my arm around her. She was crying, with one hand on the bed to steady herself. She didn't want another confrontation. She didn't want to end her purgatory with Dad on this kind of note. This isn't why she asked me to come over. I was always the son she could count on to be diplomatic, to hold his tongue and ride the rough waves with her.

That night, Mom and I shared a room at the Holiday Inn near the freeway. I ordered room service, including a glass of the house red for me, and we moved the coffee table over by the window so we'd have a view. The sun had dropped behind the Cascades, forming a kind of aurora borealis that backlit the service stations and fast food restaurants on the horizon. I could still make out the pattern of air conditioners and vents on the roof below us.

"I've never done this," she said.

"Hospitalized Dad?"

"Ordered room service."

"You're kidding. All those driving trips you took?"

"Lee always preferred to buy sandwich-makings at a grocery," she said. "He liked to have something he could munch on during the Johnny Carson show. Johnny Carson was the only person who could make him laugh."

I shook my head in amazement, both that my dad could laugh and that my mom could still revere him. "How have you done it, Mom?"

A piece of her peach started to slip off her spoon as she was ready to slide it into her mouth and she daintily guided it with her little finger back onto her spoon and into her mouth. She chewed and waited until she'd swallowed to dab the corners of her mouth with the maroon cloth napkin. "He's not always the bear he makes himself out to be with you boys. My mother told me marriage required faith, hope, and charity." She read the skeptical look on my face. "Don't scoff."

I stabbed another piece of prime rib and a green bean and wiped them both in the puddle of sour cream for my baked potato. I couldn't remember ever having a dinner with just Mom and I was enjoying it immensely. She was finally speaking. "I'm listening."

"Hope and charity were easy because I could do those on my own." She set her spoon down and folded her hands in her lap. "But faith has been the hardest."

"I don't get it."

"It's always just out of reach," she said, extending her hand toward the giant galvanized hoods and exhaust vents on the roof below us. "And you never know whether it's real."

"Isn't that the same as hope?"

"No." She was adamant. "Hope is desire. Desires are easy. We all have desires. Faith is believing it will happen even when all the evidence says it won't." She dabbed at the corners of her eyes, then straightened her posture and took a deep breath. "Oh, my, I'm sorry."

I took a sip of wine to let her gain composure. "Don't stop."

"I'm not a very good dinner conversationalist, am I?"

"You're perfect." I reached over and rubbed the top of her hand.

"You must think I'm a simpleton." She looked up at me and a trace of the gold light from the neon letters in the pole sign in the parking lot streaked her cheek. "You should have known your father back when he proposed to me on the Sausalito ferry."

"He proposed on the ferry?"

"He'd just finished his training and I met him for a weekend furlough in San Francisco. We were next to the railing at the front of the boat. I can remember the wind beating against our faces." She had a far-off look but her voice was strong. "We married in a little church in the Mission District before he shipped out."

"I don't remember you ever telling us this."

"We weren't always old, you know. We had dreams just like everyone else." I tried to imagine Dad's Navy bell-bottoms fluttering on the deck and Mom without the worry lines that had worn into her face. "You boys are the most important thing in the world to him."

I shook my head. "Now there's an act of faith."

Her face drooped and she closed her eyes as if to say a silent prayer right there in the glow of the Holiday Inn sign.

"Sorry. I'm not trying to rag on him, Mom. It's just that we've always seemed like such an afterthought."

"He's just hardest on the ones he loves. That's been his job. To teach you boys to be prepared for the worst."

"Like a divorce."

"He's sick about it."

"I wasn't sure until today that he even knew about it," I said.

"He always liked Jude, you know that."

"They seem an unlikely match."

"You need faith too, Cyrus."

"Kind of late for that, I'm afraid."

In the morning, the duty nurse said Dad was worse and I told Mom I'd wait outside his room so that I wouldn't get him riled up again.

"He'll want to see you."

"Really, Mom, it's better."

There was a big, cylindrical coffee pot in the waiting room with a stack of styrofoam cups, sugar cubes, and powdered creamer on the table. I fixed myself a cup, stirred it with a red plastic swizzle stick, and grabbed three or four magazines from the top of the pile. The best I could manage was to look at the picture ads for skin creams and booze. The same models seemed to pose for all of them, men with wavy hair and women with big eyes, long lashes, and slits up their skirts.

In the recesses of my brain, I'd always known this day would come. Even Dad couldn't defy the life expectancy tables. I also knew that when it happened I'd be grief-stricken and fly to his side and seek forgiveness for all the thoughtless, shabby things I'd done or thought. Now that the moment was upon me, I couldn't do it. I was too composed and on guard, too emotionally stunted, and I wished that my brothers had shown up. They were always so much better with Dad. They'd be able to console him. I tried to rationalize that his death, if that's what was happening, was a private thing, something between him and Mom, the same way their engagement and marriage was. They didn't need the aggravation of a son who hadn't sorted out his own affairs.

"He wants to see you." Mom was clutching the remote control for the TV that she'd absent-mindedly carried out of the room.

"How is he?"

She choked. "Not so good."

I took her in my arms and the elbows she'd pulled in front of herself as a shield poked me in the ribs. "Are you coming with me?"

"He wants you."

I helped her to a seat as two young boys in jeans and collar shirts stared at us. Their own parent was probably down the same hall. Mom and I didn't offer them much hope. The news coming from that direction was bad.

I dreaded seeing him alone. One of those morning news shows, where the anchors sit around in soft chairs, was playing quietly on the TV overhead when I entered the room. Dad was flat on his back, motionless. Creases of light coming through the blinds made a bamboo curtain pattern on the sheets. When I was practically standing over him, our eyes met.

"Good morning, Dad."

"We need to talk." His voice was anemic but gruff, and I wanted to crank up the handle on his oxygen so he could feel the vigor of a full dose of air. "I know you think I'm a horse's ass" — he straightened his arms against his sides to raise himself up off the bed — "but I wanted to explain something before I kick off and go to the grave without you and I talking." He closed his mouth and sucked in a deep breath through the tubes in his nostrils. "When we won the War, I thought the world owed me one. That's probably where I got the chip on my shoulder, but that was the way it was in those days." His voice was a whisper, and I looked over at the gauges to see if anything was falling. "My objective was to make a good living for your mother." He was putting too much energy into this and I was afraid he was going to strain himself. "I should have bought the store from Harold. I know that. Your mom and I could have taken one of those Hawaii vacations, maybe bought a Winnebago and toured the country."

"You always wanted one of those rigs."

"I'm worth more dead than alive right now."

"That's not true. Mom would be devastated if you . . ."

"She'll be better off without me." He pounded his chest with the palm of his hand the way he used to pound the top of the TV to straighten out the picture. "God damnit, listen to me." He blinked his eyes and the strangest thing happened: tears started to puddle in his eye sockets. "I need you to do something." He was trying to get rid

189

of the tears, will them away. "That's why I called you in here. And I'm not asking 'cause you're a lawyer. It's 'cause your mom trusts you." He rotated his head as if he were looking for something. "I don't want them to keep me alive with a bunch of tubes hangin' out of me. You understand? No miracles."

"Have you talked to Mom about this?"

His eyes flared in the way I'd learned to recognize. "That's why I'm talking to you."

The man who'd never trusted me to mix the oil and gas for the power lawnmower was asking me to help him die. "Dad, you might still pull out of this."

"There's no such thing as something for nothing . . . and I've run out of trading material." He was retired, he was at that point in our lives we all worked for, when we could tip back and cash in our reserves. Nobody had worked harder than my dad for this reprieve. "Get me one of those papers to sign. That's all I want. Where it says I don't want to live hooked up to wires. There's a name for it. You know what I mean."

"Most of these expenses will be covered by insurance. You're not going to bankrupt anyone, Dad."

"Listen to me. This is all I've got left to give her."

As if in a dream, my dad was finally saying something I understood, something I had an opinion on. There was a pressure building behind my eyes that I was trying to diffuse. It enraged Dad when I used to cry. I didn't want to disappoint him at the very moment he'd shown such confidence in me. "Dad, I'm sorry I sounded off on you yesterday."

He waved me away with his hand. "Don't grovel. You were great."

I turned my head away and scrambled to find my handkerchief. I could hide my eyes but I couldn't hide the shuddering. Then I felt my dad's finger tugging at my pocket like a kid trying to find a nickel for a piece of licorice.

19.

I'd entered the King County Courthouse hundreds of times in my life, to do battle over construction projects gone sour, property trespassed upon, a ship's anchor that severed a power cable, real estate transactions that cratered. I was sworn in as a member of the bar in this building. This was the palace of disputes, where every imaginable kind of civil and criminal wrong was laid bare. The people you rode the elevators with were the plaintiffs and defendants, their counsel, their witnesses, their supporters, their judges, and their jurors. I'd never entered the courthouse for a case in which any member of my own family was a party. And I was terrified.

I got off on the seventh floor and turned right to find our courtroom in the west wing. Just ahead of me was a man in orange overalls with his hands cuffed behind his back slouching toward his arraignment in the company of two corrections officers. The same judges who decided the custody of good kids presided over the felonies as well. The hallway near the courtroom was surprisingly crowded with people who I assumed were waiting for their cases to be called.

A man reached out of the crowd and grabbed my wrist. It was my old neighbor Mr. Sweet in a string tie with an imitation ivory slide over a blue plaid shirt. "We know what you're fighting, buddy. Me and the Mrs. here can testify for you." How did he know about the hearing? He was either reading Jude's mail or Mr. Washington had told him. My eyes went to the discolorations where chewing tobacco had darkened the spaces between his teeth. The man who flossed his lawn edges had ignored his dental hygiene. "You got the whole neighborhood in your corner."

I looked around and, sure enough, there were three ladies sitting on the bench next to him who looked like election poll watchers from the basement of St. Patrick's, and then I recognized some of the others standing there—parents of kids who used to babysit Derek and Justine, and the manager of Don's Grocery. Who would have thought that the first trial for the block watch group I once headed

191

would be mine and Jude's? The neighbors wouldn't be allowed in the courtroom, unless they were witnesses or the parties had consented to their presence. There's no way Jude would have consented. Nor I for that matter. I was doing this for the kids, not for the mob.

As I entered the sour light of the courtroom, my eye immediately caught the purplish haze of Mrs. Leonard's bouffant hairdo, the lady from Child Protective Services. She was in the same row as Mrs. Perryvan, the school district's counselor, and Mr. Washington, who gave me a thumbs-up sign from behind the back of his pew.

I took my place at counsel table with Larry Delacord, who was wearing a good white shirt with no stains on the collar. The plan was to put on the investigators and experts first and finish with my testimony. Jude was sitting next to Gloria Monroe at her table and she turned to look at me as my chair shuddered into place. Her shoulders were stooped, her face washed-out, the swagger gone. She looked scared and I had to look away, back at the kids, who were in the front row next to a studious man with a bald spot resembling a monk's tonsure. He must have been one of Jude's experts. Justine was pensive, but I could tell that Derek wanted to wave so badly that his wrist hurt. Lill was absent. Gloria Monroe had probably advised her to stay home and bake cookies. She was going to make Jude pretend a little.

The case had been assigned to Judge Purnell, a good draw for my side. He was a retired army colonel and considered a hanging judge, with unwavering notions of right and wrong. People shuffled in their seats as Larry delivered his opening statement. Then Gloria Monroe stood up. She seemed so much more the attorney with her gold wire-frame glasses, smooth delivery, and trim sand-colored hair.

"Your honor, we would ask the court for the opportunity to defer opening statement until the beginning of our own case."

The judge granted her request and she sat down. Although I had the perfect profile view, I knew I couldn't look at her. Jude had helped break me of that practice by telling me how easy it was for a woman to tell when your eyes were on her body. Besides, I could feel Jude's hollow eyes on me.

Larry Delacord called Mr. Washington as his first witness, and the floor heaved as the Seward Elementary principal lumbered past me in a natty dark suit that looked too hot for him. After a lengthy recitation of Mr. Washington's stellar record as a school administrator, Larry moved to Derek's capture under the mowing machine and then to the follow-up investigation.

"It was like following a ball of string that someone had unraveled. One thing led to another until we found the source of the problem."

"And wha . . . what was that?"

Mr. Washington spit out his answer. "Their mother's sexual orientation."

"Move to strike the last response," Gloria said. "There is no foundation. It calls for the opinion of an expert which this witness is not." Her voice was measured as she enunciated each word like a veteran stage actress.

The judge licked his upper lip and bobbed his head in sync with the mallet tapping against his hand. "This man is an educator, he's spent more hours in the school room than the rest of us put together. I'm going to let the answer stand."

Gloria showed no outward disappointment but whispered something to Jude as Mr. Washington continued with his testimony. Jude remained inert. The first time Mr. Washington said "unfit mother" she objected again.

"No foundation. Calls for a legal conclusion. Non-responsive to the question." There were no wasted words, no histrionics, just three quick darts into the target.

The judge sustained the objection and directed counsel to ask the question again. This time Mr. Washington went straight to his point.

"The school district operates on the principle of *parens patriae*." He looked up at the judge, as if to make sure the judge caught his highfalutin phrase, as if to demonstrate that the judge's opinion of his education wasn't misplaced. "We're the parent of last resort. When the family breaks down, we're there to catch the kids who fall through."

"Had the Sta . . . Stapleton family broken down?"

While Gloria was making her objection, Mr. Washington was answering the question. You didn't need to hear his answer; his jutting chin said it all.

When Larry was finished, Gloria stood, pressed the lap wrinkles out of her skirt, and approached the witness stand. Mr. Washington glowered at her. Although she wore heels, her step showed the balance of a dancer. "Mr. Washington, where did you grow up?"

"Hattiesburg, Mississippi," he said proudly.

"And where did you go to school?"

"Howard University in Washington, D.C."

"What was your major, sir?"

Mr. Washington looked over at the judge with a perplexed look on his face. The judge nodded for him to answer. "It was history. I took down a B.A. in history." Gloria had obviously pulled his file.

"Then you've heard of the Jim Crow laws?"

"I sure have, M'am." Mr. Washington answered before Larry could register his objection on the basis of relevancy, which the court waved off. It was obvious that the judge thought this witness could handle himself. The mere mention of the South, however, seemed to have caused a transformation in Mr. Washington's demeanor. He was more tentative and Gloria Monroe was suddenly a madam.

"And in 1896, didn't the highest court in this land say that Louisiana's Jim Crow car law was legal and constitutional?" Larry squirmed in his seat and looked at me as if to ask if I knew where this was heading.

Mr. Washington scratched one side of his face with a cluster of fingertips and scooted closer to the front edge of his seat. "I don't remember the year, but those laws have been thrown out."

"Are you familiar with the miscegenation laws?" Gloria was a pitching machine. As fast as Mr. Washington answered, another ball appeared in her hand and she fired it before he had a chance to think.

"Sure, but they've been thrown out too."

"In some states, quite recently, isn't that right?"

"What's that have to do with anything?" He unbuttoned his jacket and searched the inside pocket until he found a handkerchief to wipe off his face.

"Would it be fair to say, Mr. Washington, that these laws, all passed on by wise and learned legislators and judges, had one thing in common? They said a black person was unfit to be educated with or live with whites?"

"So?"

"And unfit to vote or play baseball on the same team with whites?"

I saw a recognition break across Mr. Washington's face as he rubbed the palms of his hands together and readjusted his feet to square himself. "M'am, those laws were a whole different thing." Gloria let him go on this time. "Those were products of deeply rooted discrimination. My God, we were slaves. We fought a Civil War over that one. If you're trying to make some kind of connection between the treatment of blacks and your client, it's not going to compute." He looked over at the judge, satisfied with his answer.

"When Orval Faubus closed four high schools in Little Rock twenty years ago, don't you think he was trying to protect the school children in Arkansas?"

"There's a huge difference, M'am. Governor Faubus, pardon my saying so, was a racist and a bigot."

"Someone who was stubbornly devoted to his own preconceptions regardless of the facts?"

"That's right."

"Governor Faubus had probably never seen an integrated school he didn't detest?"

"Probably not."

"And Jude Martin is your first encounter with a lesbian mother?"

"That's true, but . . ."

"Isn't it possible, Mr. Washington, that you and the school district have jumped to some conclusions about my client that are based on fear and intolerance?"

Larry was rising to his feet to make an objection and trying to scoot his chair back at the same time.

"Sit down," Mr. Washington said. "I'll answer that."

The judge smacked his gavel down. "Nobody's going to answer that question. You can all save your breath. Miss Monroe, the objection is sustained. Ask another question."

She seemed almost to have expected the judge's ruling because she already had her next one ready. "Let me put it this way, Mr. Washington. What *fact* about being lesbian is harmful to Ms. Martin's children?"

He readjusted himself and tugged on his lapel. "Well, for starters, it's immoral."

"That's an opinion. What fact?"

He looked at the judge for assistance, then back at Gloria. "I think the fact of how her kids have behaved is harmful."

"Are you saying that you've never experienced that kind of behavior in the child of a heterosexual mother?"

"I don't think it's mere coincidence, M'am. We've got experts to back me up."

"I'm asking you to speak from your own knowledge, Mr. Washington. Can you give me a fact, an action taken by my client that has been harmful to those kids?"

"You're twisting it around, that's what you're doing. It's obvious to everyone in this courtroom what's going down here." Mr. Washington's voice deepened as he became more righteous. "These were perfectly good kids. They had outstanding records until their mother turned into a lesbian."

"And how do you know it wasn't the result of the divorce?"

"Because our interviews with the kids showed they were scared to death of what their mother had become. Don't ask me, ask the kids." Justine and Derek were looking into their laps.

"Are you aware that the kids chose to live with their mother?"

"That was before they knew. Besides, they're kids, they're just kids. If their mom was a sword swallower, maybe they'd swallow swords, but that doesn't mean we should let them. I'm not here for my own health. I'm here because I think those kids are in danger and I refuse to stand by and let something happen to them. I may not be able to give you the technical ins and outs of it but I've got a pretty good nose and my nose says get her away from them now."

Gloria wasn't a fool. She'd gotten all she was going to get out of this witness. Mr. Washington had found his groove and the judge wasn't going to let her knock him out of it. He inhaled far enough to button his jacket before exiting the witness stand, winking at Larry Delacord as he strode back to his seat. He may not have won the battle on the facts but he'd succeeded in creating an aura of concern for the kids and that, after all, was the core policy driving this custody hearing. He'd also won the heart of Judge Purnell, who followed Mr. Washington with his eyes back to his seat.

Jude must have been picking up on the same vibrations because she had her hands cupped over her face. I knew this was her worst fear. A male senior military officer with a crew cut was going to decide whether she was a fit mother. She didn't even look up as Mrs. Perryvan took the stand and started her testimony.

"It took me a while to draw Derek out," Mrs. Perryvan said. "He

196

was very protective. But he finally told me how he'd gone into his mother's bedroom with one of his nightmares." Her face twitched with the same tic I'd noticed in my interview at the Alhambra as she drew her knees together and pressed her gloved hands down on her thighs. "They were on top of the sheets, he said, in some form of coitus. Derek, of course, used his own words." For this kind of testimony, I would have wanted Derek out of the courtroom, but then again, he was the one who'd seen it first hand in the raw.

"Your honor," Gloria said, "I don't see how this is any more relevant than Mrs. Perryvan's sexual behavior." Mrs. Perryvan put a gloved finger against her lips and bit it.

Before Larry could respond, the Judge spoke. "As far as I can figure, sexual behavior is about all this case is about, counsel. Overruled."

"How . . . did Derek react to this?"

"The children fled to their father's. I think Derek was shocked and deeply embarrassed. For himself, for his mother, for his whole family." Derek had told me he'd seen them kissing and I was naive enough to leave it at that. No wonder it was easier to tell his friends his mother was dead. When I tried to catch Derek's eye, he turned the other way.

All Jude's lawyer could do on cross-exam was get the witness to admit that an eight-year-old might feel some disgust at any form of adult sexual conduct. "But," Mrs. Perryvan added, "the child would learn over time that heterosexuality was normal and accept it. The image of your mother with another woman, I suspect, would be quite another thing."

Mrs. Leonard from Child Protective Services concentrated on Justine when it was her turn, describing to my dread the suicide attempt. I'd debated with Larry whether it was necessary and, of course, it was. The specter of that incident and the possibility that her staying with Jude could trigger another try was one of the main reasons we were there. "The poor girl's desperate to be recognized as attractive," she said. "Her mother's condition has caused her to question her own sexual identity. She wilted, thinking there was something genetic and nothing she could do about it. I think she temporarily gave up on herself." Mrs. Leonard patted her hairdo to make sure nothing had slipped.

"How is she . . . she doing now?" Larry asked.

"When I interviewed her, I sensed an ongoing desperation to prove something. She joked about becoming a prostitute. I think she perceives promiscuity as a way to prove that her sexual desires are normal." More shame, and I almost welcomed Ms. Monroe's objection.

"Your honor, this is highly speculative. The state's witnesses shouldn't be allowed to make flip asides about the private lives of these kids."

Judge Purnell ground the mallet head into the palm of his hand like a pestle and mortar. "I'm here to protect the interests of you kids." He nodded in their direction. "That's why I want to hear everything, but maybe I should have cut this off a little sooner. Mr. Delacord, isn't this kind of stuff all in the reports?"

"Your honor," Ms. Monroe said, "I don't think it's relevant if it's embossed in gold."

The judge ignored her comment.

"Mo . . . most of it . . . is in the reports."

"Thank you. I look forward to reading them. Now let's move this along. It's time for lunch recess and you're not finished with your case yet."

Larry put on our two psychiatrists after lunch in anticipation of the two that we knew Jude's attorney would call. Numbers gave weight but in this case there was another reason. One of our psychiatrists was a school district employee and, seeing how frail she was, it was easy for someone to imagine Mr. Washington browbeating her.

"The mother's lesbianism is like trying to jumpstart the kids' sexual identity by connecting the negative cable to the positive terminal," she said. "If someone doesn't stop her, it'll destroy the whole electrical system."

The other one was more gaurded. "A child's sexual preference is developed early in life," he said. "The mother's homosexuality won't necessarily change that unless she's flaunting it."

When Gloria was done with her lengthy cross-exam, it was also evident where her witnesses would be coming from. Neither of our experts could cite a single long-term study that showed academic or emotional deficits in children raised by a lesbian mother.

Larry surprised me by calling the neighborhood snoop, Mr. Sweet. He'd already called out his name when I grabbed his sleeve.

"A favor for Mr. Washington," he whispered.

I glanced over at Jude and she was shaking her head in disbelief. I wanted to signal that it wasn't my idea, but that would be a cop-out. I was the client. This whole petition was my idea. But I was ticked off at Mr. Washington for not checking with me first.

From hiding behind bushes, peeping through his mariner's telescope, and rifling through Jude's garbage can, Mr. Sweet had pieced together his own unique contribution. "The kids are home alone after school," he said. "There's arguments with their mother. Nudity is rampant. Other lesbians come in and out of her place like a revolving door." I was almost as disturbed by Mr. Sweet's disregard for Jude and Lill's privacy as I was chilled by the possibility that his story might be true.

When we recessed for the day, I was the only witness for my side who hadn't testified. Larry Delacord, Mr. Washington, and I huddled briefly in the hallway afterwards as the neighbors crowded around trying to get in on it with their hoorays and atta boys. One of them, a former member of Jude's Sunday night women's group, told me very solemnly that she thought Jude and Lill had gone too far.

"We've got 'em on the ropes," Mr. Washington said.

I steered us away from the crowd so I could say something to Mr. Washington privately. He was enjoying the adulation and took a couple more handshakes before I had his full attention. I glared at him. "Sir, I didn't appreciate you bringing in the neighbor. This is my case and these are my kids."

He looked over at Larry, then back at me. He was the linebacker scowling at me from across the line of scrimmage. "I'm here to win this, counselor. What's the matter, you afraid of a little smash mouth?"

When Jude walked by, it was the closest I'd been to her all day. She looked bushed despite the makeup she'd caked on her face to hide the lack of sleep. I had a massive headache and wished it was over.

20.

I felt like I was wearing a hairshirt that night. Everything itched. Ever since the kids had run to the Alhambra in panic, our family had been bouncing off the walls like a handball. I had to step into the court and pocket the ball. Jude would be peeved for a while but she'd thank me when things settled down. With their behavior, the kids had practically begged me to do something. Scuttlebutt around the courthouse had it that a lesbian mother had no chance of keeping the kids if the father objected.

"It's a no. . . no-brainer," Delacord said.

I called Mom. She said that Warren's visit had perked Dad up and that Carl was flying in tomorrow. I told her I'd be back by the weekend. I poured a Cutty Sark over ice to help me review my testimony notes on the kitchen table. For moral support, I also skimmed the chapter in the book that the Group Health psychiatrist had recommended on the harmful effects of parental homosexuality, but something didn't feel right.

I went to the closet in the kids' bedroom and found the unmarked Mayflower box that Jude and I used to throw in report cards, letters, newspaper articles, drawings, notes, and anything else potentially memorable. Most of it was stuff by the kids. In fact, we'd encouraged them to put things into the box on their own. Someday we were going to sort it out and mount the best of it in the official family scrapbooks. We'd laugh our heads off showing it to the grandkids. When Jude and I split, I took the Mayflower box and she took the envelopes of unmounted photos but neither one of us had followed through on our promises to divide them up.

I brought the box out to the living room and dumped it upside down. Homemade valentines, school pictures, theater programs, and finger paintings spilled onto the rug. There were lots of C&H cane sugar notepad pages with the familiar printed pink and blue Hawaiian flowers, pineapple trees, and ukeleles that had been the staple for our family notes and grocery lists. Dad had given us reams of it that we kept on a shelf in the fruit cellar, which the kids had converted into the McGovern Club using Jude's old banners and bumper stickers. Dad wouldn't use the stuff for fear it would show disloyalty to the local U&I sugar plant.

In a sterling silver frame with a lacy metal border, I picked up our mounted wedding invitation:

Mr. and Mrs. Raymond Martin
request the honor of your presence
at the marriage of their daughter
Judith April Martin
to
Cyrus Lionel Stapleton

We'd had the wedding reception on the Martins' lawn, which Jude's mom had hired painters to spray green.

There was a Polaroid photo with a cellulose membrane backing, darkened with age, that Jude's father must have taken. Jude was in a rocking chair, pregnant with Justine, holding up a light blue blanket she was knitting and Martha was next to her with a pink one. Both of them were beaming with expectant smiles. We were still living in our apartment in the University District then because I recognized the radiator in the background. That was the weekend Jude's father took me aside and asked if Jude and I needed a family loan and I declined, telling him how thrilled we were at the prospect of this child.

"We could live on fumes," I said.

He shoved a hundred dollar bill into my pocket anyway. "Buy something for the baby, then."

I iced and refilled my glass with Scotch and spread the pile of memorabilia into a wider circle. The things with kid writing interested me the most. A note in pencil read:

Reasons Why We Need Kids Lib

> *1. Adults take advantage of kids too much. They think just because kids are small they can order them around.*

> *2. If an adult tells you to do something and you don't want to do it don't. Ask them what will happen if you don't do it. If they say a punishment, say fine I'll take the punishment unless it is something really bad.*

I remembered when Justine taped that note to the refrigerator in defiance of and next to Jude's rules for the household chores.

There was a file card with a note underlined in pencil that said:

Derek's club rule book: 1. don't let anyone identify.
2. act pretty normal. 3. say you are a spy. 4. have your
shoes off and do not carry much food. 5. don't laugh
or talk when spy.

Stuck to the scotch tape on the back of a black construction paper silhouette of Derek's head was a note from Justine:

Dad, what movie do you and mom want to go to? I
want to go to that one about people who die. PS.
Write me back.

That note had come from the confinement of her room and was probably slipped under our bedroom door.

A postcard from Pocatello when Derek was staying with his cousins said:

Dear Dad and Mom, I played soccer today. Then
we went swimming. And a movie. I miss you
millions and trillions.
Love, Derek

I remembered how he didn't want to go on that trip and I made him. He called every night saying how homesick he was and I was angry and embarrassed because it felt like he wasn't being a man. When my brother Carl came on the phone, I apologized for him. Derek had been right all along; we were all homesick.

Another C&H note with creases where it had been folded into a paper airplane the kids sailed down the stairs said:

You don't understand KIDS!! They get full at
dinnertime but they get hungry later.
Signed,
YOUR KIDS

In my print below theirs, it said: *You don't understand parents.*
You can eat but it has to be something good for you. Followed by their response: *Is raison bran good for us?*

A large red booklet that was folded in half said *JUSTINE'S LIFE* in crayon on the cover with a picture of a two-story house with window frames that looked like prison bars. On the first page, it said *See my family*, and there was a view from the ceiling of our kitchen table with a man, a woman, a girl in a triangular dress, and a baby around it. The drawing looked as if the table top was resting directly on the floor, without legs, and the four stick figures were lying prostrate with their heads and shoulders on the table.

At the bottom of the pile, which meant it must have been near the top of the box, there was a hand-printed poem in Derek's writing:

> *If your a father*
> *stay a father.*
> *Don't be mean*
> *stay keen.*
> *Love your children*
> *and don't fight.*
> *Then things will*
> *turn out right.*

There was no date. I'd never seen it before. Derek must have slid it into the box one weekend while he was at the Alhambra. I read it again and the stab was just as sharp. Derek's logic made a joke out of the sociology books.

When the last ice cube in my glass had melted to the size of a lozenge, I downed the drink and decided to get some fresh air. I headed north along Federal Avenue, one of my favorite streets, with stately colonial and craftsmen mansions large enough to hold the families that people raised before the pill and zero population growth. When I reached Miller Street, I realized I was close to the old house and shuffled along until I found myself sitting on the curb across the street from it. The house was dark, except for the yellow bug bulb in the lantern porchlight and a nightlight in the bathroom upstairs.

There was a peacefulness about the house that was missing in me. I felt like a terrorist. That wasn't my wife in there, whom I'd slept with and trusted with my kids for fifteen years. She was the enemy, and tomorrow we'd duke it out in a courtroom. If it worked as well as Larry Delacord and Mr. Washington assumed, I'd be here tomorrow night stuffing the kids' clothes into suitcases and shopping bags.

The bathroom light must have been left on for Derek, who was still afraid of the dark. I used to tell him that the only thing that changed at night were the colors. The same shrubs and sidewalks and cars were out there; they were just blacks and grays instead of grass blade greens and metallic blues. I told him that as long as he was in the same house with the people he loved he didn't have anything to worry about, that we'd protect each other. Except tonight it wasn't true. There was someone lurking on the curb to be wary of, someone who was going to take them away from their mother.

My dad had always scared me with stories of people who'd died, seemingly oblivious to the living relationships around him that had become terminal. His punishment for a lifetime of not listening was to produce a family that had stopped talking about matters of the heart. There was something in what I was doing that mimicked my dad. When I tried to see myself through the future eyes of the kids, I didn't like what I saw. I had my foot firmly on Jude's neck like a prison guard; I was someone who made his way by holding everyone else in their place. And I was getting weary because part of me was down there on the floor with her.

I'd let Jude become a caricature. I'd probably helped goad her into that role to rationalize the disintegration of our marriage. But there was another Jude whom the kids knew, the barefoot mother in Patchouli oil who was trying to do what mothers have always done, to help her children stand up in a spinning world that ground you down to look like everyone else. They probably still knew, but I'd forgotten, the woman who could get sentimental over *Stopping By Woods*.

I picked up a chestnut still trapped in its prickly shell and closed my fist over it, then squeezed until the thorns drew blood to make sure I wasn't dreaming. Then I held my head still until the shuddering stopped and I could feel the cold hardness under my butt. I looked up at the house again. Derek was right and I was wrong. The dark did change things for the worse.

When I got home, I wrote in my journal for the first time in months, about how Dad had bartered his labor for simple affection, how he believed that manhood meant doing instead of emoting, and how he was willing to trade the remainder of his life so that Mom could survive in decency. I remembered something Lill had told me, a quote from an ancient rabbi, the only thing she remembered from her Jewish upbringing. The simplicity of it had moved me at the time, and I paraphrased it as best I could recall. *Don't do to your fellowman what is hateful to yourself. That is the whole Torah; all the rest is commentary.*

I was tired of dealing with the commentary.

"Here Comes the Sun" was playing when I woke up and rolled over to look at the radio-alarm. My journal was still open on the nightstand. It was eight-forty and I was going to be late to court.

I nicked the underside of my chin in two places shaving and the cuts, still oozing when I put on my shirt, stained the collar. It was my last pressed shirt so I did my best to dilute the stain with a cold washcloth smeared with bar soap. Once in the car, I realized I'd forgotten to put a hankie in my pocket and, at the light, I rummaged through the glove compartment until I found an old napkin to daub the cuts in the rearview mirror.

I found a space with a meter a block from the courthouse but didn't have any change and parked there anyway. In the bigger scheme of things, what did it matter if I got a ticket? When I crashed through the big door at the rear of the courtroom, the first person I saw was Lill in a mauve cape coat and I slid into the pew next to her.

"I thought you weren't supposed to be here."

"So did Jude, but I decided this was my business too."

I squeezed her hand. "I'm glad you're here." I'm sure she had no idea why I'd say that but there was no time to explain.

Judge Purnell was already on the bench. Larry Delacord was pacing in front and looking back at me. It was nine thirty-five and we were late. "Petitioner calls . . . Mr. Stapleton."

Everyone turned to watch me come to the front. Mr. Washington, seated with his cadre of experts, nodded approvingly and I knew that I probably should have tried to call him and Larry. On the other hand, didn't the inscription over the courthouse door say *Justitia est Veritas*? Without really hearing what the Judge said, I raised my right arm, affirmed the oath, and backed into the witness chair. As I looked at Justine and Derek in the front row, I knew that I'd made the right choice. It was about time they knew where I stood on something other than Beatles music or NFL football. This had to be public.

Larry carried his questions on a yellow legal pad, letting his weight rest on one leg as he leaned against the empty jury box. He asked introductory questions to establish the dates of the marriage, my education, and the fact that I'd been timely on support payments. Everything was proceeding according to script.

"Are you a . . . ware of the relationship . . . of your ex-wife with Miss Epstein?"

"Yes, I am."

"Wha . . . what is it?" His eyes lit up.

I was hearing his questions differently than I had in his cramped office. That's what this whole case was about, the *it*, and I could feel fear of the *it* rising out of the middle pews in the courtroom like the stench from a shallow drainfield. The two lady investigators sat upright, confident that the weight of centuries of Judeo-Christian ethics was about to waggle my tongue in their favor. Mr. Washington leaned on his forearms and I imagined him mentally beating his fists into his palms, urging me to give Jude the roundhouse. Then I blinked and there were the kids again, waiting to see if I was going to be part of the mob. I took a deep breath and looked Larry straight in the eye. "As far as I can tell it's a very loving relationship."

Larry searched his yellow pad, then looked up and scowled. "Wha . . . what else?"

"They have problems like any other couple trying to make a go of it, probably a few more." I looked at Jude, who had a skeptical look on her face and was rubbing her thumb hard against one of her fingernails.

"Your . . . honor, may I . . . take a recess?"

The judge looked up at the oversized Bulova mounted over the jury box. "Counselor, we've just started."

"But . . ."

"I've scheduled a phone call for ten forty-five and that's when we'll take it."

Larry looked out toward Mr. Washington, who'd folded his arms across his massive chest. The door in the back creaked open and it was Warren, slipping his Johnny's Flowers cap into his pocket, like he'd just stepped into church. Larry scratched the inside of his collar, flipped his page over, and I could see his eyes running down the tablet. I'd just become his worst nightmare. "Cuh . . . can you tell the court . . . why . . . this woman"—he pointed toward Jude—"should not retain custody of your children?"

"No, I can't." There was a murmur from the audience and I looked over to the judge. "Your honor, let me explain." Larry's shoulders slumped, his yellow pad drooped at his side, and the judge urged me on with the whisk of his fingers. "I've been tormented by this thing. Stupefied really. The only thing I knew was something wasn't sitting right with the kids. So when the school district did their investigation, I slipstreamed behind their recommendations. I thought they were right. I wanted the kids with me and this was the chance to get them."

"Your . . . honor." Larry stepped toward the bench. "Ma . . . may I ask to wi . . . withdraw this witness?"

The judge glared at Larry. "You can ask anything you want, counselor."

Gloria jumped up, bumping the table with her hip as she raced to get into the judge's view. "Your honor, I have the right of cross-examination. The witness has already testified. If he steps down, the defense will recall him. One way or the other, you can't excuse him. He's the father of the children. You have to hear from the father of the children."

Judge Purnell had a twinkle in his eye, maybe it was just a twitch, as he looked down on Gloria. "This is very interesting, Miss Monroe." He twisted the head of the gavel like a pepper grinder. "Didn't your brief say he's not a fit parent? Now why would you call someone like that as your witness?"

She flicked her hair back and raised her chin. "Your honor, the defense is entitled to change its mind. I can assure you we will scratch, bite, and kick if we have to in order to prove that my client shouldn't lose her children. If Mr. Delacord doesn't want him, I do."

Larry seemed bowled over by Gloria. She could spit out whole sentences between his stuttering monosyllables. And, of course, there was the added dilemma: I was his client. "I don't have any fur . . . further questions, your honor."

The judge waved the attorneys away. "Sit down then, both of you. I have a few of my own. In cases involving children, it's my responsibility to make sure the facts get out and I'm not going to be shy about it. I don't care who brought the petition or who supports it." Larry slunk back to his desk like a kid who'd just drawn the wrong equation on the blackboard. Gloria pivoted on the heel of one shoe and returned to her seat. "Mr. Stapleton, I don't know what you're up to but I'm about to find out. Your wife is accused of being lesbian. Is she or isn't she?"

"She is, sir."

"To be honest with you, Mr. Stapleton, her condition is of grave concern to me. And if I were the kids' father, I'd be breaking the door down to get them out of there. What do you think I should do?"

"I think you should dismiss the petition, your honor." Justine and Derek practically bumped their heads together trying to trade whispers.

"Please go on, I'm all ears."

I lifted my legs and I could feel the bottom of my pants unsticking from the witness chair. "Your honor, I was looking at this whole thing through my own eyes and I was missing it. Then I tried to see it through theirs. Sure they were freaked out when they learned about their mom. So was I. But what's going on in this courtroom is their worst fear. The danger isn't Jude and Lill. It's how the rest of us react to Jude and Lill." My voice was starting to tremble. "A decent father doesn't take his kids' mother away. It's that simple."

I looked down, searching for a place to hide my weakening face, closed my eyes and then let my breath out slowly, following it with my mind's eye. I felt the kind of childhood rush that came from unexpected gifts, like the time my dad said I could shoot his thirty-aught-six out at the dump. Through the blur in my eyes, I looked at Justine and Derek. "There's something about the world that panics when a woman chooses to live without a man. But there's nothing wrong with your mom." I was afraid to look at Jude but it didn't matter what she felt. I was doing this for me.

"Are there any more questions, Mr. Delacord?"

He shook his head. He was stutterless.

"Miss Monroe?"

She cupped her hand, said something to Jude, and Jude cupped back. "No, your honor."

He looked at the big clock; we were early. "After my phone call, I'd like to meet with counsel in chambers." He banged his gavel and exited, clutching his robe as he found the steps with his brown oxfords.

I'd just given a big yank to the rug under Mr. Washington, probably aggravated Larry's speech impediment, and confounded the judge, but I felt blissful for the first time in a year. In some small way, I hoped I'd lived up to those scrapbook wishes on the C&H notepaper. It was easy to identify my friends because they moved forward into the space between the judge's dais and the tables. Derek, in his white shirt and clip-on bowtie, made a beeline with his head for my belly button, and I rubbed the back of his neck and folded his collar down. Justine moved more slowly but, despite her teenage detachment, couldn't hide a faint smile. I reached out to her and she came close enough to let me pull her against us.

Gloria and Jude held each other in a sustained embrace and, when they broke, it looked as if Gloria was coaxing Jude towards me. Jude whispered something to Gloria, then glanced sideways at me. *That's all right, Jude, you don't have to do anything. There's too much history.*

I watched Larry Delacord drift into a huddle with the school district team in the back of the courtroom. I was wrong-way Corrigan; they'd lateralled the ball to me and I'd just run it across the opponent's goal line. From the jerking up and down of Mr. Washington's head, I guessed that he was chewing out Larry.

Lill strode up the aisle with her cape draped over her arm and a sly grin on her face. Confirming the neighborhood's worst fears, she gave Jude a quick kiss on the lips and the two of them hugged. As the kids let go of me, Lill came over.

"That's powerful karma," she whispered.

"I changed my mind."

"You didn't change anything," she said. "You were always on the kids' side."

Warren stood at a distance, alternately crushing, then puffing out the top of his Johnny's Flowers cap, looking like he'd just lost his job.

"Cuh . . . can you come here?" Larry was tapping me on the shoulder.

We marched past Warren and back to Mr. Washington's coterie. The Sweets and the poll watchers had entered the back of the courtroom and were staring at me like my feet were cloven. Mr. Washington's brow was sweaty and his breath stale. The wider he opened his eyes, the whiter they became.

"When friends of mine made lawyer jokes, I always stopped them," he said. "They reminded me too much of black jokes. But you want to know something?" He stabbed his thick finger into the space between us. "Your testimony was a bad lawyer joke."

"Slow down, sir. Those aren't your kids. What business is it of yours to lynch their mother?"

"Don't talk to me about lynching." The veins on his neck were like ropes. "Or didn't you notice? I'm not some blackface clown." He unbuttoned his shirt and spread it open to show his skin. "You're a coward, Mr. Attorney, and I don't know what's worse, a fairy mother or a castrated father."

I started toward him, I wanted to slug him, push him ass-backwards over one of the benches, but someone grabbed me by the shoulders.

"Cyrus, cool it." It was Warren.

"Don't you eyeball me," Mr. Washington said, pressing the tips of his fingers against my chest. I struggled to get free of Warren's grip.

"Back off, sir, right now," Warren said, "or I'll let him go and the two of us will lay you out. Understand?"

I yelled. "You're a dangerous man, Mr. Principal."

"Hey, what's going on here?" Someone must have called security because a deputy sheriff in a beige and green uniform stepped between us.

"This guy's an asshole," Mr. Washington said.

"This guy's threatening my family," I said.

The deputy put a stiff arm against each of us, and I was relieved that I wasn't going to get the chance to swing at him. Washington had a four-inch height advantage and about forty pounds on me. "What kind of case are you involved in here?"

"Lesbian mother," Mr. Washington blurted at the same time I said, "My kids."

The deputy looked around, surveying the participants. "What's your role here, sir?" he asked Mr. Washington.

"I'm a principal in the Seattle School District."

"And you?"

"I'm the father."

The deputy rolled his eyes. It was clear he didn't get it but he didn't care. "You stay on this side," he said, pointing Mr. Washington to his seat, "and you come over here." Gripping me roughly by the arm, he set me down in the front row. Not sure who or what Warren was, he made him sit alone on the other side of the aisle. Then the deputy walked toward the door to the judge's chambers, his holster drooped off one hip, his rayon pants so tight in the butt they were shiny.

After a minute or so, the deputy emerged and took a seat about five rows back so he could watch all three of us. Then the bailiff announced that the judge wanted to see counsel in chambers. As they reached the door, Gloria opened it and let Larry enter first.

I'd been grounded and I motioned for the kids to sit with me. When I'd told them stories as object lessons about the fights I used to get into playing basketball and football, Justine said she couldn't imagine me fighting with anyone. The truth was that this little scrap with Washington was nothing more complicated than male ego. Just when I thought I'd evolved to the next level, I'd suffered another relapse.

"Were you going to hit him, Dad?" Derek said.

"Probably. Maybe I'll get him at parents' night."

Derek looked over my shoulder, hurling malevolence at the principal.

"He's just fighting for what he believes in," I said.

Clients always hated conferences in chambers. It confirmed their suspicion that the system was rigged, that the attorneys all knew each other and play-acted for the benefit of the clients while the real deals were made behind closed doors. Judge Purnell was a cigar smoker and I imagined he was most of the way through one of his stogies by now; the attorneys would be begging for air. Larry was at a definite disadvantage in this format, where there were no assigned turns and you had to just blurt things out.

Then the door opened and Larry emerged, followed by Gloria, who was shaking her hair like she'd just broken loose from a wrestling hold. The aroma of Havana wafted into the courtroom. Just as the hydraulic pump on the door was about to let it smack shut, the Judge appeared and everyone stood. He gathered his robe in his fist and trudged up to his chair.

"Sit down."

The judge wiped the cigar juice out of the corners of his mouth, fumbled with a piece of paper, then looked out at the audience. "This has been a first for me, folks. I've seen parents fight over the china, the station wagon, the woman next door, but I've never seen a custody hearing where the husband testified for the wife. It's probably a signal I should be getting out of this business. Let me get to the point." He looked at the clock again. "Miss Martin's attorney has moved in chamber for a dismissal of the petition and I'm going to rule on her motion right here. I don't know if Miss Martin can be a good mother or not. I've read all the reports and, as usual, no help there. Four experts, five opinions. But I'm not going to play God." He glared at everyone at the front tables before continuing. "It doesn't sound like the kids are squawking. It's not my brand but then I don't have to smoke it. Here's what I'm going to do. The petition to take away Miss Martin's rights as custodian of these kids is denied. As cockamamie as it seems, I'm going to change the dissolution decree to give the parents joint custody. You two can divide up the time any way you want. Miss Martin, you owe him one. I want the parents and the kids to appear before me six months from today. If necessary, I'll play God and the devil both if things aren't right." He looked out at Mr. Washington and his people. "If things go to hell in a handbasket before six months is up, somebody better speak up. Case dismissed." Jude had accused the law of being blind, and maybe she was, but she could sure find her way around in the dark.

As the judge gathered up his notes and whispered something to the bailiff, Jude and her attorney shook hands under the table. I spread my arms to cover the laps next to me, and Derek and Justine grabbed on. I had no hand to wipe the rebel tear that trickled down my left cheek.

212

21.

The court's decision didn't cause so much as a ripple in the world at large. There was no article in the paper, no TV or radio story, no change in the price of local stocks.

In the smaller world in which I dwelt, the decision was a veritable tsunami. Rather than pummeling the shoreline, though, it had a remarkably cleansing effect. Derek insisted on staying at Seward even though I'd offered to transfer him to Stevens. His grades, which had slipped badly with hand-written warnings at the bottom of his cards, started inching back up. All to Mr. Washington's dismay, I was sure. His first playground fight was with a kid who'd called him a fag.

I'd always dreamt of Justine getting into ball sports but instead she tried out for a seat in an eight-woman novice shell for her age group on the Green Lake Rowing Club. I'd get up at five, bike over to Green Lake, and watch her skim across the mist against an Orange Julius sunrise. She was developing callouses on her hands and muscles in her shoulders. One night she left a folded note on my pillow.

Dad, I'm finally into respect for the body.
I never thought I'd enjoy the company of just girls.
Love, Justine.

It was remarkable that she could say it and that I could hear it without panicking.

Just when she'd been promoted to a paying position at the ACLU, Jude announced that she was quitting and going to law school. I knew exactly what was happening. The law represented power and she wanted a piece of it. I didn't know why she felt she had to, though; she could already out-lawyer me. The only problem was money. She didn't have any and neither did I because, on Memorial Day, I took a leave of absence from the firm. It wasn't the law I was leaving as much as the institution of the law. I wanted a break from the whispering and tittering at the office and a reprieve from the purgatory of tracking my life in tenth-of-an-hour billable increments. It made it easier to tell everyone that the leave was temporary so that I could teach at Seattle Central Community College in the fall. Meantime, however, it was June and I was unemployed for the first summer since sixth grade.

At bottom though, I was no different than every other child born. I needed to know what my parents thought, which now was only half-possible because Dad had passed away before I could tell him how I'd finally taken the bat off my shoulder. I wasn't sure how pleased he'd be but I wished I had him back for another try at it.

He would have certainly despaired if he knew what I really wanted to do: open my own coffee house, a place with daily newspapers and literary journals on a rack where people lingered to play cards and chess or just drink coffee and shoot the breeze. There would be New York cheesecake and bagels and an open mike in the evenings for folksongs or readings. Justine and Derek would work there washing dishes and waiting tables. I'd always regretted that I had no place to employ them the way Dad had done for us at the Thriftway. When things were slow, I figured I could sit in the corner and read or write in my journal.

I covered the Plymouth with a tarp to protect it from the weather and bird droppings, and to save money. When I had to go anywhere, I rode the bus or used the Raleigh ten-speed that I'd pulled out of the storage locker and chained to a pipe in the laundry room. It was surprising, though, how few places I needed to go, especially when the kids weren't with me. There was no one asking me to meet them at construction sites or fancy restaurants anymore. I'd strike up conversations with other unemployed people in the donut shop and we'd bitch about the Mariners, maybe even talk about religion and politics. I was Billy Bigelow, the irresolute carousel barker who couldn't hold a job. But at least my life wasn't linear anymore. I could skip the newspaper whenever I wanted to and it no longer made me uneasy to use a pants hanger for a shirt.

Warren was still disturbed at the results of the hearing. He accused me of taking a dive and, for a while, whenever I asked him to play handball he said he was busy. I finally realized that, for him, the two of us were twins who were supposed to speak with the same voice on the big issues. When I spoke up for Jude, I'd changed course without warning, leaving him running hell-bent in support of a charge that had been called off. Most of all, he was hurt because he wasn't in on it. But his turn was coming. Mandy took him back and her due date was less than a month away. One evening they came over and we propped Mandy up sideways on the couch with pillows under her stomach and between her legs and talked about the child birthing classes they'd been taking at Group Health. Warren went around my apartment child-proofing everything within three feet of the floor. When Mandy had to go to the bathroom for the third time that evening, he pulled me aside in the kitchen.

"She's going to be a good mother, isn't she?"

"Salt of the earth."

"We're gonna get married too," he said, and for a moment I thought my little brother had finally undergone the sea change we'd been hoping for. Then, with a perfectly straight face, he asked me if I could co-sign a loan for a station wagon. "Something big enough for the three of us."

By mutual agreement with Jude, the kids rotated every other month between us. Finally, there was a chance to share a life with the kids that had weekdays as well as weekends and disappointments that didn't have to be purged by Sunday night before they returned to their mom's. I found Derek a summer job at St. Joseph's cutting the grass and walking the pastor's arthritic Irish wolfhound. He put half of his proceeds into the peanut butter jar for my movie money.

"Till you're working again," he said.

Derek's soccer coach quit and Derek recruited me to replace him.

"They just need someone's name on the form," he said. My son, the lawyer. "We're old enough to coach ourselves."

Wrong. When I arrived at the first practice, they were shaking bottles of soda and spraying each other with fizz. I made them run laps around the perimeter of the playground, something Derek said their real coach would have never made them do. At the first game, I didn't let him start and he was flummoxed.

"You don't want people to think I put you in 'cause you're the coach's son, do you?"

Even the characters in my dreams changed. No more Leo Pescaras who belched and bragged like they owned the town, and me. I'd regressed to earlier periods in my life, beer keggers at the river with guys standing on rocks and howling like wolves, asking Dad if I could borrow the Buick for an outdoor movie or a golf game. Old girlfriends showed up in my dreams, but they were always with other guys. Someone walked by with Margaret Miller on his arm and gave me an upside-down finger from behind her bum. I started writing my dreams down in a stenographer's tablet that I kept under the bed with a pen in the spiral. In case the kids found it, I named all the girls Jude. It wasn't a lie. I was physically, if not whimsically, celibate, still building up steam to find the new Jude in my life.

The months off without the kids were a little depressing. When I walked by Boondock's in the evening and saw men in pinstriped suits and loosened ties leaning over their tables in spirited conversation I experienced a fleeting grief. That used to be me in the candlelight with something or other on the rocks, still fired up with the adrenaline of a day in court or a settlement I'd just inked, needing someone to pat me on the back and admire my work. I was in the appetizers-with-dinner-and-a-bottle-of-Bordeaux lane then. But the world I didn't think could survive without me had already forgotten me. I was just a guy in a pair of jeans and a baseball cap who passed unnoticed outside their window. And I was grateful that the law forbade the poor as well as the rich from sleeping under bridges.

The most frequently asked questions from the few friends I'd held onto were why did I quit my job and when was I getting married again. For those who knew Jude, but had lost touch with her, they also asked if she'd remarried. That was still her mother's hope, who told me she'd offered to pay for Jude's therapy to get her over this condition. Jude refused and her mom went instead.

Whenever I ran into Lill while we were handing off the kids, I tried to act as if nothing had happened between the two of us, which was hard because she was still the only woman beside Jude who held any interest for me. But now she was the boat fender that kept me and Jude from bumping into each other when the water got choppy. On one of our handoffs, she whispered that she and Jude were intimate again, a concept I still hadn't fully digested.

Jude's and my lives were back on parallel tracks. We didn't see that much of each other and the kids gave me periodic reports of what was happening on the other rail. Neither of us had exactly melted our swords into plowshares but we engaged in certain forms of cultural and economic assistance. Jude passed along joint custody articles from *Ms.* with notes in the margin that said, *Thought you'd be interested.* She'd still never said anything to me about my testimony in the hearing. For a while, I looked for a note in the mail from her and left spaces in our telephone conversations hoping she'd say something.

For Justine's birthday, Lill wanted to organize a surprise party at the Alhambra. She'd make all the arrangements. "All you have to do is pick up an apple-shaped cake with a *16* on it," she told me. "Chocolate with cherry frosting."

I walked over to Pacific Desert and had coffee and a croissant while they finished the decorating. It was amazing how many other people were sipping refills at one-thirty in the afternoon. Justine thought the party was going to be a dinner for her, Derek, and me followed by a movie (I let her choose *Grease* over a Woody Allen film). Dinner with her dad and brother was no big deal; she'd already planned the real birthday party with friends.

The night of the dinner I picked the kids up at their mom's and stopped by the Safeway for some Haagen-Dazs on the way back to kill time. Justine blushed as pink as the streamers when she stepped into my apartment.

"Dad, you did this?"

Derek and I played our parts right to the end. While I was putting the dinner on for the three of us, I asked her if she'd get the candles out of my closet. That was supposed to be the trigger. I'd thought about how stubborn she could be and decided it had to be something innocuous enough not to raise suspicion yet important enough to warrant the energy of a sixteen-year old.

Derek smirked.

"What are you looking at?" she asked.

"Nothing."

We tip-toed behind her as she walked down the hall and into my room. The paneled door coasters rolled in their trough. Then Justine screamed as Jude emerged from the closet in her peasant dress, and Lill, barefoot, in a lime-green jumpsuit. Finally, a third person came out with a paper sack on his head, groping toward Justine.

"That's Warren," she said, and she was right.

Derek looked at me as if to see if I was okay with all of this. I wasn't sure. When Lill first mentioned a family get-together, I was skeptical: it would either be total silence or a name-calling donnybrook. The six of us, including the wife who'd left me and the woman who'd refused me for my wife, stood there in the narrow space between the end of the bed and the closet. Jude and I shook hands.

The dinner conversation was surprisingly animated. It was like we'd been lost and suddenly came upon each other in a glade, everyone trying to talk louder than the next person. I watched the kids' faces as Jude told the latest story about Mr. Sweet.

"They wouldn't dare try that kind of crap if Dad lived there," Derek said. I looked at Jude to see if she was going to correct this residue of sexism.

She swigged another gulp of the zinfandel before commenting, her voice starting to get a little sloppy. "Don't expect him to join us soon. Your dad's not so keen on communes."

"That's old news, Jude. Unemployment has changed my perspective."

When we finished eating, Lill volunteered to take lead on the dishes while Warren and I walked the dog. We took the route toward Volunteer Park, Magpie working both sides of the sidewalk. When she found a smell she wanted to study, she spread her legs and became as immovable as a butcher block, an annoying habit that had often irritated me. I figured if we were going for a walk, let's cover the allotted distance and get back home. It was the same thing I'd been doing for the past year—trying to change everyone's shape to fit the pigeonholes I'd created for them. Tonight, the rubber was starting to resume its natural shape and it made me giddy.

"You know something, Warren? I *could* actually live with Jude in the same house. I mean I wouldn't do it, but it means I'm not scared of her anymore."

"I didn't know you ever were."

I slipped my arm around his shoulder and pulled him next to me so I could feel the rhythm of his step. "You know how you don't know how hungry you are till you sit down to eat? Well, I didn't know how much I was trying to pull away from her until I felt it was safe to be in the same room together."

"One piece of advice and then I'll butt out," Warren said. "Don't move in with your ex-wife. It'll be death to dating."

When we got back to the apartment, Lill was playing scrabble

218

with the kids on the floor, the three of them lying on different sides of the board. Magpie waded into the formation to get some recognition and Derek had to hold her back by the collar. Justine tried to cover the tiles with her hands when she saw me studying the words. *Crap* and *dammit* shared an *a* and *tush* built off the *t*.

"Cuss scrabble," Lill said sheepishly. "Sorry, Cyrus. I just wanted to see what words they knew."

I smiled to myself, the kind of hidden crack in the heart that makes you feel momentarily lighter. "Where's Jude?"

"Stomach cramps," Lill said. "She's in the kids' room."

"Too much vino."

"I think she's just tired. I hope it's okay she's using their bedroom."

I hung up my coat and draped the dog leash over its hook in the closet. A headache was advancing from the horizon of my skull toward the crown. The cheaper the wine, the bigger and quicker the hangover. I heard Warren asking if he could join the scrabble game as I walked down the hall toward the kids' room. I didn't even know why I was doing it. Jude was Lill's to administer to now. I guessed it was curiosity, wanting to know what she thought of the evening. The door was ajar and the room pitch dark. If she was asleep, I'd just leave her be. I made a warning tap on the door with the pads of my fingers as I went in. There was no answer. The light from the living room provided enough candlepower to see the lump under the covers. I knelt down next to the kids' twin bed, my knee resting on what must have been one of Jude's shoes. The room smelled of dirty clothes and sheets that needed laundering. As my pupils dilated, I could make out the hair on the back of her head. Judging from the shape of the lump, she must have pulled her knees up to her chest.

"Jude, it's me."

She drew her head further under the sheets like a turtle, then the fingers of one hand reached up and combed the hair back over one ear. The box springs creaked as she stretched her legs toward the footboard. An elbow emerged and pushed the bedspread and blankets away from her head. She rolled onto her back and looked straight up at the ceiling. I studied her familiar profile, the generous eyebrows, the Roman arch in the bridge of the nose, and the parted lips that were dry from breathing through her mouth.

"Can I get you something?"

"I feel sick," she whispered, still not looking at me. "Maybe you better get me a pan."

I almost put my palm on her forehead to check her temperature. "Sure, just a minute."

I went to the bathroom and checked the wastebasket, which had a flattened toothpaste box and some crumpled toilet paper on the bottom and a used string of dental floss caught on the rim. With my bare hands and bar soap, I scrubbed the drinking glass that we kept our toothbrushes in, rinsed it, and filled it with cold water. I rolled up the bath mat, grabbed the wastebasket and water, and reentered the hallway. There was laughter and clapping at the scrabble board. Somebody yelled, "'Caca's' cussing," and I turned into the bedroom and pushed the door shut far enough to muffle the noise.

When I'd finished setting up the vomit basket in the center of the mat, Jude had turned herself over and was facing me. "They're having a good time," she said.

"Yeah, do you believe it?"

Her face glistened with sweat. "Not much has changed, huh?"

"What do you mean?"

"You're still taking care of me."

"I don't ever remember you sick. I kind of like you this way."

She started to laugh, then grimaced as she pushed a fist toward her abdomen and doubled up. I resisted the temptation to give her a pat on the shoulder. She looked the way I felt the night I had appendicitis in college, when I played shuffleboard at the Century Tavern and thought it was just gas pains from the beer and pepperoni sticks until the pain localized to where it felt like someone had left a jackknife open inside me. "Maybe I've got a bleeding ulcer."

"That's doesn't come until law school."

She grimaced again. "Maybe I'm not as tough as I thought."

I didn't want to say anything else that would make her laugh, which was a new idea, worrying that she'd laugh too much. "I can't believe I ever seriously considered the kids living without you."

The side of her head sunk into the pillow so that her lips rubbed against the pillowcase as she spoke. "I did. Remember when Justine was a baby and I set her down behind the wheel of that car in the parking lot and she was almost killed? For years, I couldn't tell anyone about it, not even my mom. I thought it meant I wasn't cut out to be a mother. I never understood why you didn't just yell and scream at me." She licked her lips. "When the kids acted up this year, that whole incident came back to me and I lost my confidence. I knew I was a mediocre wife but I was scared to death I was going to turn out to be a crappy mother too. That's why I couldn't believe what you did."

"You mean . . ."

"Testify for me. You had me by the balls, Cyrus."

She was drained of the bravado I'd come to fear, and it felt as if she'd hear me if I answered in my own voice. No more spitting into the wind. "You'd have won without me."

"I'm so tired of wasting energy changing pronouns to hide the fact that I'm living with a woman and worrying about whether my mother will approve."

I remembered the vet putting my dog to sleep when I was a kid and holding her until she went still in my arms. Something was expiring between Jude and me and I wanted to hold on to her until it was gone.

"You're a scrapper, Jude."

"I didn't plan this, honest."

I listened to the voices arguing in the next room. The words were indistinguishable and the people seemed so far away. They weren't around when this thing started and would never know what it meant. There was a pride rising in me, though, the kind my mom must have felt, to know that she could still believe in someone who mattered despite all evidence to the contrary. Jude's and my union may not have been tender, but it had proved stubborn. Something in it didn't want to die. I brushed the hair off Jude's clammy forehead and searched for her eyes.

"I never thought you'd be waiting for me on this side of our marriage," she whispered, and slid her hand across the sheet to grip my arm.

ALSO BY JOHN E. KEEGAN

Clearwater Summer

Piper